Mabel Esmonde Cahill

Her Playthings, Men

A novel

Mabel Esmonde Cahill

Her Playthings, Men
A novel

ISBN/EAN: 9783337027452

Printed in Europe, USA, Canada, Australia, Japan

Cover: Foto ©Andreas Hilbeck / pixelio.de

More available books at **www.hansebooks.com**

I HAVE FELT IT IN THE TREMBLE OF HIS HAND AS HIS DARK EYE
MET MINE.

Page 18.

HER PLAYTHINGS, MEN

A NOVEL

BY

MABEL ESMONDE CAHILL

—◦—

NEW YORK
WORTHINGTON CO., 747 BROADWAY
1891

Press of J. J. Little & Co.
Astor Place, New York

CHAPTER I.

IN LINCOLN GREEN.

Let me carry your thoughts, Reader, to a woodland scene in the heart of England, where, but a few years ago the royal oaks stretched far above, and the mossy green sward was soft to the horse's hoofs which trampled it; where the mottled lizard and the glittering adder glided in and out of the tangled underbrush of rhododendron and sweet briar; where the lovely coltsfoot and the waving pines mingled their perfumes in early Spring, whilst above, in the wind-swung branches the gentle wood pigeon cooed her soft love tale to her mate. There on a dewy morning in the Spring of 188—, four days prior to the great race meeting of Darcliffe, we might have seen galloping over the springy turf two proud crested animals, the one bestridden by a young man of some twenty-two summers, the other, riderless, but bearing upon his glossy shoulder the trappings for a lady's use. This and much more yet could we have seen as onward dashed that bold, reckless young rider, looking not back to yesterday's peaceful hours, looking not forward to the dark possibilities of to-morrow.

Onward he dashed with the lady's charger by his side, until the park lands of Darcliffe had been left far to the rear, until fields of stubble had been galloped over and their neat hedgerows crossed, until at last arrived at the grand, old ivied wall marking the boundary between the equally important estates, attached respectively to Darcliffe Castle and Cumberwold Abbey, when the panting steeds were suffered to draw breath.

A long, low rambling wall this was, with its ivy crested buttresses, its massive earthworks, meant to withstand the ravages of centuries; full of weird memories for the little unkempt rogues of long gone generations, who had so often climbed its ledges to find where the wood-birds loved to build their nests in early Spring; full of vague terrors for the timid little girls who ofttimes wove the daisies and kingcups into fantastic chains beneath its cooling shade.

And now, as the young horseman reined in amid a cluster of poplars fringing the boundary wall, a low, clear whistle broke upon the still air and an arrow shot up against the blue sky. A pretty little arrow this, shot from a lady's archery bow, feather tipped and fleet to do its mistress' bidding, as, bearing on its sharp point a note, it landed at the young man's feet. A note, the opening of which caused the young man's cheek to blanch and his hand to tremble, whilst having read it and re-read it apparently to his satisfaction, he proceeded—with the delightful idiocy of his twenty-two summers—to crush it many times against his lips.

Blind mortal, who cannot pierce the impenetrable stretches of futurity, could you but understand that in the note you hold there is contained a message pregnant for you with subtlest poison, such as in the unknown to-morrow will blight your manhood's sweetest hours, leaving you naught but ashes and dead sea fruit behind, your cheek would blanch, but from a different motive to that which prompted it but a moment ago to grow more deadly white than the drifting clouds above you. But the young man thought not of to-morrow, as he sprang towards a buttress of the old ivied wall and waited,—yea waited for what possibilities that "to-morrow" held for him.

Not long had he waited ere there sprang into view from above the figure of a young girl in the first blush of lovely womanhood, with form and face fresh and voluptuous as the bursting rose-bud culled from its parent stem but a moment back. Especially lovely this young wood-nymph looked in her riding habit of darkest green, which by its perfect make betrayed the rounded curves of a generous figure, whilst, with a rippling laugh as full of soft music as the tinkling of goat-bells amongst the Alpine gorges, she sprang from her vantage ground into the readily extended arms of the young man. A passionately linger-ing kiss, and a little cry, a few tender greetings, eyes looking into answering eyes, and then these young people turned to where the horses stood trampling the mossy sward in a corner of the fragrant pine-woods.

It took them but a very short time to get settled once more in their saddles, and in a moment more they were riding onward together, to ruin and to heart break, such as seldom engulfs years so tender as theirs.

CHAPTER II.

A LIFE'S WRECK.

A trial race. The grooms and jockeys, scattered here and there in groups of twos and threes, admire Lady Adelaide Heathmore, the dashing young heiress of Cumberwold Abbey, as she canters leisurely towards the course.

"She's goin' to ride the race on Blackwater. I'm d—— if she's not a rare plucked un !" ·

"See her go! My eye! What a jock she'd make! Steady as a rock over the hurdle !"

"She'll do ; and if she was to ride in the big race I'd back her !"

Such were the enthusiastic comments uttered within earshot of our lovely wayward heiress; comments that, for all her wealth and high-breeding, brought a keener tinge of pleasure to her cheek than did in after life the subtlest flatteries of the many princes of Europe who kneeled before her beauty.

But though this Diana seemed an object for their unlimited adoration, still amongst the jockeys "the favorite" was "the favorite," and he was carrying Rutland Borradale quietly down towards the starting point.

"So I am going to ride a genuine race!" said Lady Adelaide enthusiastically to her companion. "I wish I were a jockey, but, Rutland dear, what is the betting to be ?"

The young man bent low in his saddle until his lips

almost brushed her loose flying hair, and whispered some words that made her blood rush to her velvety cheek.

"Be it so," she says with a ripple of laughter and a toss of the proudly turned head.

"So that is why you are mounted on the favorite, is it? Well you shall not win if I can prevent it."

Rutland had not been fearful of trusting the great racer of his uncle's stable to his fair companion, whose hands on horseback were sympathetic, and whose riding was very perfect and finished, but he had had his own views with regard to winning this race, and they were very dear to him, so he smiled at the toss of the proud girlish head, but said no more.

One, two, three, and they urge their horses to a racing speed along the resounding turf, Blackwater leading, Blackbriar, the favorite, second, as they clear the first and third hurdles. Blackwater, although esteemed the better horse by most outsiders, was known amongst the trainers and stable men around Darcliffe to have done as fine things in the way of trial races as his stable companion, and he was a horse, which, when handled gently, as he was being to-day by Lady Adelaide's finger-tips, he was pretty sure to strain wind and limb to their utmost at her urging.

Over the fourth hurdle they sailed, neck and neck, whilst the enthusiasm of the on-lookers became clamorous.

"She'll have it, the young lady! There's none like her to ride a thoroughbred."

"Nonsense," came from another; "the favorite is only holding back while she does the running."

" You're mightily mistaken, young man; that riding doesn't mean anything but dead earnest. But doesn't she ride, though; and he is pressing her hard."

" Yes, she has it! No, they're over the last together. She pulls ahead! She has it! She has it! She has it! No, d—— me if it isn't the favorite by a neck! Well, well, I must back the favorite and win some money."

Wild cheers rang out now for the favorite. He was going to win money for them all, for every one of them had backed him for the great race.

" Never beaten—he's a clipper, and has every penny I own on him."

The speaker was a burly farmer, who had since he was a small boy considered it part of his religious creed to back and uphold the horses produced by his own shire, and Blackbriar he knew to be one of the finest he had ever had the pleasure of risking his money on.

" Hedge a bit is what I am going to do," said a cooler-headed Southerner. " Every man in England has his pound, shilling or penny on Blackbriar, so the odds are too short to make anything, and I wouldn't trust him anyhow too much."

" Ye know precious little, then, an' ye don't know our Darcliffe horse."

Whereat, with a groan for the skeptical speaker, the crowd dispersed to rush to where their idol was pawing the turf and fretfully champing his bit, as though meditating another scamper over the field of his triumph.

One and all secure whatever prices remain at that late hour in the betting market, and all feel happy about their investments.

Lady Adelaide and Rutland in the meantime have

drawn up side by side, with the velvety glow of health
on their cheeks and lips, but in the young man's sparkling fresh dark eye is an especial flash of triumph, as
with ineffable tenderness and love breathing in his whole
demeanor, he bends his looks on his adorable companion.

"Do you understand, darling, the race is mine?" he
whispers. "The race is mine, you are mine, the world
is mine."

"Does it make you very happy?" she retorts saucily,
and then recoils a little timidly, as would the frightened
fawn in the gyves of its captor.

"Adelaide," he murmured, his eyes full of passionate
adoration, "I love you."

"And I you," was breathed softly in return.

A deep draught of love they drink from each other's
eyes; then they slowly come back to realities, and turn
their horses' heads towards Darcliffe.

As they left the race course with its crowds of trainers
and jockeys considerably to the rear, and emerged once
more under the fine old oaks of Darcliffe, the sun was
rising to its zenith, the rooks had spread their wings in
search of some distant pasture lands where the worms
and succulent roots were particularly tasty, and all in
the woods was silent in the noon-tide.

"You said your uncle was away, did you not, Rutland?
But he might be back by an early train."

"Yes, darling, he might, but that is improbable."

"Still he will be very angry if he hears of this, so we
had better hurry homeward."

"His anger will mean nothing to me, darling, when by

incurring it I shall have procured the slightest pleasure
for my Adelaide."

Again in one clinging kiss of youth, and love, and
pleasure their lips met under the wind-swung branches
of the oaks, and then they dashed forward, anxious to
place their horses safe in their own stalls at Darcliffe.

For a few happy moments they cantered side by side
avoiding now a projecting bough, now a blasted tree-
stump overgrown with moss and dewy primroses, until,
in the very heart of that quiet wood the slumbering
wood-pigeons were startled into timid life by a lady's
wild cry, mingling with a deep angry bellow, loud and
terrible to them in their peaceful groves as is the angry
roar of the lion in his native forests. A crashing of
underwood and a galloping of heavy feet was heard,
distinct from the flying footfalls of the horses, and the
lady was conscious of having for a moment beheld dash
ing full upon her flank, a lordly steer that had broken
from some shambles not far off, with the gash of the
slaughter-axe gaping wide in his massive neck, whilst
the blood gushed in torrents from the huge rift, maddening the brute with pain and terror.

However, fear lent the swiftness of the wind to Lady
Adelaide's horse's hoofs, as with a startled snort, Blackwater sped onward, gaining steadily before his pursuer,
though the latter was goaded by fury to an alarming
speed.

"Darling, you were always a brave girl, but now you
must show your courage more than ever. I do not think,
however, there is real danger."

Side by side they galloped, the gentleman reining in
slightly, and directing his movements according to the

lady's speed, whilst behind them, and not so very far, the savage brute came thundering along with ponderous hoof-stroke and an occasional fierce bellow which froze the blood of the riders.

Each moment, however, he was losing ground, and when next the lady turned in her saddle she knew that danger was past.

"By Jove, the bridge over the torrent is broken!" cried the young man in startling tones, "and it is an ugly spot; we must let our horses look well at it and take time."

Yawning now at their feet was a ravine whose sides were steep as a precipice, and studded at the bottom with huge rocks, over which a torrent was rushing.

They knew their horses, however, to be steeplechasers, daring and active enough to clear a wider or an uglier leap than this, and the riders were not alarmed. But some time was necessarily lost in creeping down the dizzy incline, whilst other valuable moments were past in finding a part of the torrent practicable for a leap. Parts were too dangerously wide, parts so bristled with slippery or jagged rocks that no horse's hoof could rest upon them to take off. At one spot at the near brink of the torrent lay a newly-fallen oak tree, a young tree of about sixty years' growth, which had been dealt foully with; the contraband axe had done part of the work, and a late storm the rest.

At the spot where the trunk of this tree lay the torrent was at its narrowest, and a tiny patch of sward stretched beneath the horses' hoofs. This was the most feasible spot for a leap, but it would still be a hazardous one, owing to the obstruction offered by the fallen tree.

"You do not fear it, I am sure?" said the gentleman encouragingly, and a proud little toss of the head was her only answer.

"Then here is the take off, and follow me. Your horse must rise high to the tree, and take a good stretch.

"Stay, darling!" he cried suddenly; "that bough will drag you from your saddle."

Dismounting quickly, he swung his full weight from the projecting bough so as to draw it slightly aside.

"Now! Pass!" cried he.

In a moment the lady was over tree and stream, as lightly borne as though it were a swallow that had skimmed the water.

In the meantime the brute pursuing then came thundering along, and a bellow close at hand told the young man he had no time to lose.

In consternation he sprang to his saddle, his horse, snorting with terror, scarce rose to the tree-trunk; he struck it heavily with his knees, and not being able to save himself, he struggled wildly in mid-air, and then plunged forward on his head into the water, where for a moment he lay stunned.

Quick as thought the young man had disengaged himself, and snatched from his breast pocket a revolver which he presented at the head of the oncoming steer.

Crack! Crack! rang out upon the air, and one bullet lodged in the steer's head, but it was too late. Ere the fallen horse could rise from the water again, the maddened brute had hurled himself with such savage impetuosity down the rough sides of the ravine, that at the bottom, in the rough torrent intersecting it, he fell power-less in the throes of death, but not before his cruel horns had torn into shreds the quivering heart of Blackbriar, the gallant racer who was to have carried the thousands of the rich, the hundreds of the poor safely past the post, only four days thence.

A cry of pain escaped the blanched lips of the lady, as she she sprang from her saddle to the ground.

"It will ruin the Earl of Darcliffe! What will he say? He has so much money on the race. Oh, poor, noble Blackbriar! How sorry I am for you! Rutland, dearest, can I not do something for you? Something for him?" she asked plaintively.

"Nothing dearest, noth——"

Ere he could finish there came from the crest of the hill above them a startling cry of horror, a cry with the ring, almost of wild despair, and in an instant the tall, soldierly form of the Earl of Darcliffe, with blanched cheek and flaming eye, and a loaded revolver in his hand, came springing down the slope.

Hatred and contempt breathed from his lips and brow as he advanced threateningly towards his nephew.

"Coward!" he hissed, with suppressed passion, pre-senting the revolver at his nephew's temple, "you deserve it more than that poor dumb brute yonder. Go, cow-ard! get thee hence quickly, and never dare to darken my threshold again! Go," he cried again, with intense and rising fury, "Go, or I will shoot you down like any dog in my pathway."

Then, whilst his ashen lips quivered with pain, he turned and sent two bullets through the brain of the noblest animal he had ever called his own; and it was a mercy, indeed, for in the pangs of expiring agony the limbs of the gallant brute were yet trembling.

"Forgive me, uncle!" was all that Rutland Borradale could murmur, as with a sob that choked him, and passionate despair in his starry boyish eyes, he turned to leave that scene of horror.

But now a detaining hand was laid on his arm, and a pale face was raised to his.

"Rutland," she cried, "you have a friend till death in me, tell me if I may not help you?"

"You cannot, dearest," he breathed hoarsely. "Believe me, it is best that we should say goodbye forever here. All must now be over between us, as you see, I shall now be nothing but a beg— beggar." It was with difficulty he framed the word which meant for him a lifelong struggle and pain.

"Rutland! not good bye!" and the plaintive dark yes anon wells of love and light were raised to his in mute entreaty, till his whole frame quivered, and his resolution faltered, but it was only for a brief moment.

One lingering look he cast towards that scene of horror where the idolized racer of his uncle's stables and of all their country round had, with his last faithful gasp stretched his gallant limbs, stark and cold, at his pitying master's feet, when naught of sorrow or despair could avail to rouse him,—and the young man dashed his hand to his brow.

"Adelaide! Adelaide! look yonder! It is, indeed good bye forever, and I hope, for your sake, I may never see you again."

"Rutland, you do not love me," she cried, with bitter passion, but seeing that the young man turned from her, she sprang towards him with a great fear in her hear

"Let me save you from one plunge in the depths of misery," she cried, as, unbuttoning his coat, she drew from its little resting place, the deadly toy, with glitter-ing muzzle, which, with steady hand, she pointed at her own white brow.

"Remember," she cried, with bloodless lips, "that I keep it always, and no sooner do you attempt to end your life than this will also stop the heart beats of your once loved Adelaide!"

Ere the revolver had been lowered, ere the blood had crept timidly back to her lips and cheeks, her lover had sped away, leaving her to face alone whatever the future held of good or evil for her.

But in Rutland Borradale's ear, as he went, came the low murmur of her voice:

"I shall wait for you! You will return and find me waiting."

CHAPTER III.

A QUEEN OF BEAUTY.

In the March of 18—, four years later than the events we have just described, there were invitations issued for a ball at No. 67 Boulevarde d'Igliamento, in the centre of the most fashionable quarter of Brussels, and all the wealth and beauty of the kingdom were expected to grace it *en masse.*

High hopes and aspirations were based upon the coming fête; it was to be one of the most brilliant events of the season, the military were to be represented by the handsome 2d Lancers and the dashing "Guides," to the thrilling strains of whose band the guests would dance ; and numerous and interesting were the conjectures amongst the daughters of beauty as to which of them should on that occasion bear off the coveted palm for unrivalled loveliness.   Alas ! many were to be the holocausts sacrificed on the altar of Venus for that event, and in consequence, many were the victims to tradesmen's bills who passed an uncomfortable cycle before and after the 18th.

All the illustrious houses of the capital had their guests, and amongst the most honored were those of the great "Banking Baron," who at present was doing the honors of his princely mansion to the Marchioness of Ripdale, one of the most renowned beauties of Europe, and to whom all conceded the title of "loveliest of her sex" wherever she appeared.   Little doubt had she or indeed any one else, that her triumph at this ball would be unexceptional, and that so long as she was present, no other beauty could be looked at. So accustomed was she to "come, and see and conquer!"

"We understand," said the beautiful Marchioness, one morning over her matinal ortolan to her host, the Baron de Rothsleind, "though indeed, merely from the vaguest rumor that there is at the Castle of Montelarde, a rather good looking girl, totally unknown in society, not presented at Court either in England or Belgium, who, in a word, is an American, and who, owing to her wealth, might be quite a feature of our little entertainment, Baron, so we might stretch a point and have her. But I fear sadly," she added, "it will be a case of too many millions, a very little of good looks, and nothing about her that could be termed 'chic.' However, we must complain of nothing, she can stand alone, as her wealth lends her ample attraction."

And while her host is dispatching the invitations to the Castle of Montelarde, the spoiled beauty turns to the satisfactory contemplation of her own unrivalled charms in the handsome pier glasses which abound around her.

The night of the 18th, and evening! Ten o'clock had struck in the old halls of Montelarde, and the party from the castle had not yet started, although the drive into town was more than sixteen miles.

"The horses will do it in no time," calmly asserted Monsieur de Montespaire. "They have had nothing to do for a week."

He might as well have been philosophical over the matter. Who can describe the thrill of excitement and delight, the bustle, the rushing to and fro, the endless adjusting of trifles; in a word, the infinite pleasure that reigns in the ladies' boudoir the hour before the ball.

Who, on the contrary, can paint, too, dismally the *ennui* of the gentlemen's apartments during the same hour; the standing in draughts, the gloomy endeavors to find cigars, the heavy penalty of arranging a cravat, the humiliation of looking for a pin, followed by the odious perplexity of not knowing what must be done with that pin.

Yes, for the gentlemen, undoubtedly this is the supremely miserable hour of their lives, whilst for the ladies it holds complete bliss.

Madame de Montespaire was still hurrying to and fro in her gorgeous attire of black velvet and silk, trimmed elegantly with a thousand pounds' worth of Brussels lace. Diamonds adorned her comely neck, and a tiara of handsome emeralds and diamonds sparkled in her hair, whilst in her bosom blazed the superb bloom of a single scarlet cactus.

And the while in her elegant boudoir sat Elra Brookley, with curl-caressed brow leaning on her jeweled hand, entirely oblivious of passing events, wholly indifferent to the coming hour and its requirements.

"I have been loved—yes, I have been adored by one handsome as a young god! Loved!" she murmured, as with dreamy eyes she looked out over the lake, where in the darkling shadows the queenly swans glided in and out among the waxen water lilies and tangled reeds. "Yes, loved! Have I not felt it in the tremble of his hand, as his dark eye met mine; felt it in the passionate quiver of his whole frame as his lips have brushed mine. Yea, have I not read it writ in his eyes—those glorious eyes which, looking solemnly, wonderingly into the chaos of the future, I have seen sublime with the dark, thrilling passion which might have lived in David's as he approached with rapturous intent to slay Goliath—those eyes which, speaking back to me, were all of tenderness and worship, as beneath their heavy shade of lashes they sparkled and glinted and kindled as the deep waters under the starlight, until they were very dangerous for lovely woman to get lost in their seductive depths.

" Yes, dangerous for others, but not for me, for we are beloved of one another—we have plighted faith to one another forever and ever !"

But here she brushed her curls from her brow and sighed.

" Could he but be here to-night ! Could he but assure me that his love is as ardent yet as it was in those happy days ! But he is not rich, and they will not have asked him. Poor Rutland !" she cried, flinging impatiently from her the diamond crescents that her maid had supposed would sparkle superbly that night in her dark wealth of hair.

" What avail to look handsome to-night ? He will not be present, and I shall be alone to enjoy my little triumphs, or to howl over my big miseries, as the case may be. Come !" she cried, as a tap at the door reminded her that however much she might fondly imagine she would be quite alone that evening, her brisk little maid intended quickly to disturb all such visions by taking absolute possession of her person in order to put the finishing touches to her ball-room toilet.

Fortunately the maid was not as indifferent on the subject as was her mistress, with the result that, after clusters of sapphires and handsome diamonds had been fastened here and there with the entire independence of a daughter of America, and when her exquisite gown of palest blue, trimmed with the softest blue-fox fur, which looked chic and decidedly handsome against the ivory whiteness of her neck, had been adjusted to satisfaction, Elra Brookley was indeed a vision fit to make many a female breast throb with indignant envy and astonishment.

It was a brilliant assemblage that burst upon their view as the party from Montelarde entered the crowded ball-room. A waltz had just terminated, and the promenade towards the supper room had begun. In a word, everybody seemed intent upon his or her own particular business or pleasure; but one magic whispered word brought again a rush and a crush, and a polite scramble to the centre of the hall, where Elra Brookley and her queenly chaperone were advancing up the polished floor to greet their hostess. Eyes were strained, heads were turned, glasses lowered, and through the groups on all sides there crept a thrill, a shiver, almost an expressed groan of entirely satisfied wonderment.

"The heiress!" was breathed from lip to lip.

"Can it be possible? There must be a mistake."

"One would be inclined not to credit her wealth with such good looks."

"However, the Banking Baron is a good voucher for that."

Such were the remarks that were rife on all sides as Elra swept up the hall, with the calm dignity of good

breeding, unconscious of, or perhaps more truly indifferent to the effect she was producing, when suddenly,
standing out from the rest of the crowd, she caught
sight of a face that brought a tinge of deeper color to
her cheek ; a face remarkable for nothing so much as a
pair of marvellously soft gray eyes, which answered hers
with all the enthusiastic adoration of a schoolboy. Yes!
Elra's eyes could not refrain from telling their pleasure
at seeing a friend of olden times in Murray Oresenworth,
for, down in Montelarde, hemmed in amongst the towering mountains and purple peaks, she had perhaps of late
felt a little lonely and just a little lost.

"He will be sure," thought she, "to have news from
Rutland. I am so glad he has come."

It was thus, as the startled light of surprise and
pleasure shone in her glorious eyes, that De Monteford,
a supercilious old roue, well known in most of the
fashionable clubs of Brussels, Paris, and even London,
with all the impertinence of his class, levelled his glasses
at the advancing form of the heiress, and professed his
marked admiration with all the savor of a connoisseur.

"By Jove," cried he, in an insolent drawl, "she wears
her wealth as another woman would her diamonds,
merely to crown her beauty. But," added he, with a
marked curl of his close-shaven lip, "the auctioneering
is low at present. She may be knocked down to an
earl.'

And forthwith he dismissed from his mind all thoughts
on so trivial a subject.

The next dance on the programme was a set of lancers,
and in this Elra took a part with some person of note
whose name she did not even care to enquire. She

knew he was an English "lord," a fact which made him
intolerable in her estimation. Now, Elra Brookley's
ideas on this subject were somewhat eccentric, and
showed an amount of old-fashioned independence, quite
incomprehensible, and sad to behold in so well bred a
young person.

She had once met a young Englishman of the genus
"lord," who in the superb pride of aristocracy had related to her how the "pork-dealers' daughters" were
having it all their own way amongst the English swells;
and forthwith she had settled it definitely in her mind
that she should loathe England's wooden swelldom.

"I almost fancy," she said to herself, "that I could
hate even Rutland if he were one of those titled eye-glass
wearing Englishmen.   And yet, if any one has an air of
breeding and of class about him, it is Rutland.   I suppose with my amount of money I shall be looked down
upon for choosing a plain Mr. Anybody, no matter how
distinguished that Mr. Anybody may be; but, after all,
other people's pity cannot make me unhappy with Rutland."

In the meantime whilst Elra, with intensely bored expression—the "lord" admired her all the more for it, it
was a sign of breeding he thought—was pacing through
the dance, Murray Cresenworth had been doing his best
to get close to Elra, and at the conclusion of the lancers
did actually contrive to carry her off—most willingly on
her part—for the following waltz, despite the looks of
hostility and entreaty respectively, succeeding each other
on the peer's face.

Murray's arm was on her waist, her hand clasped his,
whilst the music rose and fell in passionate or languishing

cadence, and away they floated, threading their way amidst clouds of tulle and laces, as free from jostle by Murray's superior guidance as though they sailed alone upon an open sea, with thoughts for nothing save the voluptuous swell of the music and the enthralling pleas- ure of the hour.

Such a pair of graceful dancers could not fail to be the cynosure of many admiring glances, and of some very envious ones.

Amongst others who watched these dancers in partic- ular were a very portly dowager, and her two rather well favored daughters, who were temporarily enjoying a rest.

" Why Marie, my daughter, what has become of your *jeun Americain!* I was beginning to imagine, and not without reason, that he was very much *epris.* Am I to understand that you and he have quarrelled ? "

Now, on the day preceding this important event, it must be told that Pauline, Odile and Marie, three sisters, and Madame de la Roche, their mother, had assembled to debate about the coming ball; they had arranged about dresses, about partners, about business. Each one had been alloted a certain line to pursue; Pauline deter- mines to attack a very rich widower, Odile is apportioned some younger prey, and, last of all, Marie is lectured.

"You, Marie," said the wise Pauline, "must secure Monsieur Cresenvort, he is immensly rich, and seems to care for you. He is, besides, young, ardent and very impressionable. You ought to be able to do it."

"I fear not," said Marie, diffidently; "he rather ad- mires Mademoiselle Berthe."

"Pooh, she is as cold and as dull as stone, and as hideous as an Egyptian mummy. She will not stand in your way with so brilliant and witty a person as Monsieur Cresenvort, be assured, Marie!"

"I like Monsieur Cresenvort very much," responded Marie, still unconvinced, "but I fear he is too gay and too charming for me."

"You are pretty," retorted her sister impatiently, "do as we advise you, or you will be very ungrateful."

And this then was the reason why in Marie's bright eyes lingered the air of the conqueror, as she sat by her mother watching the latest arrival, which happened to be Madame de Montclarde and her beautiful charge; she, Marie, had been dancing since she entered the rooms with that *ravissant* Monsieur Cresenvort.

"Three dances in succession," cried her sister Odile enthusiastically, "and see how wickedly those girls yonder are looking at you. You are a darling wicked little coquette, Marie."

"Mamma," said Marie deprecatingly, "I trust it will not look too marked but as Monsieur Cresenvort has asked me for the thirteenth dance, which is one of the evening's prettiest waltzes, I suppose I may stretch a point and dance it with him?"

"Then," came the quick rejoinder, "be sure you secure the fourteenth and endeavor to sit out the fifteenth with him."

"Perhaps," said Marie, with a quick gasp of horror at sight of their proposed victim skimming past on the polished floor with his arm on the waist of an unutterably lovely girl, wholly unknown to her or her sisters.

Yes, away glided those two happy dancers, dreamers

they were then, up and down and around they went as though they could never tire; till at last among the fern-decked archways and the dim lights, they disappeared altogether; and, I would not like to say positively, but I am inclined to fear, that the thirteenth waltz and its engagements were totally forgotten by some one, who as the outraged Marie presumed, with much indignation, ought to have known better.

"How decidedly frowsy our dancers are beginning to look, Baron;" remarked the Marchioness of Ripdale to her host, as they sat at the reserved supper table at the end of the great dining hall, whereon nothing but silver and the richest cut glasses sparkled under their wealth of vine-leaf and fruit, quaking jelly, cheese cake, and marron-glacé; and where in quick succession, pate de foie gras, chicken salads, cold duck, ortolans or wood cock, chased each other at the behest of the apparently unappreciative gourmands.

"But there is a complexion yonder of pure alabaster; how refreshing it is in its positively dazzling whiteness, after all those horrors of the ball room. My brain may have been softened by your excellent wines, Baron, but it appears to me impossible to explain, why people will dance if it mars their beauty."

"Oh, easily explained, dear Marchioness, they have none to lose. There are but five perfectly beautiful women in the whole of Europe, and of these only one has deigned to grace my rooms with her presence to-night. She however will ever be more esteemed than all the others.

"Baron, you are a Parisian, and you wrong your guests, especially she of the Grecian brow and marble-white skin; and, positively, if I am to enjoy another morsel of your excellent supper, I must have that refreshingly perfect face opposite me. But who is the goddess with the handsome shadowy eyes and keen eagle brows? The type is so decidedly new that I wonder where she can have brought her good looks from?"

"From the other side of the Atlantic, I presume."

"Ah, the handsome heiress!" she exclaimed languidly as she toyed with her marron-glacé; it will amuse me to make the acquaintance of a Texan or a Nevada goldmine girl, they are said to be original."

Beauty is almost always attracted towards beauty, and the English marchioness and the American heiress, after a pleasant conversation over their dainty suppers, were prepared to offer to each other as sincere and pretty a little hand of friendship as could be exchanged between two ladies reared under such widely different circumstances.

Had Elra Brookley been an Englishwoman she would have enquired the maiden name of the young marchioness whose beauty was inspiring the fashionable world with wonder; she would have placed herself in possession of the antecedents, the past history, and, in a word, all that was known about the young peeress both before and after her marriage.

But not being English, Elra Brookley lay languidly back amongst the soft cushions of the carriage as they drove homeward in the cold gray light of morning, and gave no more than perhaps a passing thought to those haunting eyes, to those lips molded for passion, to that brow of snow; but the recollection of them came to her mind coupled always with an indefinable dread rather than with any real pleasure.

"Thank heaven," she murmured, "he has been spared having ever had her beauty near him to tempt him to madness and passion."

And yet as she thought thus, she trembled, for simultaneously came to her the recollection of a strange event which had happened that evening.

During supper, Elra had noticed that the Marchioness of Ripdale wore a very handsome bracelet, to which was suspended a very small locket. This locket, unperceived by its owner, had become detached from the bracelet, and slipped among the cut glass ornaments of the table. As Elra picked it up and handed it back to the Marchioness, her face grew, for a moment, deadly pale; for in that pretty, jewel-trimmed locket she saw a face startlingly like that of the man she loved to distraction, though more boyish, with his curly locks and starry eyes, than her Rutland; but looking again, she found the face in the locket distinctly different from Rutland's, and she breathed more freely. And yet she could not put the thought of that face in the locket from her mind.

"What if it should be his face after all, hanging there at that beautiful peeress' wrist, perhaps placed there by himself! But no, it was not his face! It was entirely different, and if it had been, how could it have come there?"

And thus, torn by unhappy doubts and terrors, she fell into a troubled slumber whilst the carriage moved onward through the fresh morning air.

At the same time the Marchioness in the seclusion of

her silk-draped boudoir, sighed as she looked at that
boyish face in her little locket.

"I wonder," thought she, "was he angry or rejoiced
when he at length sought home expecting to find me
waiting, and found me —— ah!" she looked down at her
wedding ring and shuddered. "I never loved but him,
and him I have myself thrown aside! Well," she continued, with a little frosty laugh, "be it so! I must
now only fill the blank in my life by making all men *my*
playthings!"

"What is that, dear?" said her husband, rejoining
her at this moment. "You seem happy for so early an
hour in the day."

"I was thinking, dear," rejoined his loving spouse,
"how well you danced that hornpipe! It is incredible
for a man of your size and age."

With this parting shot, which she knew would prove
spicy to the middle-aged, rotund marquis, she threw herself amid the satin cushions of the lounge and exhibited
a reprehensible determination not to vouchsafe another
word to her lord and master.

CHAPTER IV.

IN THE PERFUMED PINE WOODS.

Many weeks had passed since Elra had been so universally accorded the palm for matchless beauty at the ball given by the Baron de Rothsleind in Brussels, and since then she had lingered on in the lovely old castle of Montelarde as the pampered guest of Madame de Montespaire and her husband.

"We had grown so old, dear, before you came, and now you are here we live once more and are young again; so, *cherie*, do not ask to fly from us," was reiterated so often by her handsome hostess who found in Elra's visit an excuse for gaieties long unheard of at the castle that Elra was not loathe to prolong her stay.

"So good of you to tolerate a humdrum existence like ours, at this dull old castle, but we must see what we can do to enliven you," her host would venture sometimes; but this really meant that he would as usual plunge into his daily paper, leaving to his wife the cares of thinking out the subject in question and of following it up, if she cared to, which arrangement met with the said wife's thorough approval.

Thus many was the brilliant *fete* where Elra wielded the sceptre of the courted Queen of Beauty, repeating her triumphs o'er and o'er, and without number were her worshippers who lingered always around her, ready to anticipate her most trivial wish. Amongst these was

Murray Cresenworth, who had gained the much coveted
privilege of calling every now and again to attend Elra
in her rambles on horseback or on foot.

Elra being in the position of a young woman whose af-
fections were engaged elsewhere was rather inclined to
ridicule his devotion and yet, like any daughter of Eve,
when all was said and done, she had, be it understood, a
kind of sneaking affection for this young American whose
enthusiastic admiration was preposterous and absurd, but
who, nevertheless, had brought her good news from *him*
on the night of the Baron de Rothsleind's ball.

That news whispered in her ear had made her to tread
on air for many a day after, and, strange to say, it was
oftentimes that the young man had to repeat those whispered words in their long rambles together, when they
so often watched the sunbeams as they shot aslant on
the waters at their feet, or the purple clouds of sunset
clustering about the falling disc of gold, or, again, the
gaunt shadows of the mountains falling dark and gloomy
across the valley.

Once, indeed, he had surprised her amongst the fern,
where couched the timid deer, with a letter in her hand
and with so soft, so tender a smile on her lip, and in her
brimming eye, that he had timidly asked the reason.

"Oh, Mr. Cresenworth, such news!" cried she gaily.
"Rutland is coming. Read for yourself," and she
handed him the letter which ran briefly as follows:

My Beloved One:

I am starting to see you at last, and I tremble with joy
when I think of our approaching meeting. Remember.
darling, your sweet promise. I shall call you little wife
three days after I rejoin you, and be true to the man who
adores you.

It was signed with his initials, R. B.

How selfish love and prosperity is apt to make the best of us. Elra, tender of thought and word to a degree at other times, now glanced at her companion, eagerly and selfishly expecting naught but gladness and sympathy in his glance, but she certainly was not prepared for the change that had transformed his ordinarily cheery face in hue from its healthy red to the cold, ashen gray of a snow-charged sky.

His secret stood revealed, and for the first time she felt in her heart a twinge of pity for her victim.

"Forgive me," she breathed, softly, with a note of pain in her voice. "I did not know—I never believed—"

What she did or did not believe, never transpired, for at that moment occurred something which strongly diverted their thoughts from the point in question.

Ere Murray could command himself sufficiently to utter some sarcastic word expressive of how very indifferent he felt as to anything that might occur to his lovely companion in the matter of her marrying Rutland Borradale or any other man, Elra's dainty parasol, whether premeditated on her part or by accident, got carried away by the wind, and ended up in the water at their feet, where they were compelled to watch it getting sucked and crushed to atoms amongst the rocks.

"How awkward of me to have allowed it to go," said Murray, with deep contrition, quite forgetting the sarcasm he had been planning, and instead he looked for forgiveness in her radiant happy eyes.

"It is not to be regretted at all," she cried gaily. "It will merely be an excuse to go to town for a new one."

All very well such stoicism on Elra's part, but now occurred the difficulty of how the heiress could possibly walk the length of three fields, much less all the way back to the castle, without a sunshade.

"It is not to be thought of," cried Murray, determinedly, and it was forthwith settled that the gentleman should hurry homeward and from thence bring the carriage to meet her, with a relay of sunshades whose number would allow for any more accidents. With a little wave of her handkerchief, Elra watched her cavalier disappearing amongst the trees, and then, with the wild buoyancy of spirits known only to youth and pleasure and love, she danced along the pathway towards the lake, humming to a sweet air, well known at that time:

> "She took three paces through the room,
> She saw the water-lily bloom,
> She saw the helmet and the plume,
>   She looked down to Camelot.
>
> Out flew the web, and floated wide;
> The mirror cracked from side to side;
> 'The curse is come upon me,' cried
>   The lady of Shalott."
>   —*Tennyson.*

"Poor thing," mused Elra, "to have her life's happiness wrecked by one glance. I wonder," she continued, "if it could ever possibly be that at one glance of mine the world and the sea and the sky will change in a moment and become everything that is horrible and bitter and miserable. Impossible! Impossible!" she cried. But she shuddered, nevertheless, as she thought of it.

It was a lovely view which burst upon her sight, as she cleared the pine and oak woods fringing the water's brink at this particular point. Beyond lay a beautifully wooded valley in the heart of the Ardenne country, hemmed in by the towering crags and lofty peaks of Brumenwœfel, bordered by the majestic forests ; a sunlit valley where nestled the little watering town of Vielsalm, guarded on all sides by its protecting centaurs.

At Elra's feet, on the placid bosom of the lake, the golden water lilies were peeping above the wave, their juicy fresh green leaves spanning the glassy surface of the mere ; water spiders skated here and there, revelling in the glowing sunbeams ; beauties melted into beauties, and all in nature breathed of harmony and gladness. She watched the shepherds on the distant hills collect their flocks ; she saw the huntsmen emerge from out the gloom of the forest trees, with their powder horns and game flung across their shoulders ; and lower down, amongst the willows near the river that fed the little lake, and scarce at a stone's cast from her side, she saw —what was it that made her start so ?—she saw a form, perfect in its manly symmetry and beauty, and the next moment she had sprung to her feet from the tangle of reeds and kingcups, amongst which she crouched, with a little half-strangled cry of delight, for she saw Rutland Borradale advancing down the pathway to greet her.

"Yet, no ! He has not seen me yet," she murmured. "He is on his way to the castle, and must needs pass this way ; so I shall wait and see his startled look with —shall it be surprise ? Shall it be pleasure ?" she asked of herself jealously, as half hidden by the clustering pine trees she waited for—she knew not what ; waited for that which she would rather she had never known.

Yes ! Her face blanched and became set as marble, as she perceived that Rutland Borradale—her Rutland—

was not alone in his quiet ramble; that his deep, tender tones were answered by a woman's voice.

And yet, after all, they were but groundless fears that assailed her, for although she had not yet seen the lady who accompanied Rutland, one glance at his curling lip and cold contemptuous eye sufficed to reassure her.

"Where have I heard that voice before?" she cried, in startled tones, as, advancing down the pathway, their voices became more and more distinct, until she could catch the very words they spoke.

"Things have fared well with your ladyship since that day," was heard, in the sarcastic tones of the young man.

"Yes; fortune has in a way smiled on me," she answered, sadly; "but you, the friend and companion of my girlhood, have condemned me to a loveless life."

"In your estimation, perhaps, to condemn you to poverty might have proved a worse sin. Yes, you may be thankful your lot is cast as it is."

"Rutland, you know I am not thankful."

"You are not thankful for anything, then."

"You are heartless!"

The unknown, advancing around a corner in the winding pathway, now suddenly emerged into view.

There in the sunshine, standing amongst the quaking reeds and shimmering aspens, she confronted the man who walked by her side, with a look brimming with reproach and—and love. It was the deep fire of a fathomless love that spoke from her magnificent eyes as she stood where the blue-eyed forget-me-nots in the marsh lands and the kingcups and golden iris made a carpet of flowers for her dainty feet.

And this lady, who and what was she? One with the lithe, willowy grace of a princess born to rule, one endowed with all the exquisite tenderness and sweet sympathy of womanhood—a woman with a neck like a swan and sweet, deep, pensive eyes, velvety and dark, and mysterious as the waters which gurgled and ebbed on the lake's flowery margin. Soft and white were the water-lilies she had plucked and fastened at her throat, but more like the driven snow was her classic brow, more lovely than all nature's other charms was the naturally rich.blush that lingered in her dimpling cheek.

Who and what was she?

She was, in a word, Adelaide, Marchioness of Ripdale.

She whom of all women Elra had most wished could never be thrown in Rutland's path to tempt him with her glorious beauty; and here she was deep in the heart of the lonely woods at Champisnay with him as her only attendant, and, whether by design or otherwise, this meeting had been effected Elra did not dare to ask herself.

"Rutland," said the woman, standing in his pathway, "do you remember the lakes at the Abbey and our happy life amongst the heathery haunts of the coot and waterfowl, where we used to catch the little fish and trap the frogs and water rats?" Then, seeing he turned his head away, she added:

"Can you forget?"

The last words were spoken so slowly, so softly, with such a passionate ring of regret that even Elra, listening, thought, with a twinge of pain, that they sounded sweet as the wanton zephyrs playing among the harp-strings of old.

Yes! alas! to see Adelaide was to love her, and slowly
Rutland's hand went out to her's in reconciliation, their
eyes met and lingered—and something there was in that
prolonged glance that made the unhappy watcher recoil
as though struck by an invisible hand.

"O God!" came in broken accents from her stone cold
lips, "I have been strangely mistaken! His words, his
looks were false. He loved me not. He never, never
loved me. How could I have imagined it so?"

"Yes," continued Adelaide, "as brother and sister
were we then and we were happy dreamers; but now
you have grown to love the light of other eyes and they
have grown for you lovely as the starry midnight.
Whilst I——"

"Adelaide!" he cried, imperiously, but now she turned
from him.

With the quick daring of a blinded, long-suppressed
passion he drew the queenly head to his breast and
looked long and searchingly in her eyes.

"Adelaide," he cried, his tall, manly form quivering
from head to foot, in every fibre, in every muscle. "I
know of no loveliness to equal the unholy depths of
darkness, the unfathomable mystery of your eyes."

"What can their unfathomable mysteries mean for
you?" she breathed, with a ring of almost defiance in her
tones.

"The fire in your eyes, Adelaide, has made the starlight of my boyhood! The passion-flame living in them
now must be the beacon to wreck or save my manhood!
Which will——"

But the strain upon that listener amongst the trees
was too much; in that moment, seeing what she saw,

something seemed to tear her heart down, down, down; and she knew that all of golden happiness and sweet love and faith had gone from her life forever. With not so much as a murmur, therefore, she fell nervelessly in the rank and tangled grasses, her senses gradually leaving her until all became cloudy and indistinct and her limbs grew to the coldness of marble.

CHAPTER V.

A QUESTION AND ITS ANSWER.

"Who and what was Adelaide, Marchioness of Rip-dale, before her marriage?"

The question was calmly addressed by Elra Brookley to her hostess next morning as that lady and she linger-ed over a late breakfast. Murray Cresenworth was also there, toying with some game pie and other dainties, and making a brave show of being ravenous, although in truth he had not touched any food that morning. He had been coaxed into staying at the Castle for the night, and could not sleep for the haunting thought of Elra's dead white face, and icy hand, last evening when he had rejoined her in the woods by the lake. Something, he told himself, had transpired to have effected so start-ling and sad a change in Elra's whole being, something very untoward it must have been, for her spirits of the morning would have enabled her to have shaken off any-thing trivial; and Murray's brain was exercised vainly to fathom the difficulty. This morning, too, the cold list-lessness of her manner would give one the idea that her very heart was dead within her, that she cared for nothing like she did yesterday morning, that in fact the world had come to a standstill for her.

Could it be she has seen Borradale, or what can have happened? thought Murray; he gave little cre-dence to her explanation of having fallen asleep in the woods, and having been awakened by his calling her by name, when he had almost despaired of finding her.

"You look cold this morning, dear," said Madame de Montespaire, kindly. "I fear that you must have taken a chill yesterday during your nap in the woods. About the lovely Marchioness, did you ask me? Why dear, she was the daughter of a man of wealth and note, whose name I don't remember, and was reared in the lap of luxury. She was a famous shot, a dashing horsewoman; and, by the way, that reminds me," she said, addressing Murray, "did she not, or was it only rumor, get a young man of good standing, Borradale his name was, a nephew of the Earl of Darcliffe, I think, into rather an ugly pickle by one of her usual daring feats of horsemanship. I never heard the rights of the story, but I believe it was risky in more ways than one. She rode in Darcliffe races in a jockey's colors and costume, pulled her horse, which chanced to be the favorite, and designedly lost the race. Young Borradale was made accountable by the jockey club for the misdemeanor, as it was he who had abetted the fraud, by giving her the mount on the favorite."

The story of any little scandal never loses its piquant flavor, so long as there is a woman to recount it. At the name of Borradale Elra gave a painful start, but seeing, or feeling rather, that Cresenworth's eyes were on her, she asked calmly.

"Borradale is then the name of this nephew of the Earl of Darcliffe?"

"Yes, dear, and I believe he has been greatly impoverished since then, as his uncle has cast him off, and it was this that induced the present Marchioness to give him up without another thought, for I believe they were rather attached to each other previously, and in fact had run wild as boy and girl together."

She might have rambled on forever, as Elra was too much crushed apparently to allow of her uttering a syllable, and Murray's breath being fairly taken away by the news, each word of which he felt drove a dagger through the gentle womanly heart beating within a few paces of him; but Monsieur de Montespaire, who despised late breakfasts in the abstract, and all who took part in them, entered at this moment with a gun in his hand.

"Ready for the chase, eh, Cresenworth? If you care to come, I have a good double barrel at your disposal, and we can have some good sport through our patches of forestland."

But our carpet knight, after timidly consulting Elra's eyes, in which he read something of encouragement, preferred to linger with the ladies. Everything that he could possibly devise was done during the course of that morning to chase the cloud from Elra's brow, and with such success that at length her little ripples of laughter sounded nearly as bright and ringing as ever. It was in this happier frame of mind, into which his gay repartee had coaxed Elra, that Murray and she strolled down the avenue with the arching trees overhead, and the wind soughing in the branches, prepared, as they were fully, to enjoy the lovely summer weather in each other's company.

However they were destined to have a slight break in the monotony of so delightful a programme, for coming towards them from the tower gate which guarded the entrance to the demense, they perceived a young man, whose steps were hastened as he caught sight of them.

It was Rutland Borradale.

They met, and Murray watched Elra Brookley's face keenly, but it was not to be read. With a happy little ripple of laughter she extended her hand to their visitor, and the next few minutes were made very bright with allusions to pleasant memories, and delightful anecdotes, and repartee from all sides. Then, in a lull of the conversation, Rutland Borradale, turning towards Elra, with eyes that softened with deepest tenderness, as he saw her fresh young beauty looking lovlier than perhaps ever before, under the swaying boughs of the blossom heaped chestnuts.

"You got my letter I see by your answer, but you did not tell me half what I longed to know," he whispered, bending towards her, but loud enough for Cresenworth to hear.

"Will you grant me a delicious long afternoon alone at your feet, dearest?" This was breathed very low, but sweet and clear as a bell rang her careless answer.

"The horses await us at the door; Mr. Cresenworth and I have an engagement to ride this afternoon."

For a moment he was staggered by her answer, and grew pale to the lips, his eyes darkening in anger, but the next instant he had forced himself to be calm, and drawing himself up proudly, he lifted his hat with all the freezing hauteur which the bluest blood of England can best assume at will.

"It must be as you decide," and in a moment he had turned on his heel.

"Ah," thought Murray, drawing a deeper breath than usual, "it is as I conjectured."

CHAPTER VI.

A WOMAN'S RESOLUTION.

How tiny, how inconceivably small is our human
nature with its aspirations, its pursuits, its little glories,
its trials, its infinitesimal sufferings. Look out through
the cold twilight at the grey villages clustering about
the mountain's brow; what a speck each hut; what
a palmful each village. Yet within. those huts live
human beings, taller, stronger, perhaps more noble than
we who survey them. Within those villages palpitates
the heart, the strength, the stir, the workings of human
life. And far, far above all, the immense Being who guides
and doubtless looks down, and if his eye were not All-
seeing, would that Eye detect us in our sufferings; if His
mind were not all perceiving, would he ken that we poor
beings lived, or groaned, or toiled?

And we, perhaps, if we sometimes soared beyond our little
lives on looking back, how much of poignancy would our
griefs and miseries lose from the far off sphere from
which we might survey them. But it is hard to rise
thus above the cruelties and griefs of life, and in the
ocean of sublimity forget them.

Somewhat of these saddening realities passed through
Elra's mind, as with a feeling of utter loneliness she stole
down toward where a line of poplars marked the progress of the brook watering the lawn at Montelarde. It
was a balmy summer afternoon; scarce a ripple of wind

was there to stir the leaves of the poplars that shivered through the calmest day. The shade of the oaks was dark and cool, and the sweet smelling hay was freshly strewn upon the sward, when, with a novel in her hand, she lay down upon the rugs and cushions provided by the attentive Cresenworth and began to read some of Madame's light literature. She had complained of headache through the morning and had entreated for a rest in the long and sultry afternoon, when Madame would be making a somewhat distant call; and now with heavy lids, which unwillingly did their duty, she crept languidly through a page of a very racy French novel. Gradually her eyelids drooped and she listened with a shudder to the dismally weird sound amongst the poplars. Those ghostly trees that in the cold twilight freeze the blood with suggestions of the suicide and midnight murder, which they appear to have seen enacted beneath their branches and for which they seemed ever to shiver and weep. Elra revelled in the gloomy thoughts brought by the tremor of those silver-grey leaves. There is always a certain pleasure in sharing Nature's gloom, very different from the endurance of one's own sorrow. Elra was awakened from her reverie by a footfall on the turf beside, and a voice ringing in her ears, a voice that was always destined to thrill her. "Alone!" She did not need to raise her head to recognize the intruder. Too well she knew the well-built frame and the face which charmed, though scarcely more handsome than manly looking. There are those who hold that grey eyes are treacherous. Certain it is they have the greatest power to soften or darken, to lighten or harden, of any color, be it brown, blue or black. Dark grey starry eyes, which

changed with every word, a well cut profile and, sur-
passing all, a sensitive sweetness of expression playing
around the full, ripe lips, about which lurked great capa-
bility for humor. Such were the features whose memory
came crowding back to Elra as she, with determined
bent head and averted eyes, caught his first low words.
"Elra," he said in sorrowful tones, which brought her
back to the happy days, when together they had chased
the pretty corn-crakes through the meadows at Offington,
irrespective of damage done to the silvery grasses;
"you are cold as an iceberg; why?"

A little tearless sob broke from her as she viewed him,
tall and manly looking, with his thrilling, soft eyes bent
in pleading to hers, and not venturing, as was his wont,
to touch her hand with ever so timid a caress, or to pass
his fingers with even the gentlest tenderness through her
braided locks. Catching no answer from her lips he bent
low over her, till his whispered words reached her ear:

"Have you forgotten your love?"

His hand was laid on her shoulder with what she chose
to deem the tenderness of an elder brother for the sister
of whom he is proud. That gentle caress as he well knew,
could not fail to thrill her, and half unwillingly she raised
her eyes to his. Yes, Rutland Borradale she knew had
power to kill all that was lovely, and sweet, and bright
in her life, to turn all things forever to blackest night.
She knew she worshipped this young man standing
above her with a love which is known but once in a lifetime, and which, when killed, drags down the heart to
bitter death or rather petrefaction unfailing with it.

"Rutland!" His name broke from her lips in a half
groan, and shuddering with pain as she looked at him,

she crouched lower on the ground at his feet. In an instant he was on his knees with his arm about her.

"Elra, what is it grieves you?" he murmured gently; but recoiling from his caress she sprang to her feet.

"By what right does your arm encircle me now?" she said with mocking curl of the lip. "By the right of love, I suppose. Elra," he cried in scathing tones, "I must conclude that you are not your usual self to-day." Then with all his manly dignity reasserting itself, he added: "I suppose you remember that you have promised to be my wife?" "I remember, ah, too well! Rutland," she said, more gently, choking back a sob, "it is only fair to you that our engagement shall from this moment be canceled. This is yours," as she drew the crescent of diamonds from her finger. "From this hour your love can fly untrammeled whither it wills.

"And the meaning of this?" "That can be told in four words, you yourself wish it." "And my answer lies in three, I do not." "You do not love me, Rutland?" The question was breathed in fear and the answer came slowly, calmly, coldly, "I do not." Something seemed to strike her as with a glove of steel and she staggered, but raising her eyes bravely to his she asked: "Then, why dare you to wish that our lives should be joined?" "Because you yourself wish it," he rejoined coolly. With flashing eye and flushed cheek she drew herself up proudly. "Coward," she cried, "I would rather see myself dead than be your wife" A dark light sprang into his eyes as he seized her hands and held them forcibly at her side whilst they looked into each other's eyes with all the darkest passions that human hearts can know. "You are mad," he cried; "what has come

to you ? You have loved me, you love me still, as only a
true, brave, loyal woman can, and you dare to tell me,
' go, I will have you no longer by my side.' " Here he
paused and his tone softened. " You have said it once;
but dare you say it again." His hand released hers,
his arm stole around her neck and his eyes sought hers
in the mute eloquence that he was perfectly aware never
failed to thrill her, and for one weak, delicious moment
hers answered his.

He had conquered ; he knew he held her captive once
again in that moment of sweet intoxication, and she
trembled as she remembered all, and thought of her
resolution so weak, so weak when his soft eye held hers
in thrall.

"Rutland, " she breathed, " you have been so cruel, so
treacherous —— "

"Anything else, darling?" he whispered, interrupting
her catalogue of his virtues. His cheek was now pressed against hers, his eyes dancing with humor, his temper unruffled as ever.

This was the man who with his pliant, ever-ready smile
had stolen the entirety of her essentially womanly heart,
leaving, alas, the dire consequences of that heft to be
learned only long years after.

The poor little struggling bird taken in the net which
her wings with all their little fluttering efforts could
not break, as a last resource, called to her help all her
resolution. She thought of all her vows, never to rejoice in
her recreant lover's smile again, never to allow her pulses
to throb as his lips met hers ; she thought of all this and
of all that was past, and with a superb effort she drew
herself away from his arms as she thought forever.

"Rutland," she said firmly, "our wedding will never take place; it is impossible! Here are your diamonds; they were, I believe, the pledges of your sincerity." This she could not refrain from saying a little bitterly, adding: "We are, remember, in future, strangers."

"That, then, is your final decision," he retorted in chilling tones, his eyes darkening in anger.

"It is!" She did not flinch as she said it.

"My wish can only be that you may not live to repent it bitterly," he said coldly; "but I would think a little before I should sacrifice my life to be wrecked as you are doing. Think! think, Elra! you are young, you are beautiful, and, alas! for yourself you love me."

"Alas! But this I remember, only when you will kneel to me in days to come and cry, 'Elra, I love you as I have loved none other; I live but to unsay those cruel words of mine; I shall die if need be to prove my love,' but it will then be too late! too late!" She covered her face with her hands as she sank on the rugs again and groaned aloud.

"Elra!"

"Rutland, leave me, I command it," she almost shrieked as he stood irresolute not venturing to approach, not wishing to go, and with the fitful fires of anger lighting in his eyes.

"Be it so!" he cried in withering tones, as seizing the crescent of diamonds which for two long years had been such an object of tenderness to Elra, he flung it contemptuously in the stream and was gone ere that independent young woman dared to look again in his face.

Gone! did I say? No, not gone; he had caught sight ere he turned away of the deathly pallor creeping over her cheek and lips, and in an instant, forgetting all but his tender feeling for her, he had flung himself down beside her, drawing her swiftly to him, and she did not resist.

She had felt the bitterness of parting with the man she loved; death itself, she thought, might perhaps come less bitter, and now that he was by her side again, she yielded up her lips to his quite submissively for such a would-be independent young lady.

"Forgive me, little darling, I cannot live without you. The words I spoke were but uttered in frenzy, for, in very fact, my manhood's noblest devotion is now, and ever has been yours. Darling, I shall give you life-long proof of it." And she believed him.

Slowly she raised her eyes, and unflinchingly as any judge, met his burning glance, but something spoken by those impassioned eyes made her own white lids to quiver and droop.

"Why do you change your mind so quickly," she retorted with a brave assumption of indifference. "Who are you, that you seem to have the privilege of moulding the course of my life to your will?"

"Elra, I am the man," he said not arrogantly, but with the inspired eloquence of a deep passion, "to whom your whole soul has gone forth and yielded submission, and who, in return, worships you, adores you, will die for you."

He had conquered indeed, doubts and suspicions were flung to the winds, for in his strong unyielding arms she breathed half in fear, half in ecstacy of love and gladness.

"Be it so!" And their wedding after all was fixed for three days from thence.

Out into the moonlight she wandered that night, Elra with the shadowy eyes and the brow stamped with intellect, which so many women had envied her; out she wandered to where, across the star-illumined lake, a tiny shallop glided, cutting with a soft and murmuring ripple the crystal bosom of the placid water, where deep down in the glassy wavelets she could see the glittering constellations shimmer like diamonds set in a sea of sapphire, whilst above in regal beauty Diana's crescent sailed, showering her floods of frosted, silvery light over smiling hill and towering mountain, frowning crag and glowering fortress; wrapping the far away blue peaks in hoary grandeur, whilst her softened beams the while descended on the dancing waters in the valleys below, playing in and out amongst the darkling shadows where the weeping willows hang forever their light tresses over the mysterious eddying pools.

"And his love, like these things, was sworn to last forever and forever," she murmured. "O, Elra! Elra! Elra! you are his slave. He loves you not! yet, as long as life is yours, you must bend and kiss the hand which masters you, for you cannot live without him!"

"No," she continued, clasping her cold hands together, " I am his slave. Come what will, I cannot live without him."

CHAPTER VII.

WHO SAW IT?

It is the morning of the wedding—a bright, glorious
morning, from whose sky the early tinges of crimson,
and purple, and emerald have scarce faded; a morning
redolent with joy and blessing; a morning which had
been looked forward to with intense feelings of awe and
dread by the proud, courted beauty, Elra, whose very
smile seemed only needed to charm all men to her feet;
a morning that had been looked forward to by Rutland
Borradale with hope and gladness, for he was very
proud and very fond, deep down in his heart, of the
beautiful American girl whom he was soon to call his
wife.

Elra at a quarter to eleven had a merry group around
her, and already much that should be done to her toilet
had been done. It was to be a strictly private affair,
but Madame de Montespaire could not refrain from asking some chosen friends to celebrate the occasion by
lunching with them after the ceremony. "You see, our
dear Elra prefers it so," said Madame to one of her pet
lady callers, "and in the existing state of relations between the groom and his uncle, the Earl of Darcliffe, it
is no doubt best that it should be so; but we shall have
our own little time for gaiety afterwards; and quite a
number, amongst others the beautiful Marchioness, have
accepted invitations to be present at an unpretending

little spread after the young people have settled all about their future. Be sure you come, luncheon will be served early, twelve is the hour fixed."

In the meantime, eleven had struck, and all was apparently ready, but faces began to look grave, and it was whispered around, "The bridegroom, where is he?"

Elra, chilled to the heart at what she deemed a slight, had herself asked it in a whisper more than once, and at last, with growing fear and horror, her lips had refused to ask it any more. A quarter past eleven, half-past eleven, and the ashen color of Elra's face was disagreeable to see.

"She and he, I suppose, have between them planned this humiliation for me. Oh, Rutland, it would have been more manly to have taken back the ring you gave, and accepted your release there and then. But no," she cried bitterly, "he would have been an idiot to have thrown away his claim on my fortune, when it is for my wealth alone he is marrying me. Murray," she stammered, with white lips, as that gentleman approached her, "Is—Has——"

Murray shook his head, but could not trust himself to say anything.

"Then," she cried, passionately, "tell everybody to go away again; there will be no wedding." So saying, she tore the veil and wreath from her head and flung them far from her.

"The Marchioness of Ripdale has arrived, my dear," said Madame de Montespaire, approaching, and showing on her good-natured face her utter perplexity as to what to think or say. "Where is Mr. Borradale? What can have become of Rutland, dear? I do not know

what to think. Something grave must have occurred
or he would have let us know. But there is time yet,"
she added, encouragingly; "we can keep our guests
waiting some little time," and she hurried away to entertain them. "I fear," thought Elra, bitterly, "there
may indeed be time enough, but there will be no bridegroom to-day. Oh, if I had but trusted poor Murray,
this would never have happened."

"Poor" Murray chanced to be by her side, and his
gray eyes, full of tenderness and love, sought hers.

"Murray," she breathed, almost beside herself with
mortified feelings and pride, "why did I say 'No' to your
whispered words that evening? Why did you let me?"

With a great wave of joy sweeping through his soul,
Murray quickly, daringly, caught her to his heart. "I
will never again let you say 'No,' my darling," and to
his whispered words this time came the answer from her
smiling lips, "Yes."

But ten minutes later the agony in her eyes belied her
words, as the procession moved forward towards the oratory of the castle. "Fifteen minutes more and what
fate awaits me? Oh, if he would but come!" She
paused, she lingered, under any trivial pretext that came
to her mind; but no sign was there of her recreant lover
appearing even at the last hour, and Elra's soul was
crushed to earth at the thought.

"But no," she cried, "events shall not conquer me.
I am the daughter of a race which has ever valued
courage, of a noble race, and I shall show them that
such an one can still be proud. The slight must not
crush me;" and with a queenly step she advanced up
the centre of the chapel with Murray by her side.

And how fared it the while with Rutland Borradale?
As a matter of form—merely empty form, he thought—
he sent word to his uncle informing him of his intentions, and asking, for the sake of his future bride, some
little token of friendliness between them. Judge, therefore, of his surprise when he received a wire back:

"I shall place Darcliffe Castle at the disposal of you and
your bride for the month following your wedding, and I
cordially invite you to spend your first happy days together there. I am going to Norway for the fishing, so
you will be entirely undisturbed, and you cannot find a
prettier retreat for your young wife. I shall be with you
at the wedding if you state what time." It was signed
merely with his initials.

No word he mentioned of what had passed between
them. It was as though he wished to exclude the disagreeable phantom of a bygone day from his mental vision.

The Earl of Darcliffe, truth to say, had been as intensely proud of his promising young nephew as an
utterly selfish nature can be, and now that he heard
that amongst all the suitors and gallants who had sighed
at the feet of this American heiress, renowned equally
for beauty, good breeding, and wealth, Rutland Borradale
had alone been the accepted one, the pride of family and
blood returned, and eagerly he opened his arms to his
long-banished nephew. This communication of the
Earl's reached Rutland Borradale only the evening before his wedding, on his return from seeing his bride-
elect, when he had arranged with her all the necessary
particulars for the morrow.

"The dear old uncle," he said with full heart, "I always knew he was a brick, and didn't mean it at heart;

and oh, won't it be a surprise and delight to my sweet little Elra! she darling little thing is too good for me. But she loves me and she is the sweetest little woman ever trod, so we might as well have things as they are."

. In the meantime he sent word to his uncle in Brussels to be down at ten the next morning so as to be in good time, as the ceremony should come off at eleven. But in the morning came a telegram from 104 Boulevarde des Espangnols :

"Come, quickly, your uncle has met with an accident. Ismay de la Roche." In half an hour he was by his uncle's side, whom he found suffering from a fractured bone in one of his feet, but who otherwise was not seriously hurt. He, Rutland, had telegraphed to his fiancée on arriving at the Boulevarde, and had, at his hostess' kind persuasion, given her the telegram to look after.

"Marie, dear," said Madame de la Roche, "tell Bogartz to take this message around." Pretty Marie as she tripped away on her mission had the curiosity to look at the address, and, meeting with her sister Odile, they mischievously determined to withhold it until the evening, when they intended leisurely to forward it.

"It is for the American heiress, and we owe her one point, you know. She can wait for her telegram."

They were malicious, these girls, and had been doubtlessly much nettled by Murray Cresenworth's behavior the night of the De Rothsleind's ball ; but they were not really wicked, and if they could but have foreseen half of the grave consequences of that unjust deed of theirs, they would have parted with Rutland Borradale's telegram more quickly than if it burnt their fingers.

It arrived duly in the evening and contained the words:

"Postpone the ceremony until twelve. I cannot be down until 11.30. My uncle has met with an accident. R. Borradale."

But in the meantime what had happened?

What was it that greeted the eyes of the groom elect when he made his late entry into the oratory of the Castle where all were assembled, accompanied by his uncle whose progress was but slow and painful, and de Montford who had always stood on terms of close friendship with the Earl, and who now wished to be present at the nephew's brilliant marriage.

At one end of the apartment was a group of four persons writing their names, and advancing with rapid strides to read these, Rutland Borradale saw but one name, and that one was—Elra Cresenworth.

A man cannot cry out when he is hurt, but into Rutland Borradale's eyes sprang the ominous gloom, the wicked fire, that darkles in pools gurgling around the cruel death dealing rocks in a wintry sea.

Elra Cresenworth quite calm now handed her husband an unsealed envelope.

"It is for Mr. Borradale," she said in a low steady voice.

Murray rather diffidently handed the envelope as bidden, and as Borradale opened the paper it contained, he saw at once that it was a cheque for a very large amount of money, the sight of which contained no particular meaning to his mind, until his eye caught his own name on the cheque. He then realized that it had been drawn by Elra Brookley, and that by it the considerable amount of two millions of dollars was to be made payable by the G—— National Bank of New York, to Rutland

Borradale, and a separate note showed the words: "Seeing it was for this he sought my hand——."

No more did he give himself time to read, but flinging back the papers at their feet, he turned to the bridegroom with flashing eyes. "You dare!" he hissed, between his clinched teeth, whilst his hand stole to his pocket. Quick as thought sounded the report of a pistol, and Murray Crescnworth lay next moment in a pool of his own life blood.

In the confusion that followed none could rightly say they had seen the hand that had pulled the trigger, and sent that deadly bullet home. But the very thought of the crime went hand in hand with the recollection of events which so immediately preceded it. At Rutland Borradale's feet had been flung the deadly weapon yet reeking with smoke and fire, and suspicion could not fail to point its grim finger at the man who had been crushed by one of the cruelest blows that could have been dealt by Fate, or rather by the hand of his now hapless victim.

But when the authorities had definitely settled in their minds that suspicion did actually point in a certain direction, and had sufficiently gathered their straying mental faculties to be able to look around, there was no trace to be found, or no tidings to be had, either of the Earl of Darcliffe, his nephew, or his friend, de Montfort.

CHAPTER VIII.

THE LADY OF THE MOATED GRANGE.

Peeping from amid the darkling cluster of rich green oak and beech and silver poplar that shelter them from the southerly gale are the ivied walls of the ruined castle of Bramber, an ancient pile, majestic still in its decay as it overlooks from its lofty vantage ground, a sweep of country wealthy in farmsteads, with their broad lands studded over with the browsing cattle, busy villages where the children play, and quaint windmills, with gaunt flappers ever rushing through the air with their dull, booming sound.

Truly may we utter our regret with Mr. Ruskin that there should have been no pencil to hand down to us the decaying beauties of this structure, or no pen to chronicle its glories while yet it towered in grandeur above the far-reaching flats that stretch away at its base.

Levelled by the Parliamentarians under Sir William Waller, in 1643, after a short but spirited siege, there is little now remaining of this once strong fortress, which in its hey-day dominated a country of some hundreds of leagues around, and whose sieurs, besides possessing large estates in Munster and part of the city of Limerick, in Ireland, claimed vassalage dues at one time from the lords of Pevensey and Knepp in Sussex, and from those of Radnor, Brecknock, Hay and Abergavenny, in Wales.

Breastworks, battlements, turrets, bastions that had

shielded generations, and the lordly keep that had
been witness to so many a deadly conflict have crumbled
long since beneath Time's cankering finger, or have
toppled over the steep bank on which the castle was
built, and lie strewn in shapeless piles of corroding rubbish in the dry moat.

Before the destruction of the castle in the seventeenth
century there was, overlooking the drawbridge, and
guarding, and containing the portcullis, or hanging-
door, a strong, square tower, a part of whose flank is yet
standing. This massive bit of masonry, though now
presenting the appearance of a dismantled skeleton wall,
thickly enshrouded with ivy, displays even to this day
great solidity of build from its broad base upwards,
measuring from some five to six feet in thickness.

Of the many picknickers—perhaps from Shoreham,
perhaps from Brighton—visiting the castle, those who
look across the wold to the South Downs skirting the
horizon, may perceive a striking bit of scenery expanding
at their feet. Yonder, sleeping amidst the trees, is the
little hamlet of Bramber, a helpless, unprotected cluster
of weather-beaten hovels and quaint cottages, which ever,
in the olden days of cruel rapine, fell the first victim to
cruel marauders attacking the castle. The village as it
is now seen, boasts of but a single street, which stretches
to the foot of the nearly perpendicular ascent leading to
the castle ruins. To the south of the castle, at a distance
of some nine to ten miles, lie the towns of Brighton and
Worthing; and on the west a darkling mass of waving
pine and beech crowns the rounded crest of Chancton-
bury Ring, making at sunset a jagged wall of gloom
against the crimson-tinted sky; whilst to the north and

east spreads a rural and sweet, if somewhat tame, landscape. Away on all sides stretch the yellow cornfields, with the waving golden grain or the rich green pastures, where through the long summer days the sleepy cattle stand knee-deep in the rank tangled grasses, or wherever it is possible far down amongst the reeds and sedge that shiver and sough in the bubbling cool water. In just such a way, perhaps, as did the poor peaceful beasts stand long years ago when the fitful tramp of horses' feet was dimly heard afar off; when the blast of the bugle and the clang of armor grew momently nearer, till the stream of mounted warriors swept across the marshy plain, and the tide of war rolled in one great devastating wave to the foot of the castle.

On the east side where the grass is vivid green and the tall-stemmed forget-me-nots interweave their growth with the nodding bulrushes, where the marsh marigolds and yellow kingcups abound; there spread at one time a deep morass which has since been reclaimed to advantage. This morass had held abundance of wild fowl for the hawking parties which, in times of peace, often sauntered from the castle, mounted on gaily-caparisoned horses, and dashed along the quaking turf, to watch the noble falcon wheeling in ever narrowing circles ere it dropped upon the prey, to engage in that gallant struggle which so delighted the old Norman barons, more especially, when it ended, as it more often did, in the death of the inoffensive heron.

It was whilst indulging in this lordly recreation that John de Braose, Baron of Bramber, met with his untimely death in 1232. Wheeling on the sedgy borders of the widespread marsh, the baron's hot-blooded Span-

ish horse took umbrage at a flight of wild fowl rising
with noisy flapping of wings and wild startled cries
close to the place where he galloped. Tossing high his
coal-black crest, the excited animal, with a terrified
snort, recoiled upon his haunches, and for a moment
pawed the air in majestic grandeur, ere he viciously
flung himself back and in hurtling descent crushed his
mailed and helmeted rider to almost instantaneous death
beneath him. It was then that the Lady of Bramber,
the ill-starred daughter of Llewellyn—a bride but two
short years ago—having repaired to the gloomy eastern
towers to watch from their embrasured casements the
gallant spectacle of the hawking party streaming away
to the westward in the valley beneath, had the hapless
fate to witness that black horse's fall, and to watch her
dead lord borne homeward to his castle and to her.

Around the brow of the knoll whereon stood the castle
and keep, ran a wall of considerable thickness, which
formed part of the outer ramparts of the fortress, and
which, towards the eastern side, where, protected by the
severity of the incline, the castle was more strongly
guarded, is to this day in a state of remarkably good
preservation; but to the west, from whence the chief
rush of besiegers under Waller flooded the castle, the
wall was entirely demolished and razed to the ground.

One of the most striking features of this ancient forti-
fication, as now seen, is the dry moat, which runs at the
base of the castle and extends over a circular area of
some 1,000 feet. Before the seventeenth century, when
this moat was supplied with water from the river Adur,
which flows through the valley bordering the east side
of the castle, the water filling it spanned some forty-

seven feet in breadth, from bank to bank, being some
thirty feet in depth at the shallowest point; and thus to
the inhabitants of the fortress affording the strongest
protection against marauding attacks. That part of the
moat facing the south, which was spanned by the drawbridge, is now filled with a dry rubble, formed in most
part from the wreck of the Norman tower, which being
added to and solidified by the covering of a coarse
earth, has since allowed of a more easy access to the
castle walls. Its deep cut sides, as also the steep banks
which rise from the margin of the moat to the foot of the
old ramparts, are thickly fringed with hazel saplings
interwoven everywhere in dense growth with the silver
birch, willow, gray poplar, and aspen, the shadow from
whose boughs sweeps a green sward farther down where
the pale bramble-rose and purple fox-glove, the thirsty
iris, and yellow marsh lilies rise from amongst the dank
mosses that cluster and creep around the spreading
roots of the young oaklings. As may thus be seen, the
moat affords a wealth of interest to the curious bands of
pleasure-seekers, who picnic under its kindly shade, and
who love well to pry into its vernal nooks and gather the
wood-anemones there, or to sit, perhaps, and listen to
the soughing of the wind amongst the quivering willows
and aspens overhead.

Most of the traditions and legends of the castle have
been swept away with time, and though it does, indeed,
possess a skeleton history—one quaintly-worded and full
of interest—it is such mere outline as to leave behind an
unprofitable wish for deeper draughts of knowledge.

There are not wanting, however, in the records, half
historic, half legendary, of this castle, tales of vindictive
cruelty and heartless bloodshed.

In the reign of King Henry VII, one Hubert de Hurst, an alien baron, having been accorded the charge of the castle during the minority of a certain William de Braose, the then Lord of Bramber, exercised much despotic sway over the country round, and was much dreaded amongst his own household for his jealous tyranny. Amongst other of his cruelties he effected the rape of Maud Willmot, commonly known as the Maid of Ditchling, a peasant girl of great beauty, and of hitherto untarnished innocence. Her he forced later to marry him, treating her for some time with all the lavish tenderness and care that love could inspire; but she, young, gay and frolic-loving, could find nothing beside her jealous elderly lord, that consoled her for the loss of her free, happy, careless life amidst the sweet green fields and shady lanes, far down in the valley by her father's hut.

Before her forced marriage with De Hurst, Maud of Ditchling had deeply loved and pledged herself to one De Lindfield, the young scion of a good old family, though poor; and this young squire, under guise of an old standing friendship for De Hurst, having followed Maud to her husband's castle, carried on with her there a secret and guilty intimacy. For a while unsuspicious, De Hurst, who was a true sportsman, admired in his guest all that was most frank and manly in manner and bearing, most skillful in dangerous exercise of arms, and most daring in feats of horsemanship, for in hunting fields and over hawking grounds none excelled De Lindfield. It was thus that, with stirring tales of dangers, happily surmounted in the pursuit of these manly recreations, the young Squire was enabled to while away the dreary hours when the old and irritable Baron was attacked by his baneful enemy, the gout.

But an imprudence on the part of the Lady Maud, led De Hurst to fear for the honor of his name, and ascertaining that his suspicions were correct, and enraged with jealousy, he determined to bide his time for a bitter revenge. Accordingly late one night, as the Lady of Bramber was returning from an assignation with her lover in a summery arbor within the castle grounds, De Hurst, who had been a witness to the scene between the deeply guilty pair, had De Lindfield siezed and conveyed to an underground dungeon, used in those days for the storage of corn, where he was thrown and locked in, never to come out again.

The grim tale has it that De Hurst with his own hands, night after night, built up a wall with plaster and stone in front of the cell containing his victim, and that once, towards the completion of his task, having looked for a last time at the unhappy young man, he found that the hair of the latter had turned to a snow white. The wretched Lady Maud, upon learning the hapless fate of her lover, is said to have entirely lost her reason. When Sir William Waller battered in the southwest ramparts of the castle, and his victorious soldiers pick-axed their way into the staunch walls of the keep, there was then found in an old dungeon the skeleton remains of the man who had expiated his crime in a living tomb.

What more is known of the castle's history affords but little interest, being principally a bare account of the alliances formed in marriage by the Barons of Bramber in their days of power.

Thus Time's wave is ever rolling on, and the walls of this once brave fortress will disappear; history will close for ever over that remote spot, leaving nothing but a bald earthwork to tell of the labors of giants, to tell of heroic deeds, of cruel deeds, and of the gallant deeds of many of England's noble sons performed beneath the shadow of those moated towers. The children will run and play amongst the clambering weeds and shivering willows that fringe the rock, and will laugh and dream not that this is hallowed ground, that every sod they press is pregnant with the story of a deeper tragedy than ever they will witness, the chronicles even of which are now lost to them forever in the impenetrable gulf of Time.

But history repeats itself, and Bramber has its mysteries yet; mysteries that produce endless trouble and conjecture in the timid minds of the little rustics running through the Grange meadows after the corn-crakes' nests; and such as even make the stolid countrymen passing the miniature towers of the Grange entrance exercise their slow minds with ever increasing wonder as to who may be the queen who reigns in that solitary mansion.

For where the grass is vivid green, and where the solitary heron stands in the dusky twilight on the borders of what was once the deep morass, where, in 1232, John, Baron of Bramber, met his death, but which is now ground reclaimed to some advantage, there stands a pretty and quaintly gabled mansion called The Grange. At about the time the story opens this Grange had been leased to a lady giving her name as Mrs. Eldmere, who wore the deep mourning of widowhood, and who gave but little explanation save that supplied by her funereal garments for thus burying herself in so remote a corner of creation as this little hamlet under the ruined fortress.

She had, however, brought with her several servants, which showed that she was wealthy, which circumstance, coupled with the retired life she led, caused much wonder, but it was very few from the village who ever penetrated to the inside of the Grange, and those who did saw little or nothing of its mistress. One thing, however, had become well known, and that was that the lady of the Grange was very beautiful and wore costly diamond rings, which alone in the eyes of the maidens and swains of Bramber surrounded her with as much mystery and romance as any imprisoned queen.

If they had seen more of her they might have pronounced her habits and ways very quiet and uninteresting for a person so enveloped in mystery as she, for nothing apparently broke in upon the monotony and routine in that household, every member of which seemed to think highly of its mistress, and in consequence was more inclined to keep from disturbances which might annoy her gentle womanly feeling.

And this strangely beautiful lady, who seemed absorbed in governing her household with care and patience, in the inner recesses of her private apartments, what was she like? What was the secret skeleton which confronted her there, and which had made her life such an apparent blank?

Ah! that secret she had evidently never disclosed to any one, even the most favored, and none save her trusted maid knew anything of her past life, and she never broke the confidence reposed in her by her mistress. But even this faithful, handmaiden did not know exactly everything concerning Mrs. Eldmere, for often-times she seemed entirely puzzled to see her mistress vainly searching among old papers which she kept on ordinary occasions carefully locked away, but which nevertheless often stole out from their hiding-place when Mrs. Eldmere was alone, or fancied she was alone. But from such fruitless searches she always rose with a sigh and the sad murmured words:

"Not yet! Not yet!"

But perhaps it may be interesting to our readers them-selves to take a peep at the Grange and its beautiful mystery-enveloped lady ere we proceed further with our story.

The Grange Bramber is the name of one of those charming country houses which are to be found in so many parts of southern England. It stands in park-like grounds, guarded at the entrance by two massive tower-gates, and is surrounded on all sides by a low stone wall, which is again surmounted by a thick bushy hedge, effect-ually prevents any possible chance of being overlooked by passers-by, and makes the grounds particularly shel-tered and secluded.

The house is a long low building, whose large bay-windows open on the smooth velvety lawns, overhung by well-grown trees and shrubs, and with its miniature lake and terrace opening onto a rose garden, it makes a pretty picture of quiet English country life. The family to whom the Grange belonged were now abroad, and it was at present occupied by a Mrs. Eldmere, who lived a most quiet and retired life, was rarely seen out-side the tower-gates, and who seemed to have for her sole companion a tall white-browed girl, whom she designates as Topsie, and who must have been a school-mate, judging from the frequent allusions they both make concerning mistresses and professors, and the general happenings of school life which they had witnessed together.

The arrival of Mrs. Eldmere and her young companion at the Grange had given rise at first to much conjecture in the minds of those few who make up the so-called society of a small country place; but as time went on, and the new-comers persistently ignored all advances, they saw that the ladies, for some reason or other, preferred to remain unvisited, and if ever Mrs. Eldmere's name was mentioned, it was generally accompanied with a shake of the head and a look that might mean many things. She was considered to be peculiar! and as the average country resident has a horror of appearing anything but commonplace, it is to be feared that Mrs. Eldmere had not found favor in their sight.

The lady's young companion was variously spoken of as her sister (although there was not the slightest resemblance between them), her companion, and her *femme de chambre;* and to account for her long-continued residence with Mrs. Eldmere, and the relations that existed between them, we must go back to some time previous to their arrival at the Grange.

One morning Mrs. Eldmere had received a letter the contents of which we shall take the liberty of reading, and which ran thus:

DEAREST OLD ELL.: My husband has been ordered to India with the gallant 10th (the Prince's Own) and I am going with him. I cannot bear to have him go out alone for an indefinite length of time, and yet I dread leaving poor Topsie to mother and sisters, who are dreadfully harsh to her. Do you know of any pleasant country house where she will be cared for, treated gently, and perhaps loved, while I am away, which will not, I hope, be for long. You will have my eternal gratitude if by any sweetness or kindness you can soften her hard road in life. On my return I hope never to have to part with my sister again, as Redstone is going to send in his resignation, and we shall be able to settle down for good. If I do not see you before we start, I am always your old university chum,

BOPSIE, *née* ARTRALE ALLESMERE.

This letter had been sent originally to the Chateau of Montelarde, and from thence forwarded by her business man in London to her present address. It was, therefore, owing to this delay of the letter that, having hurried to London, Mrs. Eldmere had arrived only in time to kiss her friend good-bye and to see her sail for India, but in that very short time she had contrived to make her friend Bopsie entirely happy by whispering in her ear the words:

"Darling, Topsie will be a boon to my lonely existence; she shall be cherished as my very own sister. But what has made her young life unhappy?"

"That is a miserable matter," answered her friend with a sigh, "but one which you have every right to know, so you will find the key to it in the papers which are waiting for you at my lawyer's; and now God bless you! dear old Ell., and may you be as happy as you have made me; and with another kiss and many hand-clasps the two friends parted, and Mrs. Eldmere had returned to her quiet country home accompanied by a tall fair girl of whom she appeared to be very fond, and who has been her constant companion ever since.

Although Mrs. Eldmere had often pondered over her last meeting with Topsie's sister and the words she had then spoken, she had never applied to the lawyer for letters which she knew contained the solution of the problem. She knew that Topsie had had some great disagreement with her own family, which rendered it impossible for her to live happily at home, but she had lived too long abroad to know much about her friends, except through occasional letters from Artrale, and these, though never mentioning the details, had at one time been full of a mysterious something that seemed to hint at shame or sorrow for some one she loved, but who Mrs. Eldmere never thought of associating with her sister.

She noticed that the girl never received any letters from her home people, nor did she ever mention them, and more than once she felt inclined to ask the reason, but a strange feeling of reluctance came over her and she left the words unspoken. They were so happy together, though their life was quiet and simple, and Mrs. Eldmere often feared that Topsie might grow weary of its monotony, but she was always bright, gay, and full of laughter, so that her friend found it hard to imagine that any deep sorrow had ever shaded her fair young brow.

It was Topsie, therefore, who (to Mrs. Eldmere's surprise) spoke first on the matter she had been so deeply pondering, and almost as if she could read her thoughts she said, abruptly, one morning:

"I know you think it odd, Elra, that I get no letters from home; I have watched your face; I know it is so. Did you never hear the why and wherefore of my banishment? I know Artrale wrote it all to you. She thought, and I, too, that you ought to know."

" I have never asked to see those letters, Topsie," said Mrs. Eldmere, with all her love and sympathy shining in her eyes. " I thought, perhaps, some day you would tell me, dear, and if not I am content not to know."

"But you must know!" cries Topsie rather wildly. Oh, Elra! let me read it out to you;" and the girl threw herself at Mrs. Eldmere's feet, and, leaning her pretty head against her friend's knee, she drew from a folded packet some closely written sheets of foolscap, the writing on which she began to read as follows:

CHAPTER IX.

"LITTLE TARTAR."

Once again I am in the old woods at Ravenstowe with Lenore by my side: unhappy, beautiful Lenore, with the genius-kindled eyes and broad snowy brow that intellect has so plainly stamped as all its own.

In family we are fourteen — seven young lords and seven young ladies — I the youngest, and Lenore the thirteenth; Lenore, with hair which has caught the ruddy tinges of the setting sun, with eyes that mirror the shadowy tints of the purpling clouds at sunset, with a soul tender, deep, unfathomable.

She had an alarming amount of brain; she was gloriously clever! This, I fear, is a rather girlish expression, but my sister, the "little Tartar," as Lenore was styled by the elders of the family, was very bright, and had always shown great promise for a brilliant after-life.

She was, for all this great promise, a strange little girl, merciless where she took a dislike, and notwithstanding the possession of a dear, beautiful petite face, she was not so much loved or admired by those who approached her as might have been expected. There was something in her manner that repelled—a something haughty and unconquerable—but she was also, by reason of her brightness and courage, the link between

the timid younger ones of our family and the domineer-
ing elders who, by reason of their having been born
ahead of us, had every right on their side, but whose
one-sided logic had been rather crumbled in a heap once
or twice by our "little Tartar." This was considered
remarkable for one of us girls, as our boys have always
been esteemed very talented, and especially powerful in
threading through an argument, the right and justice of
which very often depended upon the fists that upheld it.
One of our boys, "Lord Cupid," took a " double first,"
and has grown very fat upon fame ever since, but then
he has since become the son and heir. A second of our
young men, Lord Dumrell, shot a man, and was not only
too talented to get hanged for it, but was acquitted with
great honor and distinction ; while a third, Lord Rancrid,
did better still, as papa has always affirmed, for he shot
himself!   One of our younger lords, on the other hand,
being dull witted, and unable to think of anything original, married an American heiress and became wealthy;
while among the girls a few of them married, and most
of them remained old maids, poor things ! living most of
their time at the dower house of Ravenstowe near Drislehurst, Sussex.

Very little was there in common between our grand,
haughty lady mother and her numerous little lords and
ladies. Never did we run to her with our tales of woes
and wants; and, after all, she may not have been to
blame. I, Lady Artrale, the youngest of her offspring,
having so often heard myself irreverently termed the
ninety-ninth, that I have begun to forget how many we
are in family.

But to return to our pleasure party in the woods,

where Leonore and I are happily indifferent to all un-palatable family problems, we are busily engaged in building up a naughty little gypsy fire, which we feed from time to time with twigs from the neighboring trees. I say naughty, because it has always been deemed irre-deemably wicked by my lady mother (and all her other offspring of lords and ladies to the number of fourteen) for Lenore and I to so far forget our rank as to take de-light in the vulgar pastime of roasting mushrooms in the woods, and this is what we are now clandestinely doing.

Lenore and I love each other tenderly, and take all our pleasures in common; but I have also other feelings with regard to my beautiful sister. I venerate her be-cause she is capable of being so much more haughty and self-controlled than myself, and she has always been so immensely more talented than any of our smart family, including even the fat son and heir.

"I wish I were a snail," cries my sprightly sister, still keeping a sharp lookout for intruders.

"Oh!" comes in an astonished gasp from me; but I suppose talent is always strongly eccentric.

"I should then have a house of my own, transportable at will."

"But, dear," I mildly suggest, "would you not be cramped for room?"

"Yes; that is why papa's miserably fat son and heir could never get in to slay my pet rats, as he did yester-day.

"Happy America! where children and rats are pro-tected by their own special laws," she continued, ram-bling on from one thought to another.

"Indeed I hope my home will be larger than a snail's,"

I say, reverting to her former idea, "otherwise I should have no room for lovely silver and things." To which vague remark Lenore replies:

"There you are, foolish little Artrale, wishing for what you will tire of in less than three days. Poor little woman!" At this I look rather humbly at Miss Philosopher, but my after-thought is to rebel.

"Lenore," I say, very reproachfully, "you are so perpetually discontented that I am sure you never know what you want."

"You are right. I shall never be satisfied—for it is a yearning for greatness and power over my fellow-beings that eats into my soul."

Another flash of genius, I suppose, but it quite crumbles my dignity into a little heap. "You do say such funny things, Lenore," I venture.

"Not at all;" you do not know how I despise silver— how I despise wealth!"

."Oh!" She seems to startle so many "ohs" from me.

"One never can dare to enjoy anything really when one is rich," Lenore explains. "I should never think of making mushrooms here in the woods if it were not for my poverty, and you know how much I enjoy them, sister mine."

So saying, Leonore flings herself prone on her fur-trimmed coat, and in her usual graceful attitude of lazy content gazes dreamily up at the rooks overhead. The sweet perfume of violets and coltsfoot fills the air, and all around is to be seen the tender green of the young larch buds.

"Nature is what I love," she continued, sententiously; Nature, whose voice comes to me in the hush of the pine

I SAW A STRANGER, A HANDSOME YOUNG MAN, WITH HAT IN HAND
ADVANCING TOWARDS US.

Page 75.

woods or the swirling rush of the river; Nature, which is Truth gloriously portrayed."

"And in the meantime, dear," I answer dryly, your mushrooms are burning. Can you not leave the ideal and descend to the real? Here is your favorite dish cooked to a turn."

A rustling in the bushes and a slight cry of surprise from Lenore caused me to look up quickly, and I saw a stranger, a handsome young man, with hat in hand and an expression of much amusement, advancing towards us.

Instinctively I feel that my cheeks are crimson from my recent exertions over the fire, that my hands are soiled, likewise that the stranger has most fascinating eyes, and is evidently a gentleman. Lenore is, however, equal to the occasion, for she rises quickly to her feet and asks the intruder, with a would-be haughty look, if he is aware that he is trespassing.

"I beg ten thousand pardons if that be the case," he replied, "but the truth is I am a stranger here, having lost my way in the woods, and seeing the smoke of a gypsy fire, as I imagined, I came this way, hoping to fall in with some one who could put me on the right path to Sir Gregory Athelhurst's, where I am now staying to enjoy a couple of his rare gallops after hounds. I did not expect to surprise two wood nymphs at their repast and must beg to be forgiven, for I see that owing to my unfortunate appearance the mushrooms are now cooked to a turn, or rather to a cinder!"

As he said this he looked at us with such a comical expression on his face that it was irresistible, and even Lenore joined in the laughter that followed. In a few minutes we were chatting as easily as if we had known each other for years, and our new friend proved so entertaining a companion that time passed all too quickly, until Lenore, who had twice warned me of the lateness of the hour, at last insisted upon our going home. Mr. de Montford (this was the stranger's name) begged to walk with us as far as the edge of the wood, as he said, "I am afraid, if you leave me alone again, I shall be lost, and the next time I may fall into the hands of the ogre of the forest instead of into those of the 'beautiful nymphs of the woods;' though I am already so much your captive," he managed to whisper to me, "that you can do with me as you will."

"Then I command you to leave us," I replied, with a smile and a blush, "for here is your road and ours lies there."

Lenore had been walking in front of us through the wood, as the paths were narrow, and Mr. de Montford had contrived to detain me at his side, by some pretext or other, till we reached the high-road which led to the village.

There was something singularly fascinating to me in this man; he was too gentlemanly to trouble me with empty compliments, but his eyes had a marvellous power of expressing unspoken words of admiration; and though I fully realized that it was wrong to feel thus for an utter stranger, I hoped that somehow we should meet again erelong.

"You must leave us now," said Lenore, earnestly. "My mother would never forgive us if she knew we had been talking to you so long. Please go."

"I will vanish at once," said De Montford with a low bow, but you cannot be so cruel as to leave me without telling me your names—the names of my rescuers?"

"I am called Lenore, and my sister is Artrale," said Lenore, demurely. Now go, sir, and do not let us find you trespassing again on our dominions. Here she bowed and turned away, and he seized the opportunity to take my hand and press it to his lips with a whispered "au revoir," while with a significant look, that seemed to plead for another meeting, he left us.

"Well, Artrale! I must say you more than flirted with the young man, said Lenore, as we walked slowly home. How would your fiancé like to hear of this?"

"Do you really think I flirted too much? I said, teasingly. Why, Lenore, I believe you are jealous of the handsome stranger's evident preference for me! Am I to receive no attention but from my future lord and master? This young man was so romantic, and he was so good to look at, I could not help flirting just a little. I must have some fun, and there is no harm done anyhow."

No harm done yet! but other and stolen interviews followed the first meeting of Lady Artrale and De Montford, and what was begun in a spirit of coquetry, induced by the quiet country life led by two high-born girls who lived in almost entire seclusion, was destined to end as sadly as it had begun happily. In a word it came to this:

Lady Artrale, before meeting De Montford, had for some time been engaged to be married to a man she really admired, and whom she esteemed highly, though a little fear was mingled with both these feelings.

Redstone, Earl de Brun, had become deeply enamoured of the lovely Artrale, whom he had met by chance in travelling; and though, owing to her youth and inexperience, her mother would have wished for no engagement, she at last consented to his entreaties, and Artrale

was to be married and presented in the following year.
She had seen but little of her future husband, but she
knew him to be the soul of honor, and very exacting
where his love was in question. She would have grieved
sorely to lose him now through her own folly, and she
trembled at the crisis that was approaching. No ray of
hope seemed to brighten the clouds that were gathering
round her hitherto bright young life. On the one hand,
she saw the iron determination of a man ruled by a
desperate passion; on the other, a pure, upright love,
believing all things noble of its object, and expecting
love and honor from the same. She almost hated the
day on which she first saw De Montford standing in the
light of the fitful flame in the woods, and she hated
herself, most of all, for fanning into flame a still more
dangerous fire than that which flickered at their feet.
But, now that she had coquetted with the wind, she must
reap the whirlwind.

"I will meet De Montford once more," she thinks;
"but it must be for the last time." And Lady Artrale
arrayed herself in her most becoming gown—a pink cam-
bric that had been much admired by her hero—and,
taking her large straw, poppy-decked hat, she slowly
walked through the grounds to their trysting place in
the woods. De Montford was already there, and as she
approached he came to meet her with out-stretched
hands and a happy light in his eyes that showed too
plainly how dear she was to him.

"At last!" he cried. "I feared you were not coming;
and now, what have you to say to me?"

"I have to tell you," said Lady Artrale, simply, raising her blue eyes to his face, "that we must not meet
again. I have only come to say good-bye."

CHAPTER X.

LOST ON THE BROW OF DAWN.

Here, as Artrale's recital becomes vague and rather drivelling, Mrs. Eldmere thinks, we shall finish it ourselves.

De Montford, a young man of good old Norman family, endowed though he be with a handsome face and great capabilities for attracting the fair sex, with a large amount of brains and a rather diminutive rent-roll, has fallen decidedly in love with Lady Artrale, seventh daughter of Edred, Marquis of Ripdale, and his wife Leonora, and over and above is determined to marry her. He therefore gets a little disagreeable shock on hearing the word " good-bye " uttered by her in so calm a way; but he is not easily baffled. "I have likewise come to say that horrid little word, Artrale," he says coolly. "I can no longer postpone my promised visit to that wretched estate of mine in Yorkshire. Don't you pity me, Artrale?" he continues, searching deeply in her limpid eyes for the emotions which he knows his words cause.

Yes, he sees it all, rather plainly, too, for he is versed in the lore of woman's looks, and he knows that his apparent indifference has staggered the vain young lady before him. He therefore meets her angry glances with a smile on his parted lips as she says:

"Lady Artrale, if you please," and draws herself up to her full height.

"As you will, Lady Artrale," says De Montford with indifference, though she fancied that for a moment a gleam of passion shone in his dark eyes. "I will not detain you now, as you have said enough to prevent me caring to; but permit me to escort you to the high-road. There I shall leave you, and you will not again be troubled by my importunity."

So saying, he struck into a field which they had seldom or never traversed before, and side by side and in severe silence they threaded their way through the broad, rich pastures, each busy with his or her own thoughts. Lady Artrale suddenly becomes conscious, however, that they are treading new ground, and with a quick catch in her breath she looks at two peaceful-seeming cows, who, with that far-away look in their slumberous eyes so much admired in the heroines of novels, are so happily engaged in ruminating that they would not sacrifice their comfort for the uncomfortable effort of tossing pretty Artrale on their horns. No, she thinks they won't harm her, but for all that, after a quick look at her stolid companion, she makes a little dash for a gate opening on to the highway. But, alas! before they can gain the gate Lady Artrale flings her arms into space with an hysterical cry, then turns precipitately and flies, followed quietly and at a respectful distance by a noble-looking charger with coal-black mane and crest. On hearing her frightened cry, De Montford's lip curls, and he mutters, "Ha! my proud but timid beauty, I have conquered. It is as I had calculated." And in a moment he has gained her side, where she stands undecided as to what point of a wide brook she should choose to jump into, rather than be trampled to death by a vicious horse.

"You can never cross there," says De Montford, feeling himself rather master of the situation. "If the horse be wicked, he will surely follow you even into the water." This is said rather unfeelingly, and Lady Artrale turns pale and sinks in an attitude of despair at his feet.

"What is to be done? Cannot you save me?"

"I do not think you need alarm yourself; the horse looks quiet enough. Besides, even should you wish it, there is no possibility of egress at this side of the field; that line of blackthorn stakes bars all hope for us."

"Well, then, I shall die here!" (this defiantly;) "and I suppose you won't care a pin?"

"How can a man care or care not a pin?" thinks De Montford, smiling stoically at her agony of despair; but he says rather softly, as his eyes look down into hers:

"Did *you* care very much just now what pain you gave me? and you gave it unsparingly."

At hearing his murmured words Lady Artrale is inclined to be indignant, but, remembering the wicked horse and her helpless condition, she becomes piteous.

"I cannot love you! I wish you would take that for an answer," she rather whines.

"That is not true, and I shall *make* you love me," retorts De Montford masterfully, as she crouches lower on the sward.

"You have heard the only answer I can give you,' murmured the lady. "I wish you would accept it."

"I cannot and will not accept any answer that you have yet given me. Artrale, I love you!" This was breathed rather than spoken in tones soft but full of feeling.

" Don't care !" says she flippantly, whereat he bites his lips and grows pale, but very determined.

" Artrale !" he repeats, " my love is dangerous and deep ; think twice before you spurn it."

" Sir !" begins Lady Artrale grandly ; then her dignity collapses, for, sailing with majestic strides towards them comes the coal-black horse she dreads so much, and as he breaks into a loud, angry whinny, she gives a little shriek : " He is so wicked ! He has already trampled two of his keepers. " I suppose my mangled bones will strew the plains to-morrow ! "

This she says with a persuasive sidelong look at the man above her, but he is as unfeeling as an oyster, for there he stands with immovable countenance until she longs to give him a little shake !

" Mr. de Montford."

" Well ?"

" Did you hear what I said ?"

" Yes, that your bones would—"

" Yes ; will you not save me ?" This is said pathetically.

" I'd not mind being reduced to powder myself," cries the young man nonchalantly.

" Oh ! oh ! oh !" Three little shrieks escape Artrale's pretty lips as the horse, who is now close to them, paws frantically at the sod, ploughing up the dainty mosses in a ruthless manner.

"Artrale, the horse is only playful ; he will not harm you when I am near," says De Montford protectingly.

" He will, he will !" cries she, desperately. " Can we not jump the brook ?"

" Do not attempt it ; you will never get over it. But,

Artrale, suffer me!" Here he clasps her slight form in his arms, and with her hair sweeping her neck, and her face very close to his, he breathes:

" Artrale, in another moment you can be safe. I can put brook and fences far behind me with Artrale in my arms; but, darling, I will not cross them without the answer my heart is longing for. Be my love, Artrale— be my wife, my adored wife!"

Now passion is breathing from his lips and eyes; his whole frame is trembling with the very strength of his resolve that she shall be his, and Lady Artrale knows that the crisis of her shallow little life is at hand—that whatever word she shall speak in this moment of her supposed danger' De Montford will hold her to forever after, if he really be the strong, determined man he looks.

· " I choose rather to be trampled to death !" cries she, with a wicked flash from her handsome eyes, which seems to make her captor doubly determined to be the winner in this little game.

" That is not the answer I am waiting for, Artrale." Here he holds her face close to his, with her form still resting in his strong arms, and looks into her eyes till he feels a quiver run through her frame, and he knows he has conquered her.

" I wait to prove my love for you, Artrale. Say you · will be my loved and loving wife."

" Yes," came in a sigh from the pretty trembling lips, which were immediately pressed passionately by him.

" The horse !" she whispered in terror; " save me !"

De Montford, with one magnificent bound, such as the most powerful of athletes might justly think of with

pride during a lifetime, cleared the wide brook, and its
fringing line of blackthorn stakes, with his promised
bride held lightly in his arms.

What passed between Lady Artrale and De Montford
after this we need not mention. Suffice it to say that
the lady reached her home in safety, and, gaining the
shelter of her own room, locked the door against all
intruders, and then gave way to a burst of passionate
tears. The Fates have indeed been unkind to her. Had
she not meant to dismiss De Montford this very day?
And instead of this she finds herself pledged to him by
a promise which she knows he will surely make her keep,
though it was wrung from her at a moment when terror
had blinded her to every thought save that of her supposed danger.

"What shall I do?" she moans, wringing her pretty
hands and restlessly pacing the floor of her room.

"Are you here, Artrale?" cries Lenore's voice at her
door, and hastily removing, as she hopes, all traces of
grief from her face, she admits her sister, who is evidently impatient at being kept waiting.

Lenore's quick eyes at a glance see that something is
wrong. Artrale's flushed face and nervous manner show
her only too plainly that her little sister is hiding something from her, and by dint of pleading and persuading
she at last draws from Artrale the whole story of herself
and De Montford, their stolen interviews, and now this
promise given; and the poor child, with many sobs and
tears, entreats her sister's help and advice.

Artrale, in her misery, notices that Lenore's eyes are
inspired with something that she cannot describe but

as a strange sublimity, but they are very sad as she remarks gently,

"I shall save you, Artrale. Have no fear, dear sister."

"Dearest, do nothing rash," cries Artrale, rather in fear of what she reads in her sister's eyes—"nothing that can possibly hurt or blight your happy career through life or in society. Promise me."

But she answers abruptly. Lenore is always abrupt, Artrale thinks.

"I do not care for what you term society. It is madness that a girl should yearn to go into society, to be stretched on the rack and tortured like any dozen of little fried oysters."

And so the subject was suffered to lapse for the time between the two young ladies.

When we next see Lady Artrale and her sister we find them busied with preparations for the former's wedding, and the old house, which had been so dull and quiet since the sudden death of their brother (by having shot himself), is now all alive and bustling with the excitement that such an important event is sure to cause.

Artrale seems joyous and full of life, her eyes are radiantly blue and happy, and the late nervousness that had been observed in her manner had almost disappeared. She had had a respite from De Montford's attentions, as he had been called away peremptorily on business, and though he had written often, he had not since appeared on the scene.

It was Lenore who brought Artrale nearly all her letters every morning, this latter young lady liking to linger among her pillows a little longer than her sprightly sister, and it was therefore with little surprise that Artrale saw Lenore appear in her bedroom on the morning preceding that of her wedding with a bundle of monogramed notes in her hand. She little dreamed of the serpent in the basket of fruit. She found it, however, all too soon, and with blanched cheek and lips handed it to Lenore, who, singing softly and happily as a young thrush in the luscious spring-time, is all unconscious of the horror written in her sister's eyes. But Lenore changes color, too, when she reads; though, seeing her sister's haggard face, she says confidently :

"It will be all right dear, don't trouble about it, I will see him instead of you to-night, since he must see some one. To-morrow you will be past his power; darling, how happy you will be then !"

Artrale's blue eyes are full of tears as she tries to smile assent, and Lenore leaves her no time to pursue the subject, which is not again mentioned between the sisters.

That evening, in the hubbub and bustle of preparation for the morrow, no one noticed the slender white robed figure which stole out through the shrubberies; no one took any notice of a light-wheeled carriage which stood waiting by the shrubbery gate, and yet those were the signs and tokens of the opening act of a tragedy as sad and bitter as ever the pale crescent witnessed.

No one missed Lady Lenore until the following morning, and then it was only because she was absent from her place as bridesmaid. This incident caused wonder in many minds, but in that of the bride herself it caused a panic which showed itself in her white face and trembling lips throughout the ceremony. Two and two were put together, and when Lenore did at last appear, she found, alas! a cruel reception.

Lenore's father, at her mother the grand cold marchioness' bidding, refused his permission to his favorite daughter to cross the threshold and mingle with the other members of his family—refused to his hitherto idolized child the protection of a parent's roof—and Lady Lenore found herself publicly lost—an outcast and homeless.

So ended the sad tale written by Artrale, now Countess de Brun, to Mrs. Cresenworth, to throw some light for her benefit upon the past career of the beautiful Lenore, *alias* Topsie.

CHAPTER XI.

SIR GREGORY'S LOVE FEVER.

Among those of her neighbors who were curiously interested in the mistress of the Grange and her quiet way of living may be mentioned Sir Gregory Athelhurst, a wealthy baronet, who, having had occasion to stop for a short time at his Manor-house, had heard something which rather tickled his imagination, and, moreover, had seen something that had still more powerfully interested him in that part of Sussex.

Adjacent to the Grange, and dominating a princely park through which the mottled deer roamed at will among the tall ferns, is this Manor-house, the much-despised country seat of the jovial Sir Gregory, who, truth to tell, preferred his shooting cottage on his Scottish moor, or his racing box near New Market, to this lonely old pile of buildings, where his man-of-all-trades, Michael Dolan by name, seemed to be his sole companion. For, excepting a few waifs who visited the well-established county families scattered here and there, there were very few strangers who ever allowed themselves to be found in that rather forgotten part of the country, and it was because of this, and the doleful stagnation around it, that the Manor-house had always held so few attractions for Sir Gregory. The latter, when he wished to entertain his friends, did so always at some other of his country places. He was an ardent sportsman, had killed tigers in India and moose in Canada, was the straightest rider in the county, and in addition to this he was a bachelor of forty-two, rich, and not ill-looking; and though the gossips said he was too much addicted to the foaming bowl, they at the same time excused this weakness as a necessary adjunct to his character of country squire. At this particular time Sir Gregory had already been at the Manor-house much longer than was his custom. He had spent his days riding across the downs and in long rambles with his dogs, while his evenings had been generally passed in the company of a large bowl of punch. But even these attractions had begun to pall, and he had already decided to make preparations for his departure to the north, when something occurred to change his plans.

One day while he was returning from a long cross-country ride, and was walking his hunter slowly down a wooded lane, he soliloquized thus with himself: "This is getting to be blamed slow. I can't stand it much longer. Glad I gave Dolan such strict orders to have my traps ready for to-morrow. The Manor is nothing but a sleepy old bat-hole. I shan't be sorry to go north."

Just at this moment his hunter shied violently, and with a half-suppressed oath the baronet looked for the cause. What he did see was a fluttering silken skirt and the glimpse of a face so lovely that at the sight of it the bachelor baronet's heart went humpety-bumpety, and his jolly face turned scarlet as his coat, while he heard a sweet voice saying,

"May I trouble you to hand me that basket?" and, looking down, he perceived a little fancy basket half full of flowers lying on the roadside near his horse's feet.

"Certainly, madam," he said, handing it to her with great alacrity. The fair unknown bowed her thanks, and disappeared behind a big oak trunk, leaving Sir Gregory with interest and curiosity both aroused as he peered anxiously between the trees to get another glimpse of his fair inamorata.

"Who on earth can she be?" he thought; "that is no mere country girl, I am sure; I wish I could have another good look at her. Turning his horse's head homeward, he saw Dolan coming down the lane, and at once put him through a series of questions regarding the fair unknown, but the Irishman was as much at sea as the baronet himself. Dolan was Sir Gregory's right hand man. A good-natured, easy going, ready-witted fellow, with a fund of Irish humor; fond of a joke and perfectly devoted to his master. The two men were about the same height and build; but Sir Gregory had dark eyes and hair, while Dolan's head was crowned with a shock of coarse straight red, that no amount of brushing would reduce to order.

That evening, after dinner, Sir Gregory called Dolan and ordered his hunting clothes unpacked, and his pink coat brought out, saying that he wished to make an early start for the meet next day.

"Why, sir!" exclaimed the factotum in astonishment. "Sure I thought your honor would be departin' be the railway?"

"Never mind, Dolan, I have decided to stay a few days longer, I have nothing to hurry for, and I want to try the roan mare before I go; besides (to himself), I must find out who my fair unknown of this afternoon may be. If she be staying in the neighborhood she will surely be at the meet to-morrow, either as an onlooker or a participant; ten to one she is a regular Diana as well as a Venus! From this moment on Sir Gregory is possessed with one hope and one object in life, and hard enough he finds the task he has set himself. He discovers his fair one's name to be Mrs. Eldmere, and that the lady is living at the Grange, but as she does not visit in the neighborhood, and is rarely seen outside her own gates, he torments himself in vain to find some means of approaching her. Thinking she may possibly play tennis, he goes so far as to handle a racquet, doing so about as gracefully and effectually as an elephant swinging a bar of iron, but without any favorable result as to his playing tennis well, or seeing the lady, and he begins almost to despair of ever making her acquaintance. Dolan is the confidant of all his schemes, and he has orders to watch the Grange from time to time, hoping in this way to discover some means by which he can introduce himself to her notice, but at last the baronet growing impatient, resolves on a desperate step. "Just take these letters round to the 'Grange' and the 'Nest,'" he tells Dolan; and the person addressed feeling called upon to answer, but being totally incapable of answering like anybody else, replies in the following manner:

"Faix an' I will thot!" as he smiles his approval of his master's boldness, and goes off stolidly with the precious missives.

Dolan is a character in his own way, and when Mrs. Dolan allows him, he rules his master with a good-natured tyranny—that is, he makes allowances for human nature's frailties in him, and even helps them on occasions. But he has discovered that a great secret of

any man's power over his fellow-man is contained in
these words of advice given him by a friend: "Control
your own wife first." And Dolan sets about doing it.
Now this at first seems not so easy, as Mrs. Dolan has a
tongue that does perpetually seem to wag at both ends,
while for mere self-defence Dolan is reduced to the sad
plight of placing corks in his ears, so as not to be dis-
turbed in his duties or his night's rest by the eloquence
of his spouse. However, by degrees his corks are made
by an unaccountable agency to disappear, and Dolan is
sorely troubled, for he finds himself completely at the
lady's mercy, till he hits upon a happy expedient that
at last enables him to gain and hold undisputed sway.
He has hitherto made it a rule to fly at the first sign of
argument, and as Mrs. Dolan generally pursues, he now
leads his spouse around the garden at a brisk walk. At
first she has it, as usual, all her own way. However,
the pace soon tells, she pants for breath, and finds
herself wishing that, for the sake of argument, she had
never been blessed with such portentous charms. Her
breath goes. She can but gasp something to the effect that Dolan is an "iggerant clod;" but that person
refusing obstinately to hear her, she sinks on a bench
that fairly croaks beneath her portly form, and relapses
into an ominous silence. This manœuvre, repeated two or
three times a day, when his madam is in her most argu-
mentative moods, has an annihilating effect upon the
discussion of politics and abstract subjects, and the said
tonic duly administered reduces the poor woman to such
a state of submission that she often hears herself with
wonder pronouncing the words, "Then do as you like,"
or, "Just as you say, but don't worrit about it." Thus

Dolan had found himself master of the field with regard to his wife. But there was some one else who was supposed to have some kind of a voice in his family, and that was his daughter Maggie, who, as Dolan *père* expressed it, "was a caution, and too knowin' for her age." Now just how Maggie had secured a voice, morally as well as physically, happened in the following way:

On one occasion of hurry and bustle, when the master had brought home some friends unexpectedly to sleep at the Manor-house, *mère* Dolan was struggling with a basket of spotless linen in the rear hall, which at the time was buried in utter darkness. Setting the basket down, she advised the youthful Maggie to run and fetch the lantern from the house-keeper's room and to look sharp about it. This produced the effect of Maggie's scurrying on her errand, and returning to the fourth landing of the stair-way, on which is situated the room designated. She then proceeded to crane her neck over the balusters, in the endeavor to throw light upon the scene of her parent's struggle with the darkness and the linens, and seeing her below she (the daughter) muses thus:

"Mar is tearin'! she'll whip me when I get to the bottom if she don't have the light quick! I know what I'll do!" This with a sudden burst of inspiration, and suiting the act to the thought, she flings one of her pedal extremities (translated legs) over the balusters and holds aloft the lantern, so as to illumine her parent's pathway. She loses no time either in turning the head-over-heels act, and for a moment she and the lantern offer the sight of a confused jumble in their endeavor to reach the ground first. On the whole, the lantern, I think, fares

worst, as it comes down with a crash and a bump at a
safe distance from Maggie, whose wide flung limbs are
deposited in the linen basket! Now on first becoming
aware that her daughter is flying through mid-air, Mrs.
Dolan, with a gurgle of horror, sinks upon a chair, and
hopes she is going to faint. But she does not; and when
next she has the courage to remove her hands from her
eyes, she sees through the semi-darkness a face peeping
from over the rim of the wicker basket. This she slowly
discovers to be Maggie, who has had the effrontery not
to have met with any personal injuries, at the expense,
too, of her (Mrs. Dolan's) newly washed table and bed
linen.

"Not even her nose broken! and my table-cloths all
spoilt, the hussy!" she cries as she makes a wicked dive
for the linen. But Maggie in her heart of hearts, as she
peeps from the basket, tells herself. "Mar *is* tearin'!"
so she makes a lively spring from under mar's portentous arm, and seeing no means of escape from the hall,
she darts like a rat into an aperture under a walnut cabinet, heavily laden with the master's handsomest pieces
of antique china; nor does she suffer even the tip of her
heel to remain open to the attack of the enemy.

"Come out of there, ye little viper!" says the afflicted
mother, but Maggie laughs to herself and remains firm.
"Such a thrashin' as ye'll get!"

Here a light appears on the scene, carried by the
master himself, who had heard some of the uproar, and
wanted to hear the rest. But the good woman had
worked herself into so white a heat that she was oblivious of everything save a desire to get at the culprit.

"Thrashin's too good fur ye! Ye'll have the dose!"

This for Maggie meant castor oil, two table-spoonfuls of which were choked down her throat each time she was particularly naughty, each time without fail to come up again, and each time to have a still bigger dose choked down again. Therefore was Maggie never more desperate than when the "dose" was mentioned in her hearing. The effect upon her in this instance was seen by the calm but determined upheaval of the china decking the walnut cabinet, of the rocking to and fro of the same, of the tottering—

"Hold! hold! come out, you little ferret!" shouts the master in an agony of uproarious mirth, for nothing appeals to him like what he chooses to look upon as a huge joke, even though his china is in danger.

"Come out, little Meg! and I'll make it all right for you. You shall not be worried or punished, I'll answer for that."

But Maggie is incredulous, and the earthquake and upheaval business continues until Mrs. Dolan succumbs in fear and trembling, falls into an arm-chair, and Maggie knows that she has won the day.

She creeps out from her rat-hole with feelings of triumph and safety, and from that day she has gained her master's protection and is never "dosed."

But from her rat-hole on that day Maggie has carried with her something more than mere feelings of triumph and security. She has also carried with her a little faded piece of paper, blood-stained and torn at one end, and which piece of worthless paper no one but cunning little Maggie herself is permitted to see.

CHAPTER XII.

IN BACHELOR QUARTERS.

Sir Gregory Athelhurst is a bachelor, and when we say that, we mean to imply that though he has now reached the mature age of forty-two, he has not yet found it necessary to change his state of single blessedness, being perfectly content to live in his beautiful, rambling old manor-house (going sadly to waste for want of a mistress), entertaining his friends and enjoying himself in his own peculiar way. Yes, Sir Gregory is a bachelor. Sir Gregory has a beautiful house all for his own. So thinks Maudie de la Roche.

What does a bachelor who smokes want with a drawing-room all gold and pale blue paneling? What does a bachelor who lives on horseback, or in his cattle-houses, know of the luxuries that can all be piled by one pair of fair, plump little hands (such as Maudie's, for instance) into the exquisite boudoir she reserves for her own private little love scenes and sorrows and novel reading? So thinks Maudie de la Roche, who is very envious of a title in general, but of that of Lady Athelhurst in particular.

So also does *not* think Sir Gregory, as, leaning backward in his comfortable arm-chair, with his large football-shaped head submerged behind the *Times*, he is enjoying a temporary lull between the business of his breakfast and his morning gallop.

Sir Gregory is a stubborn bachelor. He persists in preferring his low pipe to the exquisite art and blandishments that the feminine mind can offer, and this morning in particular he hugs his lonely state; but then he is essentially unamiable. This state of solitary rejoicing is produced by a letter which he has received this morning from Maudie de la Roche:

"DEAR SIR GREGORY: We are giving an entertainment," etc., it runs. "You must, must, must come!"

"I must, must, must come! Must, must, must I? We shall see about that, little Miss Fattie! (That is what I fear most of her men friends called Miss Maudie.) And forthwith the wicked—*the wicked* baronet shoots the would-be love letter into the cuspidor, then calmly returns to the contemplation of the *Times*, giving the while an occasional pat to his favorite cats. Of these, being a bachelor, he has two—Larkie and Scotchie, and they enjoy their mutton chop every morning with their master, whom they rule. When the latter retires behind his newspaper, it is the cats' especial time for enjoyment, and this morning they are having their usual boisterous sparring match at their master's feet, who himself actually begins shortly to purr with content. And shall fat Maudie, the wicked temptress, come in to disturb his happiness? Never!

_____

If Maudie does not come to disturb his dreams, something else does in the shape of a greyhound puppy, who means no harm, but whose appearance causes, quite unnecessarily, a great pit-pat-patting to begin suddenly in the gentle feline breasts, whose owners, with angry grinning jaws, jump among the china and cut-glass arrange-

ments so copiously covering the breakfast-table, while
the bachelor looks calmly on from behind his newspaper, and gently remonstrates with the units of his
menagerie.

What Sir Gregory next sees is his handsome puppy,
of whom he is especially fond, trying to follow the
cats.

" Down, Trevor, down !" cries Sir Gregory, the twinkle
in whose eye tells the puppy plainly that his master is
enjoying the fun.

Trevor has a gallant heart that is not to be conquered
by mere cats, and since his master ordains that he shall
not skip over the table after them, he is determined that
those cats shall come down to him from their strong-
hold.

This end he calmly effects, with a twinkle of mischief
in his roguish eye, by giving one short sharp jerk to the
corner of the damask table-cloth, which gives to his pull,
and next moment comes to the floor, with its litter of
cats, china, cut-glass, and silver, at the same time burying Trevor, like Samson, in the ruins.

Next there is a dreadful howl and screech and hiss,
followed by the rolling about and cracking of china and
glass on a large scale ; and in the midst of this charivari
the bachelor baronet stretches his arm calmly and pulls
the bell almost from its socket.

" Dolan," he says, rather red in the face from anger,
to the woman who runs hurriedly to answer his call,
" what the d—— is the use of a house-keeper who does
nothing but eat her head off in wages and fine feeding ?
I give you a month's warning for letting that puppy in
here. That will teach you, I hope, that my dining-room

is not a kennel. Pick up those things, and you pay for everything that is broken!"

With a sullen growl, and an angry dive for the cats and the puppy, Mrs. Dolan stoops over the debris of the breakfast-table.

"And it's all his fault, it is. He should have stopped the fight, and not call for a poor helpless woman to do everythink for him; but men is such arrogant good-for-nothing creatures."

The month's warning did not trouble her in the least. She had been six years with Sir Gregory now, and every fortnight of it had she received, without fail, the same month's warning. In fact, it was a problem now whether she or Sir Gregory ruled at the Manor-house.

That afternoon, as Sir Gregory was returning from his daily gallop, with his thoughts in a flutter at the remembrance of a certain vision which he has seen but a short hour ago, and which rather shakes his allegiance to bachelor life, he is surprised to find, as he turns a bend in the road, that two horsemen in pink are riding down the high-way, only a little way ahead of him. Seeing that one of their horses had gone lame, and being a keen sportsman, he rides quickly forward to see if he can offer aid, as the Manor-house is quite near and the village at least four miles distant.

Upon hearing the sound of horses' hoofs behind them the two strangers turn to meet the new-comer, and there is a general murmur of astonishment from all three as Sir Gregory rides up. "Well, Borradale! Hello, De Montford," he cries, with a genuine ring of pleasure in his voice, "how in the name of goodness did you come here, and why, being here, did you not let me know your whereabouts? Don't you remember that the Manor-house is in this neighborhood, and that you have both promised to put in a few days there, if ever you were in this country? I see that you can't get much farther with that poor beast of yours, Borradale, so, as the Manor is close at hand, I must insist on your both putting up there for the night at least, and when I have once got you safe in Liberty Hall, you will find it such comfortable quarters you won't care to move."

"It's awfully good of you, old fellow" says Borradale. "I shall be glad to accept your offer; it isn't much fun riding an animal that is dead lame, and we were consulting just now as to what were best to be done, for we can't possibly get back to Shoreham in this plight."

"Well, come on now," says Sir Gregory, cheerily, I will send a man over for your traps in less than two hours, and if you want any other inducement, you can shoot all day if you like, drive or ride my thoroughbreds, besides having the chance of seeing some of the finest heads of cattle in the shires. The coverts are in fine condition just now, and it will be a godsend if you two fellows will help me shoot over them during the next few days My cook is not to be despised, and if you are as fond of good wine as you used to be (with a sly look at De Montford) you will find the Manor cellar equal to the occasion.

"You offer us such a list of good things," says De Montford, gayly, "there is no resisting you. My only surprise is that you have been allowed to enjoy these good things unmolested for so long."

"Eh! what?" said the baronet, coloring a little under his friend's determined gaze.

" I mean, is there no fair Lady of the Manor? or are you sure there is not one hidden in this delightful retreat? Has Cupid never troubled you, my dear fellow? or is your heart adamantine, and given wholly to your beasts and cattle?"

" Well, well, all in good time," replied Sir Gregory, sheepishly, but " here we are at the house, and now, before we go in, I want to show you the stables." Thereupon the three men stroll off in that direction, having given the horses to a groom with minute direct-tions from his master to bandage and attend to the suffering animal.

While visiting stables and cattle sheds the conversation between the three friends degenerates into a genuine masculine gossip, and who will dare to say that of the two genders the masculine will not be by far the more voluble and searching a gossip than any chattering that could be gone through by the feminine crowd? The conversation having veered from horses to cattle, and from these latter to lovely woman, Sir Gregory finds himself in a corner.

" You have not yet answered my question," continued De Montford, rather enjoying the baronet's discomfiture on this topic. " Now tell me, isn't there a woman in the case?"

" Wait until you see her," says Sir Gregory incautiously; then, having betrayed himself, he continues, in a stage whisper, " I am rather struck just now by a beautiful and mysterious lady, a widow, I presume, as she dresses mostly in black, and lives alone with a beautiful young girl for her sole companion. Her name, I find, is Mrs. Eldmere, and she has taken the Grange for a year,

lives there in style, must have money, is a divinely
lovely woman, and a perfect horsewoman," he continues
warming up to his subject. "I tell you, my dear fellows,
she's thorough-bred every inch of her, and I swear I will
make her acquaintance, however difficult or improbable
that may seem. As she and her friend both ride, I am
looking forward to seeing them with us over grass
and fallow, and if I can't make the lady's acquaintance
then, somehow, why d——— it, my name isn't Gregory
Athelhurst.

"That's right, old fellow, go in and win !" cries Rutland
Borradale with a quiet smile. "Young, beautiful, and
a widow ! what more could any man desire ? and I suppose, as you have no designs on her pretty friend, one
of us poor fellows might have a chance there. No wonder
that you are getting tired of bachelorhood, with such a
tempting prospect as the handsome widow presents, for
of course any woman would think twice before she refused a title (this is said rather satirically), and if she is
fond of country life and sport, you will have no difficulty
in persuading her to a change of name."

"I am growing quite curious to see the fair lady, says
de Montford, and hope you will manage it while we are
here."

But in the meantime, after Sir Gregory had with great
pride shown his friends all the various beauties to be seen
in the stables and out-houses attached to the Manor, he
took them both up to the house, quite ready to be introduced to the good comfortable quarters he had promised ;
but alas ! at this early hour in the afternoon he is apparently not expected home, and he finds that the angry
Mrs. Dolan reigns supreme to the exclusion of outside

authority. The gentlemen are therefore prepared to be astonished at nothing, and are not even startled when, issuing from the direction of the drawing-room, they hear the most lugubrious sounds.

Thump, thump, thump! and with the loud pedal well down, fall the clumsy fingers of the ambitious Daddy Dolan on the keys of Sir Gregory's grand-piano, and as the gentlemen enter the room unseen, she raises her voice in a loud, unmusical wail, whose tune is, alas, unrecognizable!

The voice of her master calls her from her dreams of bliss rather unfeelingly:

" Why don't you get a sledge-hammer ?"

With a scream and a kick which reduces the piano-stool to a lowly position among the flowers of the carpet, Daddy flies, with her head hidden under her apron, and the three gentlemen laugh heartily, though Sir Gregory, as he picks up the fallen stool, mutters audibly: " This is what comes of being a bachelor. I am not even master in my own house."

Here Mrs. Dolan reappears, and in a very aggrieved and dignified voice murmurs, with her hands folded before her:

" Well, Sir Gregory, what's for dinner ?"

"Dinner !" cries the baronet, looking as thunderstruck as though he never expected to have any that day.

" Yes, sir, dinner," in a still more aggrieved way.

" I thought dinner was cooked long ago."

" Cooked !" retorts the house-keeper, " when no *hor*ders was given, and no one to give 'em."

" Couldn't you have given the orders ?" shouts Sir Gregory, in a towering temper, " or what do you do all day?" This looks hopeful for Mrs. Dolan, and she triumphs secretly, but outwardly she wipes away an angry tear with the corner of her white apron.

"You know very well, sir, that I have resigned *h*all *h*authority in this 'ouse, since I'm engaged packing to leave at your orders next month."

"Tut, woman! In the mean time I'm d—— sure I'm not going to do without my dinner every day. So put off the packing and go about your business, and that quickly!" thunders Sir Gregory, knowing in his inmost heart that he is, as usual, going to be the loser in the argument.

"What do you wish for dinner, Sir Gregory?" pursues the relentless house-keeper.

"Oh, anything," scornfully; "anything that I can carve—chops, steaks—and be quick!" for Sir Gregory, being portly, remembers to have suffered severely from over-exertion on one occasion when he carved a turkey for twelve persons, and he thinks it detracts from his pleasure in dining to have to mop his brow in the very middle of dislocating the drumstick.

Mrs. Dolan, I think, likewise remembers the occasion in question, for later, while a generous dinner is being served, there appears on the table before Sir Gregory a magnificent bird, something of the description of the despised turkey; and the baronet finds ample reason to curse his house-keeper for being so clever.

"If I don't settle that woman!" snarls Sir Gregory. "I'm hanged if I don't be married just to get the better of her!" And so on, and so on, until he gets actually wearied of the hanging business, as applied to Mrs. Dolan.

" Well, De Montford," cries jolly Sir Gregory late that night, as they are retiring after a long evening spent in dining copiously, and quaffing of the oldest vintages offered by the Athelhurst cellar, and that very apparently to no sparing amount, " I have your promise to bring the earl down for the big meet at Drislehurst, and we shall have a royal day, or rather week of it, I hope. Borradale there loves pretty women and fine horses as well as the best of us, and I am sure he will stay with me till then."

" That, I fear, is impossible," begins Borradale, but is summarily interrupted by his host.

" Tut, man! you are my prisoner now in these ghostly old halls, and as such I declare you to be incapable of deciding for yourself in any matter to-night. So, until to-morrow, just yield to the inevitable, which at this moment, as I see your eyes are blinking, is sleep. I could be an all-nighter, but you young ones can't be expected to stand under all I can."

Whereat Sir Gregory, on his way to his own particular sanctum, endeavors to describe the ever-widening circles of a hawk on the wing.

The last thoughts that present themselves to the minds of De Montford and Rutland Borradale, ere in sleep they lose all power of unravelling problematical questions, are somewhat similar.

" This beautiful *inconnue* of Sir Gregory's," thinks the former, " who may she be ? She has rather interested me. I declare to heaven I think I'll stay and solve the mystery. It may turn up something to my advantage, and it can't harm me ! Who knows if I might not even win an heiress, and that, faith, will be acceptable ; for if

I don't do that pretty soon I shall have to look up New York, with its own peculiar style of thinking and its more peculiar style of marrying. To win a pile here will be to save an odious journey, so here goes for it!

"They say she has a husband somewhere!" The fact looks rather important, but it does not have a very dampening effect upon De Montford's resolutions. "No matter," he thinks; "she will, no doubt, be willing enough to go through the courts if the inducements be made sufficiently fetching, or if the thumb-screw be applied with sufficient determination; and— I think I have mastered lovely women before."

With a contented expression he falls asleep, and in his dreams he has a wealthy heiress at his feet hungering for his smiles, which makes him happy.

Not less interested in the beautiful unknown is Rutland Borradale, but his interest in the matter is more or less unselfish, as it springs entirely from a feeling of *camaraderie* towards his host, and an intense appreciation of the humorous side of the question. He therefore falls asleep promising himself, if he be persuaded to make a longer stay with Sir Gregory than had been his intention, to witness at least some rather ridiculous and spicy love scenes.

CHAPTER XIII.

TRACED IN RUBIES.

Next morning, notwithstanding the revel overnight, all is bustle at the Manor-house. Sir Gregory has offered the two young men each a fine mount, and the meet being at a distance, they have to make an early start; so, after partaking of a hasty breakfast, all three ride off in the best possible spirits, anticipating the day's enjoyments.

But Fortune does not favor them; the hounds do nothing in particular, and after a rather disappointing day they find themselves leisurely riding homeward about three o'clock that same afternoon. They are a somewhat silent party; the horses are tired and jaded, and Sir Gregory is not in the best of tempers, as he had promised himself a fine day's sport, and looking upon their continued ill luck as a great want of consideration on the part of Providence, he is greatly disgusted at their nonsuccess.

As they ride onward, the country begins to look familiar, and at last they reach a low stone wall that borders the Grange estate. Here Rutland Borradale falls a little behind his companions and allows them to get several paces ahead; he is riding in a listless kind of way; his face looks dark and sad; perhaps thoughts are running in his mind of a day long ago when he had hoped all things of woman's love, and had seen his hopes wrecked.

As he and his companions proceed, however, the country grows to look a little more like home, and this rather cheers the riders, as, man-like, they promise themselves something warmly comforting when they shall leave their saddles.

As they find themselves passing along under the shadow of the Grange walls, from which to the Manor-house is but a step—otherwise a quarter of a mile—they are startled at sight of the lithe form of a greyhound which, leaping from behind to the top of the Grange wall, lands on the road near them, as graceful and light as a feather wafted by summer winds. Rutland Borradale's eyes followed the retreating form of the handsome hound rather indifferently; while the dusky shadows thrown by the trees, interweaving overhead, prevented him from observing the dog's points more fully as the latter disappeared over a neighboring fence, to reappear, however, lower down. Here the hound stands revealed in a full burst of sunshine, and Rutland Borradale, as he spurs his horse forward, is observed by his companions to change color.

"Whose is he?" cried Borradale, disconnectedly (apropos to them of nothing). "Whose? I do not think. I think some— No, I think—"

Here sir Gregory breaks in with "Do you often think aloud, my dear fellow, in such disconnected language?" which remark has the effect of making Borradale subdue some powerful emotion, which has come near mastering him; and with a light remark he turns the tables on his opponent.

"My incoherency was owing to an eagerness on *your* account. Is not that your adored one's hound?"

"Why, so it must be," cries the baronet in astonishment, noticing the dog for the first time.

"And therefore the object of your courtly admiration cannot be far away."

"By Jove! if you aren't right." And here Sir Gregory, with a heart that seems to go up and down like a field of mangold-wurzel in autumn, with a bump here, and a hollow there, and all turned higgledy-piggledy, proceeds to do some earnest prowling for the longed-for sight of a gate cut in the Grange wall, but none appearing, he turns by way of pastime to watch the hound, snuffing among the fallen dried leaves, probably for a hedgehog (ladies' dogs are good for rooting out pig-headed little hedgehogs and making a fuss about it). Then Rutland Borradale, gently pressing spurs to his horse's sides, proceeds calmly on his homeward way, but not without having first whistled to the hound, calling him by name in a masterful voice:

"Lion! Lion! to heel, sir!"

Suddenly the dog, to the astonishment of Sir Gregory and De Montford, lifts his noble crest, pricks up his ears, and in the flash of a thought has passed them with a loud yelp, and has thrown himself madly upon Rutland Borradale. Astonishment is succeeded in their minds by fear for their friend's safety, as the only explanation to them of the matter is rabies in the dog! but, soon, however, they find that the gallant hound is covering Borradale with canine caresses, licking his hands, toes, leathers, cords, everything, with an occasional little yelp of delight, even rubbing the clay and leaves off his own nose onto that of the gentleman.

"Quiet, Lion! quiet, old fellow!" mutters Borradale,

and seeing that he has turned a bend in the road, which hides him from his companions, he lowers his head over that of the hound and examines the dog's collar. This is a beautifully elaborate piece of workmanship, bearing the mythical inscription that he has seen somewhere often before, executed in tiny diamond chips, "With my heart forever!"

He reads still further, something that makes his lips quiver, it is the word wrought in glittering red stones, "Never!"

"Elra! Elra! she loves me still, she will not dare deny it," and unclasping the rich collar which opens only to the pressure of a secret spring, he gives the dog a tender, long, maudlin hug, and then, sitting erect once more in his saddle, after having placed the collar in safety, somewhere about the region of his waistcoat, looks as emotionless as though his heart was not throbbing in wildest rebellion against his breast-pocket.

"Hello, Bor.! we thought you were home by now," says Sir Gregory. "Sly dog, who knows all about the lady of the Grange, and won't tell others who might like to know. Well, well!" he continues, putting spurs to his horse, "we'll get square; but first we must dine side by side, to show there's no ill feeling, you know!" and he gives a knowing wink, which Borradale does not appreciate, and in reply to which he denies all knowledge about Mrs. Eldmere, although the hound, he maintains, is one he has once sold at a very high price to a dog fancier, previous to starting for a tour on the European continent. A silvery whistle interrupts the knowing laugh with which Sir Gregory answers this "yarn," as he terms it, and at the words "Get back there, hound,"

HE UNCHAINED THE RICH COLLAR, WHICH OPENED ONLY ON THE PRESSURE OF A SECRET SPRING.

from Borradale, the dog skims lightly over the high
moss-grown wall back again into the Grange meadows.
There he is greeted by a little murmur of delight from
his mistress, and a little cry of astonishment from her
companion, Topsie.

"Why, what has become of his collar?" cries Mrs.
Eldmere in dismay. "Oh, it could not have been a
tramp who stole it! he would never find the secret
spring. Who could it be? I remember but one who
ever knew the secret, and he—"

"Oh, Elra, that lovely collar!" says Topsie, regretfully,
"I always knew it would be stolen some day! the only
thing you can do is to offer a very large reward for its
recovery—"

"Perhaps! I don't know," is Mrs. Eldmere's answer to
her friend's amazement, but the latter cannot hear the
muttered words, "If only it were he!"

"Elra, dearest, I have an idea!" cries Topsie suddenly,
as they are walking slowly back to the house followed
by Lion. "Let us go down to old Peter's cottage and
tell him about your loss; he is crazy enough sometimes,
I think, but he might make inquiries in the village for
us, and I know that he will do anything for you or me."

"It's not a bad idea," said Mrs. Eldmere thoughtfully;
"let us go across the fields; the sooner something is
done the more chance there is of finding the collar, and
old Peter knows all the country folks for miles around.
Come, Lion, we will take you with us;" and turning
briskly in the opposite direction the two ladies are soon
out of sight across the fields on their way to old Peter's
cottage.

This individual being somewhat of a character, de-

serves a few words of introduction, which are here
given:

Peter Long had been one of the old family retainers
in the house of Ravenstone during two generations. He
had seen the old marquis grow up and die, to be succeeded by his son, the present owner of the title; and old
Peter, as huntsman to the Marquis of Ripdale, considered
himself as much part and parcel of the family as the
gloomy old mansion-house of Ravenstone itself. He had
lived there, man and boy, for over fifty years, and could
as little bear transplanting as any of the sturdy old oaks
upon the place. So that when the present marquis, a
man of fast life and dissolute habits, came to his own,
and Peter found himself curtly dismissed, he obstinately
refused to leave, and gave the marquis to understand
that he intended to live and die in his old home at Ravenstone. This obstinacy so incensed his new master that
he gave peremptory orders for the old man's removal,
and old Peter was turned out bag and baggage, no one
daring to oppose the cruel power of the proud and
haughty marquis. This blow nearly broke old Peter's
heart, and for a time it seemed as if his mind was weakened, but he had some kind friends left, and by their help
he was established in a little cottage in the woods,
where he now lived on the small pittance allowed him
by the ladies of Ravenstone, who, though they were
powerless to prevent his dismissal, contrived to assist the
poor old fellow unknown to their brother. Peter's hut,
or cottage, stood in the midst of the woods, and often
the passers-by could hear him cheering on the dogs, imi-
tating the bugle call, with loud cries of "Tally-ho! tally-
ho!" as he roamed through the woods, for in his crazy

moods he was once more the gallant hardy huntsman of
former days, and the sound of a horse's hoof or the bark
of a dog would often be enough to rouse him when
nothing else would. Topsie had known old Peter from
her childhood, and she it was who had done the most for
him in his lonely exile. He would never want while she
could help him, and Peter loved the very ground his dear
missie (as he called her) trod on. Twice in her life had
he been at hand to save her from great peril: once as a
child, when riding, he had caught her from the saddle as
her pony, mad with fright, had leaped into the quarry below; and again, when the doors of her own home had been
closed to her, she had crept to old Peter's cottage and
passed two days in hiding there; so that Topsie's love
for the poor crazy fellow was only equalled by her pity
for his lonely condition and wrecked life.

Mrs. Eldmere and Topsie, meanwhile, had crossed the
fields and were entering a little glade in the woods, which
now stood in the budding beauty of approaching spring.
It was carpeted with moss, greener than emerald and
softer than velvet, and the faint sweet perfume of violets
mingled with the soft breath of a light breeze which
played around them, ruffling the plumes of Mrs. Eldmere's dainty hat and tossing the red-gold locks of the
young girl into still more picturesque confusion.

"Hunting will soon be over," said Topsie with a sigh, as
she drew a long breath of the fragrant perfume which now
filled the air. "I always remember how Peter hated the
violets when they came, and I never could bring him
to admit any beauty in flowers. 'Drat them vilets!'
was his usual reply; 'they spoils the scent for us, and
that's all I care about.' However, it's a good thing there

won't be much more hard riding, for Irish King is getting
very tender on his forefeet, and I am afraid he won't be
good for much after this year."

"That reminds me, dearest," says Elra with a loving
smile, "I never told you that I was negotiating for a new
horse for you. Such a fearless rider needs a better mount
than the poor old King, and I mean you to have a steed
worthy of your equestrian powers."

"Oh, Elra !" you darling," cries the girl, impulsively
throwing her arms round her companion's neck and giving her a fond kiss. "How good of you to think of it;
but please don't buy the horse now ; it would only be
idle, eating its head off in the stable all summer, and the
King carries me beautifully in our country rides ; he is
only found wanting on the hard dusty road."

"Well, we will see," is Mrs. Eldmere's answer. "I
haven't heard of a suitable animal yet, so it may be best
to wait, as you suggest, though I will tell Robert to keep
his eyes open, and if he hears of a lady's hunter being
for sale to let me know of it."

They found old Peter in, and after fully explaining the
lost collar to him Topsie said :

"Now, Peter, this collar must be found, and if any of
the villagers know anything about it I am sure we can
trust you to find it out"

"That ye can, missie," says the old man with a chuckle
of delight. "I'm spry enough still, and if that there
dog's collar has been stole by any one as lives within
ten miles o' here, I'm bound to hear about it. You trust
me, missie; they all thinks I'm daft, and takes no care what
they says afore me, so I'll just go down and have a mug
of ale at the Hare and Hounds, where I'll likely hear all
ye want to know."

"That's right, Peter; we knew you would help us; here's the money for the ale, but mind you don't stay too long or drink too much;" and with this injunction the ladies left him and returned to the Grange by the same way as they had come. As they reached the house Mrs. Eldmere said: "We had better renew our search now, Topsie—I am so determined to find that missing link;" and they go up to an old lumber-room and are soon pouring over a collection of dust-begrimed papers which lie hidden in the depths of a worm-eaten oaken chest.

CHAPTER XIV.

LION FINDS A MASTER.

Yes, there is no denying it, life at the Grange is dull, very dull, and its quietude is beginning to tell on Mrs. Eldmere, though she scarcely dares to admit it, even to herself. But to-day, somehow, the ghost of the past has risen from its grave, and, sitting there in her quiet boudoir, with hands idly folded and eyes gazing listlessly out on the lovely glowing landscape, which seems but to mock her with its brightness, Mrs. Eldmere thinks of those happy days now past and gone. As the lovely American heiress, who had there been so courted and flattered as she, when in the zenith of her girlish beauty she had queened it at ball and reception—when her name was upon every lip, and the homage of every man was laid at her feet? Society had chosen her for queen, and for two happy years she had reigned; her life had been full of gayety and brightness; now all was changed, and she felt herself left lonely and deserted, though in burying herself at the Grange she had volun- tarily cut herself off from all society, and her hiding- place was even now unknown to many of her friends.

"It is not only for myself," she says, as she rises and impatiently paces the floor of her pretty room. "That poor child who shares my exile; what must this dull life mean to her? I was wrong to let her come, and though I doubt not her love and fidelity to me, I must not suffer her sacrifice to be too irksome.

" Life," she continues plaintively, " is a sorry problem. Yesterday a reigning queen; to-day a solitary, despised hermit. But, oh ! better so. Better to live alone and die unnoticed than to count hours of lingering torture by the side of Murray Cresenworth.

(For Mrs. Eldmere, the lady of the Grange, is indeed Elra Cresenworth—who, having vainly tried to yield loving allegiance to her adoring husband, has at last fled from him in despair, and buried herself in the loneliest little nook in Sussex, hoping that her lord and master may never see her again.)

"After all, the human heart grows accustomed to changes, and I shall live my sorrow down, I suppose. Things might be infinitely worse, for I have Topsie, with her glorious intelligence and her darling gentle ways.

(As she is speaking, a clock in the room strikes eleven with silvery tones, and Mrs. Eldmere starts with a cry of surprise.)

" How late already; and we are to ride this morning."

So, hastily gathering up some letters which lie open on the table before her, she turns and leaves the room to don her hat and habit.

Half an hour later finds her standing in the hall, whip in hand and with a smile on her face, for as she knows the sharp eyes of Miss Topsie would quickly search her soul, she is determined to hide, even from her, the unsatisfied longings and vain regrets that she has lately indulged in.

" Come, Topsie dear, aren't you ready ?" she cries to her young companion (who was in herself somewhat of a mystery to the people about, being known as Topsie to all her friends, and apparently possessing no surname by which to distinguish her). "It will be a glorious morning for a ride, and Irish King is getting so impatient."

"Coming! coming!" cries a fresh young voice, and Miss Topsie appears, clad in a smart, well-fitting habit and jaunty hat, from under whose brim her bright, dark eyes glance mischievously, and, with a smile that shows every one of her brilliant white teeth, the young lady runs down the steps to fondle her horse and give him his accustomed lump of sugar.

"You will spoil the king," says Mrs. Eldmere smiling, "and you should always give him his reward when the ride is over, not before the start."

"That's just where I don't agree with you," says Topsie, brightly. "'Duty first and pleasure after' is a stupid saying. I make it pleasure first. Perchance *après* one may have to do the duty, but I always get out of it if I can."

"Well, where shall we go?" says Mrs. Eldmere when they were both mounted and indulging in a preparatory canter down the avenue with Lion at the horses' heels.

"Let's go round by Chancoubury Ring, and see if the fairies have finished their revels. You know they always have a good time at midsummer, at least the story-books tell us that, and I would dearly like to have my three wishes fulfilled."

"Well, what do you wish for, dear?" says her companion, amused at the girlish chatter.

"First, a pair of wings, which would fly with me wherever I wished to roam; a purse like that of Fortunatus, never empty; and last, but not least, to be a brilliant financier or statesman with the world at my feet. I am restless, ambitious, extravagant, and these three longings would then be gratified. Now what do you want, Elra?"

"Oh, I!" said Mrs. Eldmere, with a start and change of color. "I want to find Lion at present. Do you see him, Topsie? He has missed us, I fear."

"Why there he is!" she cried, pointing to a solitary horseman in the field ahead of the riders, towards whose knee the dog was leaping with spasmodic efforts. There is Lion springing on that man. Can he be going to attack him? What can be the matter? Why, he is caressing Lion!"

"You must be mistaken, Topsie," said Mrs. Eldmere, growing suddenly pale, "Lion has never suffered any one to caress him but one man, and he— It cannot be." Hastily crossing the fence they came up closer to the horseman, who did not even turn in his saddle, but acted as if he were totally unaware of their presence. Elra called Lion to her side, but for once he did not respond, and remained gazing up at the rider, his very beautiful head almost touching the tips of the gentleman's patent leather boots.

And now Topsie receives somewhat of a shock as she concludes that the man before them is a total stranger, if she might judge by the greeting he received; yet, on glancing at Mrs. Eldmere, she sees her trembling with vexation or some other indefinable emotion.

But here the gentleman, at whose knee Lion persists in trotting, wheels his horse round, giving Mrs. Eldmere room to pass. They exchange a long, steady look, charged with defiance on both sides; a deep, dangerous glance, which stirs their very souls and bridges over many a weary month, and which, in its very intensity of pain, is intensity of keenest pleasure, but passing, it leaves the lady looking very haughty and unsubdued as she advances with an almost imperceptible acknowledgment of his salutation, and does not even offer to call Lion to her side.   But Borradale, for it was he, with fully as haughty a glance, watches their retreating figures with some muttered words, the spelling of which would be very difficult to accomplish.

He remains, apparently rooted to the ground, in the middle of the field, like some old statue of some older king, transported there to frighten the preying rooks, until he catches a glimpse of one of the ladies' skirts fluttering to the ground.

She has descended, ostensibly, to unbar a five-rail gate, but she seems to find it so pleasant on the soft mosses that carpet the banks fringed with blackthorn that she has suffered herself to sink down among the golden kingcups and mosses, and seems to think she is going to remain there.   A few powerful strides brings Rutland Borradale's horse alongside, and then he sees it is Mrs. Eldmere, who, with the tears of mortification and anger frozen in her eyes, and with a face colorless as her kerchief, has sunk down pale and trembling as the aspen in the breeze.   Topsie is beside her in a moment, and offers remedies none of them half so effectual as the reappearance of the (to her) strange gentleman on the scene.

"What secret misery is the cause of this emotion?" thinks Topsie, with a sad shake of her wise little head; "I have never seen her ruffled yet."

As Mr. Borradale looks at her something soft and pitying creeps into his eyes and he says a few gentle words,

which, however, do not seem to have at all the desired
effect. Elra thinks she hears a triumphant ring in his
voice, and hastily rising, with proudly erect head, she
springs into the saddle, disdaining his proffered help
and taking that of Topsie. "Come, Lion!" she says,
commandingly, but Lion lingers by Borradale.

"He has had a master before he acknowledged a mistress," murmurs the young man, with a challenge in his
eyes and voice.

"Then he can still lick the hand of the master, and
bend to his sovereign rule, for no mistress will whistle
for him again!"

"Mrs. Murray Cresenworth is mistaken if she thinks
that Rutland Borradale reclaims that which he has once
given, be it so insignificant a gift as that of a dog, or
even that of his own heart's affection. He never takes
back what he has once given!"

Entirely calm he stood there as those quietly spoken
words, surcharged with painful meaning, fell from his
lips, and with one quick, frightened look she turned
away—not, however, before a little telltale quiver, one
rapid, rebellious heaving of her bosom, had given him
the answer that he sought. In a moment more her met-
tlesome horse, having felt the sharp sting of her tiny
spur, springs away over the heathery fields, bearing a
mistress whose form is very light and supple, but whose
heart is strangely heavy, and will be so for many a day
to come. When they reach the Grange Topsie notices
the cloud on Elra's brow, and sees what she thinks looks
like great tears standing in her eyes; so, subduing her
natural curiosity about their late encounter, she chatters
gayly till they reach the house, when Mrs. Eldmere,

pleading headache and indisposition, retired to her own room, and was not again visible till dinner-time that evening.

"Oh dear, what can the matter be?" sighs the girl, as she takes up a favorite novel after her solitary lunch and throws herself down for a quiet read, "I would give a great deal to know who and what Lion's master may be, and what he has to do with Elra. I hate mysterious men!" and she sighs again.

CHAPTER XV.

SIR GREGORY AT THE GRANGE.

That same evening, had we chanced to turn in at the Grange, we might have seen that Sir Gregory has at last effected his entry between the tower gates of its avenue, and has been bold and fortunate enough even to penetrate to its divinely appointed little drawing-room. But once there, to his bitter chagrin be it said, he finds that the object of his intensest interest is gone out; or more likely, Sir Gregory thinks, is in her own sweet little boudoir, but won't be worried out by him.

He therefore keeps a careful eye on the door-way, to cut off her chance of passing it unobserved, while he settles himself to the task of charming Miss Topsie, whom he has surprised over a volume of Erckmann-Chatrain, and who now finds herself in for a dismal interview. "So glad to make your acquaintance," says the baronet, blandly smiling, and advancing to shake hands with his victim. "Such charming ladies and good horse-women are an acquisition in a country place like this."

"What do you know about our riding, Sir Gregory?" says Topsie, mischievously; "I am not aware that you have ever seen us, except at a great distance." (Mrs. Eldmere and Topsie had on more than one occasion surprised Sir Gregory in hiding behind a tree or fence to watch them as they rode past, and Topsie had often

joked her friend on the supposed passion of the baronet
for the fair lady of the Grange.

"There is one thing in which I should like to claim
your help," she continued, calmly, "and as you are one
of the magnates of the place, you can doubtless be of
great assistance."

"Delighted, I am sure," smiles the gentleman urbanely,
"to be of any assistance to the lovely Mrs. Eldmere and
her beautiful friend;" this is said with a low bow, hand
on heart, and with a would-be killing glance, that looks
more like a leer.

"Well, Sir Gregory, I will tell you we have been
lately much annoyed during our rides, even walks, by
the movements of a mysterious man, who evidently
wishes to shadow us; for we have seen him crouching
down behind fences, and hiding behind trees, as we
have passed, and though we have never actually caught
sight of his face, we are becoming alarmed by his persistently following us; Mrs. Eldmere has even grave
thoughts of employing a detective to watch the man,
and find out if he is only a harmless idiot or a dangerous
lunatic, in which latter case it would be better to im-
prison him at once or deprive him of his liberty.

Sir Gregory's face had been a study during this recital, turning from red to crimson, and the desperate
efforts he made to appear a calm and interested listener
delighted Topsie's wicked little heart.

"Hum! You say you have never seen his face, my
dear young lady?" he asked, taking out his handkerchief and mopping his brow with the same, while he
fidgeted on his chair and cast a look of deep anxiety on
his tormentor.

"No, Sir Gregory," says Topsie, sweetly, "but I am sure I should know him again. He is tall and stout—a man about your own size, I should say."

"Oh, indeed; about my own size," says the baronet, growing, if possible, more crimson than before. "You don't say so! Why, how unaccountable," Sir Gregory laughs, or rather tries to; while Topsie is delighted to indulge in a little burst of merriment on her own account.

"Well, well, it's too bad! something must be done; I will look into the matter myself," says Sir Gregory, pompously, and then the conversation languishes, while the young lady disappears into the recesses of a bow-window.

"Why, here comes Maudie de la Roche," cries Topsie, in a tone of joy, eying the baronet with a sidelong glance that means more mischief. "She is coming up the avenue. How fortunate! She and you get along so well together, Sir Gregory." Here she sees his face grow a shade paler and his eyes darken, while cautiously, and with the defiant look of one driven to bay, he draws two corks from his pockets, à la Mike Dolan. These, on Maudie's entrance, he places in his ears, and then retires comfortably into the recesses of his arm-chair, feeling safe.

Maudie's garrulous tongue is in glorious form, and, conscious of the advantage of her position, she rattles on to Sir Gregory about her fat dog, her fat pony, and her fat self.

Stealing a glance round she finds that Topsie has glided from the room, and, seeing an encouraging smile on the baronet's face, she deems that a little dash of the sentimental will not come amiss.

"It's such a long, long time since I saw you last, Sir Gregory, she begins. I have been quite ill lately with a cold and sore throat and haven't dared to go out! But perhaps you did not know of it?"

"Delighted to hear it," says the baronet with a bow and wave of his hand.

Maudie thinks the answer strange, but is not yet subdued.

"Why didn't you answer my letter?" she says, imploringly, "I waited so patiently for an answer, just one tiny word!" reproachfully.

"Bless me, I give it up," he cries testily, "its no good asking me for the word, I never could guess a riddle!" Then seeing Maudie's astonished face, and imagining that his reply had not been satisfactory, he added, "Of course not, I never intended to, I thought I told you that some time ago. A man in my position cannot afford to take part in amateur theatricals, and, besides, I'm no actor."

"I don't think you are listening to what I say, cries Maudie rather angrily; can you hear me speaking?"

"Yes, yes, I quite agree with you; I am sure you are right."

"But what are those things in your ears? how can you hear me with those there? But perhaps you don't?"

These questions have broken from Maudie in quick gasps, and in another moment, realizing the position, she draws herself up grandly, stretches out her hand to him in a dignified and freezing good-bye, and sails from the room.

As soon as Maudie is well out of sight Sir Gregory rises from his chair, and taking the corks from his ears restores them to his pocket with a satisfied air of triumph —for once he has got the better of his *bete noire,* Miss Maudie de la Roche.

In another moment Topsie reappears and looks greatly surprised to find him still there.

" I thought you would have escorted Miss de la Roche home," she says, "knowing what friends you are; it was very unkind of you not to do so."

" I could not leave before I had seen you again, he says gallantly, and you are grea*ly mistaken if you think Miss Maudie and I are on such friendly terms."

"Oh, come !" says Topsie, archly, " I won't allow you to say one word against her, I know you were longing to accompany her when she went, and if you go at once, you will soon catch her up, for she doesn't walk very fast !"

"No, indeed, I could not think of it. I must stay and see Mrs. Eldmere. I have an important project—"

"Oh, then, if you wish it," retorts Topsie, certainly; stay as long as you like! you are most welcome! But I must run away from you for a short time. Make yourself quite at home in my absence, and in case you wish to leave, there is the door! in case you think of staying all night, there—is the door-mat for you to lie across !"

But not even this little ruse of Topsie's would have gotten rid of the baronet, had not something rather un-accustomed happened just at that moment.

This was the appearance of a young man on the car-riage sweep, leading a horse, and dragging in his hand the tire of a wheel of the dog-cart to which the horse was harnessed.

"There must have been an accident somewhere," says Sir Gregory, watching the new-comer with great interest. A card is next moment brought in by the servant, and Topsie, catching sight of some number, and "Fifth Avenue," in one little corner, she waits no longer, but dashes off in pursuit of Mrs. Eldmere, who turns pale on seeing the card; and then a bright color suffuses her face, with a strange hope dawning in her eyes.

"He is a friend; he will be kind," she murmurs, and forthwith descends the stair-way to bid her guest welcome.

In the drawing-room she finds a young man, tall and debonair, talking gayly with Topsie, whom he seems to have taken very kindly to, notwithstanding the freezing little air that this young lady seems to keep in store for strange young men.

An American has a strange propensity for ices of all kinds, and Roanwood Offington did not think the ice in question, flavored as it was by rose-leaf lips, very terrifying. Even an iceberg may melt, and Topsie certainly did.

"I am afraid you will think my presumption very great," says the gentleman, as, hat in hand, he is ushered into the room; "but I hope that my appearance here will justify itself. My carriage broke down just outside your gates, and being a stranger here, and not seeing any other residence in view, I was bold enough to enter, feeling sure that English hospitality would not refuse to help a stranger and a foreigner in distress. I was told that the house was occupied by a Mrs. Eldmere. Have I the pleasure of speaking to that lady?" with an inqiring bow.

"No, sir," says Topsie, demurely, "I am only her friend, but as Mrs. Eldmere is herself an American, I am sure she will be glad to see you. I sent her your card, and she will doubtless soon be here. In the mean time, please consider yourself among friends, and allow me to give you a cup of tea."

"No, thanks. Miss—er—"

"Topsie," she says, abruptly.

"Miss Topsie," he continued, with an almost perceptible smile, "I never indulge in that beverage."

"Oh, then you haven't been in England long," cries the young lady. "It's quite English to love tea and scandal—the two always seem to go together; but I dare say you are not too fond of the English, and Americans, being a superior people, are above those little weaknesses!"

"There you do me great injustice, Miss Topsie," replies Mr. Offington, "though I have hardly been long enough in England to appreciate its hospitality and its many beauties—as I shall do after to-day," he adds, with a meaning glance.

Upon the entrance of Mrs. Eldmere a sudden change comes over the face of Roanwood Offington, and with a cry of mingled surprise and pleasure he comes forward with out-stretched hands.

"Mrs. Murray Cresenworth," he says—"what an unexpected pleasure! They told me a Mrs. Eldmere lived here."

"And they were right—you are now speaking to that lady. There was no mistake. I am Mrs. Eldmere," with a glance at the young man's face that seems to command or entreat his silence. Then turning to Sir Gregory with

a gracious smile and a few words of welcome which reduce the inflammable baronet to a state of exquisite delight, she explains: "Mr. Offington is an old friend,"
and upon her introducing the two men the conversation
becomes general.

"What an unexpected pleasure to see you again!
says the hostess to Mr. Offington (who has not yet recovered from his surprise, but gives no sign of the same).
"It must be quite a lucky accident that has brought you
so near us."

"A very fortunate one for me" (with a glance at Topsie). "The Grange must be a kind of loadstone; and
who can wonder at it, considering the many attractions
it contains?"

"You need not compare us to *stones*, Mr. Offington,"
says Topsie with a delicious pout.

"No, indeed," says the baronet, gallantly coming to
the rescue; for in his present state of beatitude, which
he has so little anticipated, he is ready to champion all
the fair sex. "Beauty is always attractive, and when
Mrs. Eldmere and Miss Topsie are the ladies in question,
every man must fall and worship at their shrine."

"How poetical you are, Sir Gregory," says Mrs. Eldmere, with a smile, while Topsie sends Mr. Offington a
coquettish glance, which is fully appreciated by that
young man.

"In this case Sir Gregory's sentiments are all my
own," he cries; "only, not being poetical, I cannot do
the subject justice."

"Hear, hear!" cries Topsie, gayly, quoting: "'And
Beauty draws us with a single hair.' Do you think a
woman's beauty is her hair?"

" Very often."

" Then you are all beautiful," breaks in the baronet.

" Yes, indeed," says Topsie, demurely. " I have a large share of beauty—but it is in my trunk; it was cut off last June!"

Here there is a faint smile of appreciation on Roanwood Offington's face, and Topsie feels his magnetic eyes searching hers. Mrs. Eldmere, who has been more or less restless during the conversation, has risen from her chair and is standing at the other end of the long room. Suddenly she turns and beckons Mr. Offington to her side.

" I want to show you these," she says, pointing to a group of photographs on a table. " You have been in Rome, I know, and I was never quite decided as to what this picture may be." Mr. Offington joins her—and Topsie, who is watching them from the corner of her eye, while she vainly endeavors to converse with Sir Gregory, sees that the photograph was only a subterfuge. Mrs. Eldmere and Mr. Offington have never even pretended to look at it; but, after an earnest whispered conversation between the two, Mr. Offington turns to Sir Gregory and proposes that he shall drive him over, as the Manor-house will be on his way homeward. The hospitable baronet is highly delighted with this suggestion, being already in a convivial mood. He proposes that they shall make a night of it together at the Manor-house. Nothing loath, Mr. Roanwood Offington accepts with pleasure, and with many adieus to the ladies they get into Sir Gregory's cart and drive off.

" By Jove! I'll go to little ' Miss Fattie's,' after all," says the baronet as they sweep under the tower gates. " I'd go through fire to see that widow again. What do you say, Offington ? Do you think she will have me in the end ? Some women, I know, like a long courtship; but, come and judge of matters for yourself at Miss Maudie's afternoon party to-morrow."

"Can't, my dear fellow, so I will only wish you every success in the matter," says Offington, with something like deviltry in his eye, "and I hope you will let me know when the happy event is to take place."

"You seem to look upon it as matter of certainty," says Sir Gregory with rather a grewsome face, and there the subject drops.

CHAPTER XVI.

MAUDIE PLAYS HOSTESS.

Maudie de la Roche is in her element, and as she bustles about the room her mother sits watching her with secret admiration and conscious pride. The "Nest" has on its most festive appearance, all the rooms are decorated with a wealth of flowers, and Miss Maudie's fat little figure trots from place to place putting last touches, giving occasional directions to the bewildered maid, and trying in vain to impress the button-boy or small page with the solemnity and importance of the occasion, for Miss de la Roche has a garden party to-day which she hopes will be honored by the beauty and fashion of the neighborhood.

"Voila mon enfant; repose toi maintenant," murmurs Madame from her chair of state; "it is *all* perfect! and you will be so hot, so tired."

"Yes, I think it is all in readiness now," says Maudie, looking round the pretty room with conscious pride; "I only hope Anatole will announce the people properly." (Anatole being the name at present inflicted upon the luckless youth who is told off to answer the door.)

"How do you like my dress, maman?" she continues, sinking into a low comfortable chair near her mother; "the dear marchioness advised it, and I really think it is quite a success!"

The gown in question is composed of bright blue silk much frilled and furbelowed, while the hat is a diminutive sailor in white straw, trimmed with blue ribbons, and now perched coquettishly on Miss Maudie's head. Her face being broad and fat, and the hat small and narrow, it is not the most becoming head-gear she could have chosen, but having vaguely heard that English girls generally wear sailor hats all summer, she concluded that it would be the most appropriate finish to her toilette.

"The color is lovely, it is like the blue of heaven," her mother replies, not trusting her own taste against that of her anglicized daughter; but tell me who are coming to-day—did Mrs. Eldmere accept?

"Oh yes, of course," says Maudie with a disdainful shrug;" I had to ask her, as she lives so near, but you know, maman, that I have heard strange stories about her. She shuts herself up at the Grange with that girl, and one would think that she thought herself too good to mix with us; but to-day she will see the Marchioness of Ripdale here, and I hope to show Mrs. Eldmere the sort of people who come to *my* parties, but who would never go to see *her*. Some say she is a divorcée, others that she has a husband living, and Eldmere is not her right name. If she wasn't rich, and didn't live at the Grange, I wouldn't invite her, for I don't admire those women who have a story like Mrs. Eldmere."

Here Maudie gives a virtuous sniff, and turning to take a look at herself in an opposite mirror, is horrified to see Mrs. Eldmere advancing with a quiet well-bred air, and dressed in creamy white from head to foot. Her face betrays no sign that she had overheard the previous conversation, and Maudie, much relieved, goes forward to meet her and several other guests who have at this moment arrived.

Mrs. Eldmere, however, had overheard Maudie's last remarks, and she feels a hot wave of anger and shame at the thought that this girl, whom she had always despised as shallow and weak, should be able to use her name so lightly. She wishes she had never come, or that at least Topsie were here to defend her; but she wisely resolves to remain for a time, congratulating herself that she ordered her carriage at an early hour. Now the visitors begin to arrive in shoals, and Maudie is quite proud and pleased at the undoubted success of her first large garden party.

The house is crowded, and so are the pretty lawns and trim walks, with smart, well-dressed girls and matrons, accompanied by their attendant cavaliers. Tennis is in full swing and some adventurous spirits are engaged at bowls and croquet; all is life and animation, for the good people of the neighborhood have few opportunities for showing off their fine clothes, and the present occasion is worthy of their best efforts, for has not a rumor been whispered that no less a person than the Marchioness of Ripdale would grace the fête with her beautiful presence.

Maudie de la Roche was a little upstart nobody, it is true, but, viewed in the reflected light of a real live marchioness, she becomes a charming hostess whom they are all glad to patronize.

Maudie is in a perfect flutter of delight, but her anxiety becomes evident when the last guest has been announced and no marchioness appears. She consults

her watch every few moments, and at last, to her
delight, with a great clatter of prancing high-bred steeds
and glittering trappings, the Ravenstowe carriage appears, and her bliss is unalloyed. The Marchioness of
Ripdale languidly descends, and is received by Maudie
with effusive thanks for her ladyship's appearance.

"Yes, I thought it would amuse me to come and see
your garden party," she remarks, coolly. "What a
crowd you have here! Where did they all come from?"
she continues, sinking into a comfortable chair and gazing with apparent curiosity at the scene on the lawn.
"There's a pretty gown rather—Pingat or La Ferrièrre,
I would swear. Maudie, who is the wearer of that
creamy-white gown? She's not a country woman, I'm
sure."

"Oh, that's Mrs. Eldmere, of the Grange," says
Maudie, and is about to give further details of that lady
when the marchioness, to her surprise, with a start and
cry of astonishment, exclaims:

"Why, that must be Elra Brookley—it's so like her!"

"She's called Mrs. Eldmere," says Maudie, pursing up
her mouth.

"Oh well, never mind," continues her ladyship—"it
may be only a resemblance;" nevertheless, in her own
mind she knows it is Elra, and determines to find out
why she is now masquerading under the name of Eldmere. It will be some sort of amusement, she thinks, to
unearth a little intrigue, and she resolves to begin on
this at once.

If the truth must be told, Maudie de la Roche is now
honored with the friendship, or rather patronage, of the
Marchioness of Ripdale for the simple reason that the

lady is now vegetating (as she calls it) at Ravenstowe, and having met Miss de la Roche at a tennis gathering, and being much amused at her posing à l'anglaise, she makes her acquaintance, promising herself much entertainment from the girl's evident simplicity and gullability.

Her ladyship's husband is now in Canada, and during his absence she has deemed it politic to spend a few weeks with his people at Ravenstowe, though she hates everything pertaining thereto with a deadly hatred, and is consumed with ennui. The life they lead is intensely dull and formal, and as her only society is composed of the ladies Psyche and Amabel Allesmere, two antiquated spinsters of doubtful age, Maudie's rill of chatter proves a welcome and refreshing oasis in the dead level of her existence at Ravenstowe, and she has even condescended so far as to honor the garden party with the light of her presence.

Sir Gregory Athelhurst and his friend De Montford were among some of the earlier guests that afternoon, and, after a few words to his hostess, Sir Gregory cleverly contrives to secure a vacant seat near Mrs. Eldmere, to which he appears to be glued for the next half hour, happy in the mere presence of his divinity, who receives all his advances with great coldness, and seems quite unconcerned by the baronet's deep sighs and furtive glances, though she is in truth much annoyed by the same.

De Montford has been introduced to her, and, with his usual keen perception and fine tact, he at once recognizes her as Mrs. Cresenworth, but does not intend to let her know that he does so. He, therefore, makes himself very charming to the lady, who is greatly relieved to be rid of Sir Gregory, and at the same time he makes up his mind to two things: one is, that Mrs. Eldmere is the wealthy American heiress who made a sensation by her beauty and riches at Brussels some years ago; the other, that he is perfectly willing to assist the lady in spending her money, being particularly hard up at the time, and he concludes that he must either marry her, or, if her husband is still living, so far compromise her that he will get a divorce, and De Montford will then make his own terms with the supposed Mrs. Eldmere.

Though these thoughts are flitting through his mind he does not forget to play the part of a polished gentleman, and Mrs. Eldmere, far from suspecting his real motives, is genuinely glad to meet him; it is such a treat to find a well informed traveller such as De Montford appears to be; and after Sir Gregory's platitudes his remarks are doubly welcome.

"May I not get you some refreshments?" he asks her, after a time—"an ice, or a cup of tea, or some fruit?"

"I think you may bring me a cup of tea," says Mrs. Eldmere; "no sugar," she adds, "only a little cream;" and De Montford goes at once to procure it for her.

Just at this moment she becomes aware that Maudie de la Roche has entered the room with a gentleman, and instinctively she feels that they are watching her. Mrs. Eldmere glances carelessly at the speakers, but as she raises her eyes, it is to meet those of Rutland Borradale fixed intently on her. One look from those eyes of love or scorn or hatred, she knows not which, and he has turned away without even an acknowledgment of her bow of recognition. Her heart is beating fast, and she feels the color ebbing from her cheeks; would De

Montford never come? At least he will shield her from the cruel coldness of those eyes, which will haunt her now for many a day.

Being a woman, and a finished actress, Mrs. Eldmere shows no sign of what she feels, as leaning lazily back in her chair she plays with a white feather-fan, and languidly swings it to and fro, while in the silence of the now deserted room she plainly hears his voice and Maudie's replies.

"Now, Mr. Borradale, you must see my flowers," says that young lady, as coquettishly as she is able. "I am proud of my orchids. Won't you please take Mrs. Eldmere through the conservatory? I see she is sitting there alone, poor thing, and it would be a charity to take compassion on her! Let me introduce you. She is a charming grass widow." This is all said in a hurried whisper, but the gentleman's reply is clearly spoken:

"No, I thank you, Miss de la Roche, I do not care to improve my acquaintance with *such* widows, but if *you* will be my partner I shall be delighted to join our friends in a game of tennis;" and offering his arm to the young lady the two pass out through the open window onto the lawn.

"Here's another man who doesn't approve of Mrs. Eldmere," thinks Maudie, with a little snigger of delight at the same. "I really mustn't ask her here again. It doesn't do to be too charitable, and men always dislike any mystery about a woman. But," she continues aloud, "there is the marchioness! How would you like to make yourself agreeable in that quarter, Mr. Borradale?"

"Here is your cup of tea, Mrs. Eldmere," says De Montford, who had quietly entered in time to hear the last few remarks; and noticing her deadly pallor and trembling lips, he adds, so significantly that Elra felt sure he must know all her secret, "This room is close and you are looking pale. Will you not accept my escort through the conservatory? The cool air will revive you, and I cannot bear to see you suffering."

Mrs. Eldmere mutely thanks him with her eyes, and placing the tips of her gloved hand upon his arm, they enter the little conservatory that opens from the drawing room, and, with a few carefully chosen remarks, De Montford puts his companion at her ease again as he points out the various beauties of Maudie's somewhat diminutive collection of flowers and orchids.

"Oh, how very beautiful!" cries Mrs. Eldmere, really pleased. "These lilies are fair as the young girl, I suppose, you will choose for your bride."

"Who could the fair one be?" laughed De Montford. "She may be very fair, but not so for my eyes. I do not know that any one is lovely beside you."

"Oh!" she says, a little sceptically, if ever so little startled, "you are learning to be a polished courtier, Mr. de Montford."

"Sunshine perfects and draws forth the beauties of the rose; my sunshine lies in your eyes, Mrs.—Cresenworth."

He said it so gently, breathing the last word with such reluctant tenderness, that she could scarcely feel inclined to resent his speech, but a little look of alarm stole into her eyes as she placed her fingers on his coat sleeve, saying:

"I think I hear the first carriages approaching the hall door. I shall be glad to have mine ordered also, so I must go and say adieu to my charming hostess."

CHAPTER XVII.

THE TEMPEST SWEEPS APACE.

Do we blame one who has been starved for hungrily devouring some delicious food which is at length offered him ? Can we sympathize with the frail human nature which, having hungered of the mind for many months, has the intoxicating banquet of love placed before it to tempt it to partake ?

Such was the allurement offered by the naughty little god to Elra Cresenworth on the day when, thinking no harm, dreaming no harm, she wandered listlessly among the hedge-rows, plucking a golden primrose here and there, rejecting it for a cowslip bell that tempted her from its nook under the pink and white hawthorns lining her way, and among whose shower of blossoms the soft-eyed wood-pigeon was cooing to its mate. Her thoughts, in sympathy with the gladsome nature around her, are pleasant ones, though sometimes, indeed, they are tinged with the more sombre of colors. Why do her thoughts fly back to that unpalatable episode of Maudie's "afternoon ?" She clinches her teeth at thought of Maudie's triumphant malice—she spurns beneath her heel an inoffensive pink-lipped daisy when her thoughts revert to Rutland Borradale's coldly calculated slight—she remembers with pleasure of De Montford coming to her rescue.

De Montford ! where has she seen or heard that name ? In Brussels; yes, but where else ? "Oh !" she cries, as a

light breaks in upon her—an unpalatable one, evidently,
as her eyes darken with something like annoyance as
she thinks: "Was his the name that Topsie read as
figuring in that sad story ? How little attention I purposely paid when Topsie read to me the details of her
sad secret! but, now I think of it, I fancy the two names
are alike. Can he be that villain ?—and yet his face does
not look very wicked. He tells me he has a brother who
is an entirely black sheep, but what must I believe ?"

Thereupon she arranges a little plan by which she
will herself find out all about it; to speak to Topsie
on the matter would, she thinks, be to torture her need-
lessly, poor little woman !

"If it be indeed he," she cries, clasping her hands,
"no hatred or vengeance of mine will be too bitter for
him. But I must go to work cautiously."

Here Lion, who has hitherto been following her, and
who thinks he has not received his due share of attention,
pushes his wet nose beneath her hand and thus compels
her to stroke his glossy head.

"Naughty Lion, who has lost his collar and cannot
recover it again, do you not know that it bears a message
from me to my only loved one ?" She continues, play-
fully, "Naughty hound, bring it to me again, for when
he comes back once more he must read the word and
solve the problem, as he alone can."

She has come by this time to an ugly looking stile,
and as she stands reflective as to whether she will cross
it or not a strong hand is put forth to help hers; there is
a meeting of the eyes, a lingering hand-pressure, and
Borradale stands once more beside Elra with the old
protective look and attitude, his arm on her slight waist

while he draws her to him. Very dangerous for Borradale at that moment is that protecting position he holds above the beautiful woman who calls another man than he her lord and husband; more dangerous still is her position to the woman who knows in her heart she has never swerved in love's allegiance from the man towering above her.

" I entreat you, let me pass," she says, pale to the lips with the emotion that is mastering her. " It is unmanly, cruel, your being here," she continues, endeavoring to brush his arm aside."

" My meeting you here was by no will of my own, God knows! Elra," he replies, bitterly—"but here by an adverse chance, if you will, I have found you, and I do not relinquish you again, as I am a man and love you."

Something in Elra's brain there was that seemed to snap, and in her mind was a wild confusion as of a world turned upside down.

" What is right and wrong ? Is it the justice of Nature to give allegiance where the heart has given love, or is it more praiseworthy to give cold friendship where devotion has been vowed ? Heaven !" she cries, lifting her hand to her brow, " My head is on fire." But to Borradale she says, coldly, " Go!"

" I will go indeed, darling, now, with the assurance that your love has never been given to any save me," and without other caress than a tender pressure of the golden embroideries of her waistband he is gone.

Elra's emotions for some days after the above scene we shall not attempt to describe, but Borradale's are as follows: Now that the overpowering influence of love has crept into his life again—for he is more than ever passionately enamoured of the woman who, in the midst of her love has insulted and scorned him—he longs to have her snowy arms placed of their own accord once more about his neck, and her lips breathing the words "I love you," till in the very wretchedness of his loss he swears it shall still be so, however he encompass it! To effect his object he has many times to elude the vigilance of Sir Gregory, whom he once actually meets prowling around the Grange walls on—he supposes—the same errand as himself, and he feels consequently wrathful with the meddlesome baronet for sinning as he sins.

However, nothing appears to reward his efforts until one morning, on which he had carefully watched Sir Gregory and De Montford ride off for a distant meet of hounds, when, strolling in the fields without even the excuse of a gun over his shoulder, he hears a little appealing cry of distress. It comes from a lady at the other side of the fence, who, unaware of the proximity of any male thing, is doing brave battle with an innocent-looking bumble-bee, and ducking her head affrightedly now and again as though a huge winged monster were looming above her. This affords him even a better opportunity than he had hoped.

"The horrid bee!" he cries, mimicking her tones of distress, when coming upon her unawares he draws her tenderly to him with one arm while with the other he wards off the monster, and he is rewarded for his gallantry by seeing that her primly pursed lips have broken into an unwilling smile.

"Let us sit here for a while," says Borradale, gently drawing her down beside him on a bank of mosses and kingcups; "I wish to speak to you seriously."

"Really," retoits she, looking a little ruffled and a little frightened. "And you cannot speak seriously walking ?"

"It is not my wish to !" says the young man illogically, the while scanning her coolly from head to foot.

"You surely do not think to speak ably or calmly or seriously with your arm where it is at present. But I presume you are above the follies of your sex." This she says in a partly mocking, wholly provoking tone, and it makes him cry, in return,

"Perhaps so, but as I do not wish to speak coolly I shall leave my arm where it is and dare all for so delicious a position."

"Pray don't speak warmly; I must suffocate if you try," says Elra, with a very attractive languor.

"Elra," he cries, in a hoarse whisper, "I would I could overpower you with the strength and depth of my great love! I would I might always have you to protect and cherish, Elra;" eagerly, "let me live—let me hope that once more I shall have you by my side !"

"I am sure," she says, rather flippantly, "you will have me much longer than you care to keep me." Why then did she appear so astonished at the passionate caress that followed ? Was it mere coquetry that made her turn her wondrous lovely eyes to his with a glance of languid, haughty inquiry and the little scornful word, "Sir?"

"Elra, why cannot we be to each other as we once were ? I cannot help picturing you in my mind as one of those dazzling flies that haunt the water's brink, no sooner touched than they vanish from your grasp. Shall we not be as we have been, Elra ?" But she evades answering him.

"Do not, for mercy sake, puzzle me with conundrums to-day, my brain is softening, the sifting of a problem would dissolve it utterly; leave me, in fact, overpowered if not seated here all night."

"Then I should be happy staying with you, Elra," he cries, pleadingly; "say with your own sweet little lips, 'Rutland, I love you!'"

Elra is silent, and in the pale twilight which is creeping on he fails to judge of the horror, the pain written in her eyes.

"We must separate, sir," she cries, coldly springing to her feet, but he draws her back to his side again by the power of his strong right arm, which is not to be deterred now.

"Sweetest, you fear to stay, you tremble for yourself because you—love—me! Say it is so and I live but to win you by my side again." And as he says it a great wave of hope and passion struggles in his eyes.

"Love you I do not," she says, coldly turning away, and remembering as she says it a scene of not so very many months ago in which it had been from his lips that those same callous words had fallen. He bites his lips as he hears them. "And yet he says it is ennobling in a woman to love."

"Not with the woman whose love solemnly plighted to one man is given to another."

."Is it thus in this case, Elra?" he says, softly. "But do not deny it; you cannot," he cries, with a flash of something very like triumph in the eyes that he turns to search hers, and with which he seems to tear her secret from her in spite of herself. She trembles with virtuous indignation and—and some other kind of feeling that we shall not

attempt to describe, but which we fear was the more
potent of the two in making her feel very much like an
aspen in the summer breezes. "Do not deny it," he repeats. "You dare not! You shall not! You cannot!"
and losing all self-control, he takes her in his arms with
a few whispered words which make her turn white as
the blossoms that heap the hawthorn sprays. "Leave
him! Come to me! It is but justice that I ask. You
have insulted and injured me through him. Let him be
the sufferer now." Recoiling from his caress Elra Cresenworth, with the grand dignity of only an offended
goddess, or the daughter of an independent race, with
lip that curls with noble scorn, and tiny foot that seems
to spurn the very ground he treads, she says, in a voice
trembling and hoarse,

"How must I teach you that I loathe you? how I
contemn you as you deserve? how I—".

"Enough," says Borradale, with a dangerous flash in
his eyes. "Yours, madam, was the fault. To you was
reserved the task of making our deep, simple, noble love
a sin—yours be the blame. To that which in my promised wife was a cowardly disloyalty must I return the
thanks that are due." As she saw him turn on his heel
in bitter scorn her white cheek was not more deadly
pale than his passion-marked features, and with a groan
of scarce so much anger as horror she sank back in a
hopless and hopeless attitude among the primroses
and kingcups.

Once again Rutland Borradale stands beside Elra
Cresenworth, and this time the victory is his, for she
trembles as she tells herself that her jealously guarded
secret lies bare before him.

"Lion has no collar now as he used to of old," he had said, "and yet I remember when he had a costly one. '*With my heart forever*' I gave him—" Here he pauses, and as she does not appear to have heard what he said, he continues: "And our compact, Elra, do you remember it?"

"I believe," she retorts, indifferently, "it was that if the parties were separated, and he should come back after many years, the word *never*, inscribed on the collar, should tell him—what he did not deserve to know—that her love had never swerved."

"And was that word ever written?" he asks, eagerly seizing her hands. But Elra has clinched her pearly teeth with the determination that the man before her shall never wring her secret from her lips, and it is therefore with the utmost seeming indifference that she replies:

"Not to my knowledge. The bill for rendering the word as agreed upon, in rubies, would have come to nearly five thousand—a sum that the lady thought scarcely worth while throwing in the dust."

Here he listens no longer, but with a little laugh of triumph he catches her in his strong arms and strains her to him.

"Elra! Elra! deny it no longer, you love me still, for here is the proof," and he unfeelingly holds before her horrified eyes the rich collar taken from Lion's neck scarce a fortnight ago. Driven to bay, with a flame in her eyes that is to him rather maddening to see, she is for all that more powerful than ever in her very weakness, for she says:

"I have loved you, indeed, Rutland, but for the sake

of that love give me your pity and do not drag me down. God grant I may never see you more!" With this she passes from his arms without—as he tells himself reproachfully—his having wrung from her dewy lips the confession : "I love you, Rutland!"

CHAPTER XVIII.

RECONCILIATION.

It is past eight o'clock, and Mrs. Eldmere's pretty profile still lies cushioned among the billowy eider-down; she is dreamily thinking of those sweet, dangerous moments that yesterday has made her live through; and "Oh," comes the thought to her, "shall I yield—shall I give myself to love and all that is glorious and lovely in human life, or (shuddering) shall I rise beyond myself? Can I?" She is gliding down-hill, she feels herself very weak to resist, and yet in her great struggle she cries aloud:

"Oh, for a staying hand! Oh, for the protection of a strong, true friend! Why is not my husband here to stand by my side and save me? Elra! Elra! it will soon be too late! Go back while yet you can to the shelter of his roof, to the embrace of his protecting arm."

At this thought she shudders and pales, but with a little clinched fist and set white teeth she mutters, "I shall—"

Here her thoughts are interrupted by the entrance of her maid, who, coming gently to the bedside, says, "Two letters for you, madam," and hands her the silver salver.

"That will do, Forbes," her mistress answers, hastily glancing at the handwritings. "I see there is a letter from my lawyer here which will entail a visit to Brighton to-day. Order breakfast for 8:30, and then come to dress me."

"I shall take the ten o'clock train," thought Mrs. Eldmere, "and I must go alone. It would not do to take Topsie with me. How I hate the business! But Mr. Barton says he must see me, so I suppose there is no help for it, and I don't want him to be seen *here*. I can't afford to have the village gossips making conjectures on his appearance, though old Barton looks more like an out-at-elbows parson than the clever lawyer he really is. Heigh ho! I wish the deed were done."

Two hours later Mrs. Eldmere was seated in a first-class carriage on her way to Brighton, and on the arrival of the train she drove at once to her lawyer's office.

. "Mr. Barton is very busy, but if you will wait a few moments he may be able to see you," says a young clerk, with great assurance, pointing to a vacant chair. This Mrs. Eldmere refuses to take, and giving the luckless youth a withering glance of scorn, which causes him to blush perceptibly, she hands him her card and says, "I wish to see Mr. Barton at once."

A moment more and she is ushered into the lawyer's sanctum, to find Mr. Barton blandly bowing and smiling, as is the accustomed method of the spiders of the law in receiving their victims or fair clients.

"Very glad to see you, my dear madam. Lovely day, is it not?" says the lawyer, handing his visitor a chair.

"Yes, indeed," says Mrs. Eldmere, or Cresenworth, as we must now call her, "but I didn't come here to talk about the weather, Mr. Barton. Now tell me frankly what you want me to do. You know I trust you to do the best for me."

"Yes, yes, my dear lady," says Mr. Barton, playing nervously with his spectacles and moving some papers in front of him as if in search of something. "Now I am going to suggest something to you—something that I feel sure is the best thing to be done." Then, after a pause, "Is there no possibility of a reconciliation between yourself and your husband, madam? That is what I mean;" and the old lawyer glanced keenly at her face, as if he would read her very thoughts.

"You see the case looks very badly for you," he continues; "I think there is no hope of its being ever understood in your favor, and a black pall of dishonor, though totally unmerited, would darken and enshroud your life.

"My dear child," says Mr. Barton, "for you are but a child to me, and must forgive the extreme interest I take in you, my advice to you is, try to be reconciled to your husband and take no further steps in this affair. His fault was but too great a love for you; can you not forgive him, and treat him with somewhat of wifely affection? He has nearly suffered death; he will never be the same man again that he was before he made that fatal mistake for love of you?"

Mrs. Cresenworth listens in haughty silence, and Mr. Barton pauses for a reply.

She is thinking of it all—the sacrifice she will have to make, the loss of esteem from all those who to her are estimable, and she sighs. Even the other day did she not quiver when listening to the spiteful words of the fat Maudie, whom she had always so thoroughly despised, and how would it be if such words were always meted out to her by her own sex? Would she always be held in light esteem by men, or be, in other words, despised by all her friends and foes alike? She shudders, and sits with clasped hands, while a sob breaks from her quivering lips.

The lawyer is not slow to take advantage of her softening mood, and clinches his argument by a persuasive:

"What shall I write to your husband, madam? Shall it be reconciliation, as he most dearly hopes it may, or must it be separation, which means a broken heart for him and untold misery for you? What shall it be, madam?"

Without trusting her voice to speak, Mrs. Cresenworth took the pen and wrote but one word, "Come!" and then, placing her hand in the big palm of the kindly lawyer, she made as rapid an escape as possible from this little den of legal horrors.

The same evening we find her again at her home at the Grange, and after a solitary meal she strolls out in the cool of the evening to wander in the fragrant rose garden, now filled with delicious perfume of June roses. As she paces through the green parterres a shade of sadness is on her brow, for she remembers the events of the day, and is haunted by thoughts of the future and the message she had sent, if only of one word. Had she done right to send it? As she paces up and down restlessly she calls from time to time, "Lion, Lion," but nothing living appears to answer her call. She has been told that since her departure that morning her beautiful greyhound has been missing, and her heart is filled with misgivings, for Lion is a link to the past. The dog had belonged to him by whom, alas, her life had been made the wreck it was, and it was the only thing left to remind her of the past. She could not bear to picture her noble hound in any one's keeping save her own.

"Perhaps he knows, poor brute, that his master is banished now forever, and that a rival will soon take his place—may be here even to-night. He is more loyal than his mistress, who is willing to bend to an unloved rule."

Leaving the rose garden, she wanders down through lawns and meadows towards the river, which, in the soft twilight, lies shimmering between its leafy banks. Here she is startled to see a lanky form crouched among the ferns and grasses, which, springing up at her approach, presents very much the appearance of a half-tamed creature. Mrs. Cresenworth recognizes in her a village girl she had often seen in her wanderings, who went by the name of Daddy Dolan, and had rather an unenviable reputation of being as wild as a young goshawk.

"Why, Daddy, what are you doing here at this time of night?" says Mrs. Cresenworth, kindly, as the girl, seeing a friendly face, had gone down again on her knees among the bracken, as if searching for something lost.

"I've lost my best friend," she answered brusquely.

"Indeed!" replied Mrs. Cresenworth, smiling. "And who may that be?"

"It isn't a 'who,'" says the girl; "it's a 'what.'"

"I really don't understand you."

"No; I dare say not. I mean it isn't alive."

"Oh, dead. Is it a pet bird you have brought here to bury?"

"I never had a live pet," says the girl, sullenly. "This 'ere's a knife."

"A what?"

"A knife. Tim give it me; brought it from the fair at Shoreham a while back. I uses it to cut most every-

'thing with; crack nuts; cut off mice's tails, and pare apples. And now I've lost him. I have heard that a knife cuts love; so I suppose Tim won't bring me home that pink ribbon he promised, or, if he do, will give it to Sal—bad luck to her! But I want to find my knife again, just to spite 'em. Tim allus liked me best."

"You foolish girl, to believe in such nonsense. Tim won't like you any better or worse if you lose it, though he may say it was careless."

"Well, here it is, lady," cries the girl triumphantly, holding up an old well-worn jack-knife. "Now, you must have brought me luck, for I've searched here nigh on an hour. Good-luck to you; and if ever you wants a friend, remember there are two of them at your service —me and the knife!"

Mrs. Cresenworth laughed at the girl's grotesque re-marks, and had almost forgotten her late sad thoughts in the quaint little episode just recounted; but as she walked back to the house she heard a rapid footstep behind, an arm was thrown around her, and, turning quickly, she sees her husband! Elra Cresenworth started backward with a cry of pain.

"I did not think— So soon!" she gasped.

"My wife! Are you not going to be my loving wife?" he says, with the wistful ring of tears in his voice.

"Can we forget?" she asks, after a long pause.

"Everything can be forgotten, if you so will it, Elra. Elra," he whispered, with his longing eyes searching hers, and drawing her gently to him, "my wife! forgive and forget!"

Closer and closer he drew her to him, till, with an un-mistakable shudder, Elra lay in his arms, with her lips pressed by his. It was not long, however, before this little scene was interrupted. A sound among the trees aroused them, and close at hand they heard the joyful bark of a hound, and in another moment Lion springs upon his mistress, while Elra, with a soft little purr of content and delight, caresses her recaptured idol.

"Why, where do you come from, Lion?" she asks, in happy surprise, and, looking up, sees that they are not alone. A tall form is standing there in the shadow, and every vestige of color fades from her cheek, while into her eyes springs the fire of desperation; for, coldly contemptuous, Rutland Borradale is surveying her with the scant mercy that the tyrant may give to his slave, the persecutor his victim, while from his lips drop words frigid as icicles.

"I have had the pleasure of saving your dog's life, and now I have the honor to return him to, I fear, his unappreciative mistress."

He accompanied his words with one long, coldly cruel look, and ere she could choke back a traitor lump that would rise in her throat to prevent her forming words as icily indifferent, as bitterly cutting as were his, he had lifted his hat with lingering politeness and turned from her without another word.

No word was spoken by the lately returned husband of the appearance of Rutland Borradale on the scene at such an untoward hour, but it had proved for him none the less a deadly shock, and it could not fail to revive old and bitter scores.

"Let us go in," said his wife, rousing herself a little later from a dreary state of stupefaction—"the fog from the river has chilled me."

And then it was for the first time that her anxious husband noticed with alarm the strangely rich color that burned in her cheek, while to his touch her hand was clammy and cold as that of the dead.

CHAPTER XIX.

A COAT OF SILKEN GRAY.

Mrs. Murray Cresenworth is leaning languidly back
among her luxurious sofa pillows looking rather paler
than we have ever seen her before, while Topsie bends
over her, gently smoothing back the masses of her dark
hair and bathing her brow with some cooling fragrant
essence. The girl's eyes are full of sympathizing compassion as she says gently:

"You have been ill, dear?"

"Yes. I have had, perhaps, cause; but it is passed,
says Mrs. Cresenworth, with a wan smile, and I am
saved from a terrible temptation."

"I know, dear," whispers Topsie sadly, "but you
would never have fallen," and the girl softly kisses back
the tears which are thickly gathering in Elra's eyes.

"I believe you are my good angel, Topsie," she says
in a faint voice, "what should I have done without that
glorious pure light, that burns so steadily in your eyes,
to help me onward over a stony pathway?"

Poor Topsie has turned away to cover the powerful
emotion which is mastering her, and she points to the
carriage drawn up at the door, with Murray as driver,
waiting for Elra to take her seat beside him.

With a sigh Elra rises, throws a wrap of costly sable
about her, and descends the stairs to join her husband,
while Topsie, from the window, watches them start with

a half unconscious sigh of "poor Elra!" lingering on her lips.

"Do you feel better now, Elra?" asks her husband, anxiously, as Mrs. Cresenworth takes her place beside him. "You are so pale; had you not better put off the drive?"

"No, no," she answers impatiently, "I am quite well, it was only a slight faintness and that has passed." And Elra settles herself amid the carriage pillows with a t red sigh, while her husband, quite reassured, and gladly welcoming this tete-a-tete, takes the reins from the waiting groom and drives off.

"Where shall we go?" he asks her; you know the country better than I do.

"Oh, anywhere!" she answers listlessly, these country roads are all alike.

They drive on for some time in silence, then Mr. Cresenworth begins, "I am sure you are dull here, Elra, this quiet country life is killing you; let us leave the Grange and go abroad again, or up to town at any rate. Here you are completely buried alive—and I want my wife to enjoy herself and have every pleasure that can be found. Will you not let me drive you to the meet of drags and four-in-hands to morrow? it will be a pretty sight and one you ought to witness, for I hear that all the county folks from far and near will certainly be present."

"And that is a very good reason why *I* cannot go," she says rather gladly. "I have nothing but such a weird collection of dowdy old-fashioned wraps—many of which should certainly be pointed out as fit for Thady O'Flynn's collection of antiquities in the village museum."

"I suppose you might make up a second edition of the petrified bundle of rags, especially in these," says Murray, touching her sables, "but dear I don't think you could possibly look to disadvantage even though the gathering be ever so *chic !*"

"Ah! you do not know anything of our little feminine weaknesses and pinings to be considered the best dressed lady of the throng. Most of us would never show ourselves if it were not for the pleasure of eclipsing some other star of beauty or note."

"I believe you," says Murray, laughing, "and as you must have the pleasure to-morrow of excelling in beauty and dress, we must see what Worth can do for you."

"But the meet of drags is to be to-morrow morning," interjects Elra!

Here Murray draws from under the carriage-seat a carefully arranged parcel, which is found to contain a lovely dove-colored mantle, trimmed with chenille embroidery and fringe of feathers and lined with soft rose-colored satin.

"Why, what a beauty !" says Mrs. Cresenworth, "and how good of you to think of it."

She is supremely touched by this small incident, and tells herself that she is cruel to give so little in return for so much love and thought for her. She longs to be gentle and womanly, to fling her arms around her husband's neck with the tender, whispered words, "I am yours, darling!" But when her dewy lips meet his a vision rises up as though to mock at her—a vision of two eyes aflame with mingled passion, scorn and hatred—and after all it is with a little rebellious sigh that she suffers the caress of her husband.

"I forgot to tell you, dear," he says a moment later, "that I have asked Offington to come and stay with us for a week. He is a bright, clever fellow, and I know you like him, so I felt sure you would not object."

"No, indeed; I am very glad to hear it," says Elra. "Mr. Offington is an old favorite of mine."

"He is quite *épris* with your little friend Miss Topsie," says her husband. "I wonder if there is any likelihood of its being mutual? It would be a good match for her. Don't you think Topsie would marry him?"

"No, dear; I do not think she is the girl to care to marry in a hurry. She has only seen him once, and I am sure I shall never bear to part with her."

"But I want my Elra all to myself!"

A look of wistful reproach steals into Elra's eyes as she answers:

"Dearest, remember all she has been to me when—when I was alone here."

"Then, Elra, you shall have her always if you wish it, if that will make you love *me* the least little bit more."

Being a New York business man he did not fail to make a bargain, even in an affair of love.

On their return, an hour later, they find Miss Topsie impatiently awaiting them, as she stands shading her eyes from the sun, and tapping the broad stone steps with a little foot clad in a smart patent-leather shoe, while now and then she pushes back a stray lock of red gold hair from her white forehead.

"At last!" she cries, helping Elra to alight, while Murray Cresenworth tosses the reins to a groom, and they all three enter the house.

"Are you tired, dear?" says Topsie, for Mrs. Cresenworth sinks into the first comfortable chair with a little
yawn.

"Yes, I am, dear—wretchedly tired. We drove too
far, I think. Fortunately, I can go and rest now till
dinner-time."

"And, in the mean time, I will go and gather some
flowers," says Topsie. "I see the roses want renewing,
and I noticed some beauties out on the front lawn just
now." So the young lady runs to fetch a pretty willow
basket to hold the flowers; and, tying a dainty bit of
lace and muslin over her bright hair, she starts out to
rob the garden of its treasures.

Her basket is now nearly full, and she makes a charming picture of girlish grace as she flits from one rose-
bush to another, softly humming a merry tune the while.
So intent is she on her thoughts that she has not heard
a carriage drive up to the door, and she gives a little
cry and start of surprise as she hears herself called by
name, and sees, coming across the lawn to meet her,
Roanwood Offington, accompanied by a young lady of
about the mature age of eight years.

"Oh, Mr. Offington, how you startled me! I had no
idea that any one was near. Have you come to see Elra?
She is tired after her drive, and resting now, but Mr.
Cresenworth is visible. Please come into the house
after you have properly introduced me to this young
lady. I am longing to meet a genuine American child,
and she looks sweet."

"So she is," he replies heartily. "Here, Daisy,
shake hands with this lady. She loves little girls."

"How do you do? I am glad to meet you," says Miss

Offington, gravely; and Topsie bends down to kiss the child with a tender, loving glance.

"What a pretty place the Grange is, and what lovely flowers!" says Mr. Offington, who has been watching Topsie's face intently all this time.

"It's all very well in summer, but wait till November or February," she replies. "The country is only bearable for six months in the year. But please come in, and let me take possession of that wee mite, as she looks bored by our old-time notions of conversation. Come along, Daisy;" and, taking the child by the hand, she leads the way into the house.

"What a glorious pair of eyes!" thinks Mr. Offington, as Topsie leads them across the lawn; "and where could my own have been when I met this girl the other day? I thought her pretty lively and interesting, but I find her a woman with soul and thought and depth shining in her eyes—lovely ones, too!" he ejaculated. "She will give some person trouble near the region of the heart before long, I expect, if she hasn't done so already. Fancy calling a girl like that Topsie! Why, it's heathenish! With that lovely face and figure one can picture her as Adelaide or Marguerite!"

At this period of his soliloquy Topsie turns to him and says:

"There is Mr. Cresenworth now, so I will go and tell Elra you are here, and carry Daisy off with me, for I know she is dying of ennui at present."

"Well, old fellow, glad to see you!" says Murray Cresenworth, as he enters the room, and the two men go off for a chat and the inevitable cigar, while Elra and Topsie amuse themselves with the quaint oddities of the extremely self-possessed and entertaining maiden of eight summers.

"All plain sailing now, Murray, isn't it?" says his friend, with a keen glance. "I heard all sorts of rumors, you know, but I am ever so glad to find that things are amicably settled, and hope you may have a long life and a happy one." Then, as Murray does not answer, he continues : "Mrs. Cresenworth is a lovely and charming woman, and her friend, Miss Topsie must be a great addition to the family circle, eh ?"

"Oh yes; Topsie is a dear little girl," says Murray, hastily, and a great friend of my wife's; but you know, Roan, or rather you will know some day, that there are times when three is no company—when one would like to have one's wife to one's self; but Elra has offered her a home here, and, of course, you will understand that though I like her very much, I rather wish sometimes we could be alone—Elra and I."

"Well, Miss Topsie may marry some day," says Mr. Offington, rather wistfully, "and then your wishes will be fulfilled. I know of one who admires her greatly— too much for his own peace of mind—but I don't know if she would have him. You see, he has only seen her twice, and that's being rather sudden, isn't it, even for a New Yorker?"

"Yes, yes," says Murray Cresenworth, absently. "It would never do to speak to her yet; and then, poor child, maybe she is happier now than she ever could be as the wife of even the man you allude to; women are such strange creatures it takes a man's lifetime to find them out, and then, perhaps, the discovery of what they really are is made too late."

"I am not sure if you are complimenting the man in question or the reverse," says his friend, with a laugh; "but I am conceited enough to think that I could make any woman happy—that I loved passionately."

"Well, well, who knows?" replies Murray. "We all think we can do that."

CHAPTER XX.

MATHILDE BECOMES ANGLICIZED.

But let us in the mean time take a peep at Maudie de la Roche in her own little home, as she tries to improve the hours of her stay in England.

Not many miles from the Grange, on the Shoreham road, stands a pretty bijou cottage, surrounded by tiny grounds, and with an air of semi-gentility lurking in its green shutters, that are now hermetically sealed against the pure breath of the September breezes, and through which the subdued murmur of voices can be heard.

They belong to a French lady and her daughter, who have taken up their residence at "The Nest," as the cottage is poetically called, and very substantial nestlings are now its occupants. The neighborhood was mildly alarmed when it was first made aware that two French ladies—Papists, as I fear the country folks called them —had taken the Nest for a year. But the new-comers had not proved themselves at all formidable. Indeed the daughter, Maudie (*née* Mathilde), appeared only too anxious to become an English girl at the shortest possible notice, and most praiseworthy were the attempts she made to copy her more emancipated sisters of *la perfide Albion*. And in the light of her good will to become Anglicized as rapidly as possible, the neighborhood had begun to tolerate Maudie, and even welcomed her sometimes at their slow tea parties, seeing that she was neither beautiful nor witty, and would never prove a formidable rival in a love affair.

If the truth must be told, Madame de la Roche had many reasons for wishing the youngest and least interesting of her daughters to be favorably received, and her admitted taste in dress did its best to hide a stout thick-set figure, which was poor Maudie's greatest *bête noire.*

" Why, *mon enfant,*" says her mother, coming into the small sitting-room one morning, and lifting expressive hands aghast to see her daughter calmly surrounded by letters of unmistakable masculine caligraphy, " who are all these gentlemen writing to you ?"

"Oh, don't be alarmed, mother. They are only the greatest racquet players of England."

" But where, darling, have you met these gentlemen ? I see the names of Mr. Hartington, Mr. Wallace, and others. Why, I don't even know them by name."

"Neither did I," says her daughter, imperturbably ; but that doesn't matter, you dear, simple old thing. I have only asked them to play in our tournament. It's allright. Many of the English girls do these kind of things."

" Oh," says Madame, toning down again, as she contemplates her clever daughter, " then I suppose it's all right. These English have strange manners and customs, it seems to me. Well, how many of the gentlemen will play with you my dear ?"

" That's the worst part of it," says clever Maude, irritably. " These horrid men ! How very distressing it is to try to do anything for them ! Here is Mr. Hartington says his doctor actually forbids his playing, and I read his name as playing somewhere yesterday, so I don't believe him. What shameful stories men can tell ! But now I must go, mother, as I am to join a paper chase to-day.   How do you like the costume for it?"   And Maudie gets up and walks across the room to exhibit a marvellous new bloomer costume which she assures her mother is the correct thing for young ladies to wear during any athletic exercise.   The dress looks oddly enough on Maudie's plump, round little figure, which is thus shown, unfortunately, to great disadvantage; and, to crown the costume, she has perched a small cap on her head, which is as unbecoming to her round, good-tempered face as anything could possibly be.   But Maudie is determined to look like an English girl or die in the attempt; and though she hates active exercise of any kind, she is now prepared for a two or three mile spin across country, which will involve climbing gates, fences or other impediments; but go she must, or she will lose the prestige it has taken her so much hard trouble to gain.

Madame de la Roche, whom we have seen before in Brussels, is at a loss what to say, she finds the bloomer costume *affreuse;* and she is lost in wonder at the unlooked for traits which their sojourn in England has developed in her daughter's character.

" What is this paper chase ?"

" Oh, we girls are the hounds, and the one who runs fastest is chosen for the hare, and he or she goes first, carrying a bag full of scraps of paper, which are dropped here and there on the road, to leave a track.   Then, after the hare has had five minutes' start, the hounds are off, following the scent or track by means of the scraps of paper.   We don't keep to the road, of course, but go across country, climb hedges, leap ditches, etc.   Indeed, we have to go wherever the hare leads us. Well, I must be off now; so, good-bye," and Maudie gives her perky little cap a few pats here and there before the mirror, takes up a pair of gauntlets and a riding-whip, and thus oddly equipped goes out smiling, and satisfied that her costume and appearance will be as English if not more so than that of the girls she is likely to meet.

"Ah, *mon Dieu!*" soliloquizes Madame de la Roche, as she watches her daughter's departure, "she is a clever girl. Who is there that knew her in Brussels would meet her now in that strange dress, and say, 'This is Mathilde!' She surprises me, her mother; and if Sir Gregory will only be at the hunt, he will find her like any English girl—though I think the men here have no taste if they say they like such a dress. It is horrible to me, *mais enfin,* one must do as others do in this country," and poor Madame nodded her head sagely, and trotted out to see her cook and arrange about their dinner for that evening.

_____

Early in the afternoon of the same day De Montford may be seen walking up the avenue to the Grange, where he sends in his card, asking to see Mr. Offington, if he is at home. The servant goes to inquire, and returns with a message to this effect: that Mr. Offington is not at home, but Miss Roanwood Offington will be glad to receive him, if he cares to wait until his return, which will be shortly.

Somewhat surprised at this, as he does not know who Miss Roanwood Offington may be, he decides to be received, and is shown into a pretty drawing-room opening onto the rose garden, where he awaits his hostess. He

is contemplating the lovely woodland scene before him
with great interest, when he hears the patter of footsteps, and, turning, sees a small child's figure, not more
than knee high to a grasshopper (as some people would
remark), graciously advancing towards him.

"Miss Offington?" he asks, dubiously.

"Yes, I am Miss Offington. Won't you be seated,
please; and by what name shall I call you?" says the
young lady, quietly, of the six foot of manhood towering
above her.

"You would scarcely know my name, madam," replies
six foot with a sweeping bow. "I bring a letter to Mr.
Offington—your uncle, I presume?"—introducing me
from the Earl of Darcliffe. "Here is the letter; but
perhaps you may not be able to read it?"

"German; no," was the reply, in frosty tones, as she
draws her little figure up; "but if it should be in Eng-
l sh, Spanish, or French, I am quite able to master
its contents."

So saying, she took the letter and demurely perused
it, while her visitor sat lost in amazement at the self-pos-
session and quiet dignity of his child hostess. With a
serious face she handed him back the letter, saying,
quaintly, "Be assured you are most welcome, sir, and of
course you must stay to luncheon; they will all be home
soon, and then you can see my uncle." Mr. de Montford
bowed and accepted, and here the conversation lan-
guished; for, for the life of him he couldn't think of anything to say to this mite, who seemed so unembarrassed
at entertaining a perfect stranger that he was lost in admiration of her ready *savoir faire*, and only wished that
he could feel as entirely at his case as she did.

"Do you read poetry?" his new little friend asked suddenly, and, before he had time to disclaim any such sentimental taste, she continued, "I recite!" and forthwith plunged spiritedly into "I had ten dollars in my inside pocket;" half singing, half reciting it, in a very extraordinary and amusing way the Englishman thought. It was a very severe trial for one whose nationality obliged him, under pain of being considered hopelessly ill-bred, never to be amused, to repress a strong inclination to laugh, but being an Englishman, a hero in some respects, and a stoic in all, he valiantly crushed his hilarious inclinations, and rewarded the recitation with "Very nice indeed; a charming piece of poetry!" which remark greatly offended Miss Offington, who had been accustomed to have her successes crowned with loud applause and much laughter, and who was secretly puzzled at this new genus of humanity whose acquaintance she had just made.

"I am afraid you must be tired of staying in-doors," she said, rising, "and would perhaps like to see the horses. I don't myself go into the stables, it is more correct not" (she was in reality afraid of the horses, but she would never acknowledge it to any mere stranger); "but I can introduce you to the coachman or stable-boy, and either will give you all the information you want." So saying Miss Offington led the way through the garden and field to the stables at the back of the house, and De Montford humbly followed, not daring to remonstrate.

On the way there she condescended to him somewhat, and showed him how a man who was not afraid could stroke and scratch the pretty gentle Alderney's ear, and showed him how the chickens loved to hear her voice, knowing in their own little minds that she seldom passed without causing some grain to drop from her dimpling fingers into their midst; grain which, in this instance, the Englishman remarked, had a noted propensity for landing on the fat and comfortable backs of the more venerable hens, where it would remain, probably for hours, safely out of reach.

On the whole, the conversation was waxing friendly, when they were startled by an unaccountable commotion at the entrance to one of the cattle-sheds, and De Montford caught a glimpse of Maudie de la Roche displaying her charms in a very startling costume, while she was in the act of disappearing from view in a neighboring door-way.

Their next sensation, and it was a curious one, was the apparition of Mike the 'herd, in a very agitated frame of mind and gasping for breath.

"Oh, yer honor, sure it was stark starin' mad she was! and I chased her all around, and the queer thing ran like crazy. Then she took and hid in the cow-house, and sure then I nabbed her safe, for I locked the door. All the same I felt curus to know what them creetures looks like, so I slides in at the windy and asks her what she wishes. Then such pitiful eyes as she raises to me, the poor thing! and she says: 'Won't you let me out agin? I won't hurt you, I'm only a hare, and the hounds are chasing me.' And sure that was the poor thing's craze, so I left her locked up, and was going for the perlice when I sees yer Honor, and thought to tell ye and show ye the poor crittur. But here comes Mr. Offington and Elra Cresenworth—sure and they might know best what to do wid her!"

Here the man at last drawing breath, Miss Offington breaks in: "Why, here's uncle and dear old Elra," cried the child, joyfully, with a feeling of relief, now that her responsibility regarding Mr. de Montford was at an end. "This is a gentleman who wanted to see you, uncle." The two men being duly introduced, she turned to the cowherd, who had now recovered from his breathless recital, and was gesticulating and pointing to a shed in the corner of the field with great energy.

"Poor thing! she must be a mad woman," said Elra, compassionately, upon hearing the details from the 'herd, whose name was Mike; "let us come and speak to her; I don't think she is dangerous."

Accordingly, the whole party walked over to the cowhouse, which Mike unlocked with great deliberation, and followed him in to see the strange creature.

"It's ne'er a man or a woman, but somewhat like both," said Mike in a stage whisper, "for I saw the trousers when it went flying around here, and it has petticuts as well. There it lies, miss," he says, triumphantly, pointing to a wet, bedraggled-looking heap crouching on some hay in a corner; "and now, ma'am, hadn't I better run and fetch the perlice?"

"The police? Oh no, no!" cries the figure, springing up and trying to make for the door. "I have done nothing! Allow me to go directly," she cries, with a would-be haughty English stare, which has the result of making Elra feel rather a choking sensation.

"How do you do, Maudie? Been out for a run? But I see you have."

For it was, indeed, Maudie, who, having been pressed hard by the pursuing hounds, had taken refuge in a

cattle-shed attached to the Grange farm, and now stood
before them gasping for breath, and deploring her lost
dignity.

"I shall never play hare and hounds again," sobbed
Maudie. "I am tired of the hoidenish ways of English
girls! I am tired of everything! And oh, that dreadful
de Montford will tell Sir Gregory, and then—oh!" This
last thought brought a little angry sob with it, as
Maudie paused to survey her own pitiful condition.
Alas, for her hopes and aspirations to conquer on sight
in an English girl's bloomer costume, for a sorrier figure
she could not have presented! Her dress, wet, torn and
knee-deep in mud, her jaunty cap crushed over one ear,
and her face burned a deep brick red by contact with the
wind, presented a whole which was rather trying upon
Maudie's dignity and good looks, and which she rather
suspected of forcing those little rebellious smiles to the
lips of the horrid English audience.

With a little injured whine of "The marchioness is
waiting for me all this time," Maudie sneaks out of the
"foreign" crowd, and is off as quickly as her short
limbs will bear her, in some direction best known to herself, while De Montford improves his chances, or hopes
he does, by lingering by Elra Cresenworth, opening
gates, and paying her those hundred attentions which
we poor women have such a weakness for.

CHAPTER XXI.

AN UNHAPPY HUSBAND.

Reduced since the return of Murray Cresenworth to her own companionship, and being in rather a dreamy mood, Topsie goes down to the lake one lazy day and establishes herself in ease and comfort on the soft cushions at the bottom of one of the boats—a favorite haunt of hers. She is lying idly, looking up at the blue sky, when a footstep is heard, and Roanwood Offington appears; then, with a scramble and a jerk, Topsie sits up in the boat, with heightened color and an assurance that she was not asleep or anywhere near the land of dreams.

"May. I take the oars and row you around the lake?" he asks; which request being granted, he enters the boat, and together they float around the island.

Who has not loved to be alone, or nearly alone, on a lake on a lazy summer afternoon, gliding over the sheet of unruffled crystal, startling the coots, who go fluttering and splashing noisily to their covert among the rushes, or watching the black-eyed swans diving their snowy necks beneath the water, to reappear in another moment glossy and smooth as if no speck of moisture had touched their downy plumage? It is cool in the shadow of the chestnuts, and along by the overhanging bank the keel of their boat cuts through the rippling water, making it rush with with a soft gurgle against the high-thrown sands.

Topsie leans forward and gazes into the water with half-closed eyes, while her companion watches her keenly and notes every light and shadow that passes over the girl's expressive, telltale face.

" Of what are you thinking ?" he says at last, and her reply startles him.

" I was thinking of the laws made by man, and how I despise them," she answered. " One day they bind the land with a band of iron ; the next day they are dissolved or laughed to scorn. Laws made by Nature alone stand."

" Well, my little metaphysician, what do you know of the making or breaking of laws ?" he asked, curiously.

" The law means might, not right. It is only the weak minded who consider that immorality consists in the breaking of laws—those tiresome people who consider that the appearance of evil is evil, and that where there is no such appearance there justice is !"

" But there is no smoke without fire," was his answer, while his honest eyes sought hers searchingly.

" No, truly ; but who can judge by the smoke whether the flame is pure or impure ? Who dares to say that beneath the appearance of crime lurks the real crime ? The wise, at least, will not dare a judgment, for there are so many little tricks of Fate, so many possible little happenings in human life, so many unfathomable motives in the human heart, that what appeared the crime of yesterday may show as the height of nobility, purity and greatness in the human soul to-day."

"Poor little woman ! What has happened to make you speak so sadly of life, when you should be so happy and thoughtless in your youth and beauty ?"

TOPSIE LEANS FORWARD AND GAZES INTO THE WATER WITH HALF-
CLOSED EYES.

Page 176.

"Alas!" she thought, "that my life was once such a continuous flood of golden sunshine, such a never-ending bubble of sparkling joy! And now I have cut myself off from all right to sympathy. I have been insane enough to part with a birthright that can never be regained." Aloud she said: "Often those who seem the gayest and brightest are those who have most to bear in silence. There are some secrets that must be kept inviolate, and even were I to tell you all, you might condemn me as others have done."

He bends swiftly over her and takes her hand as he says: "You may never enlighten me as to what has left this blight of melancholy upon your young life; but I shall never believe aught of you save that which is pure and true and sweet."

"You may be promising too much," cries Topsie, with a tremor in her voice, and without waiting his answer, as the boat has now touched the shore, she springs past Offington, and, without touching his out-stretched hand, runs swiftly through the garden and is soon lost to sight.

As days spread out into weeks, and Offington still lingers on near her, hoping he knows not what, Topsie feels a chain linking itself around her heart which she had never known there before, and she trembles at the thought of sounding the depths of her own heart, which she knows she must do soon.

But about this time a change comes over Elra's volatile husband which affects matters rather strongly in the Grange household.

The effect upon the neighborhood caused by the sudden changing of Mrs. Eldmere's name to that of Cresen-

worth, and the startling appearance of that lady's husband, had been great indeed, and rather confusing to
rural minds. If Sir Gregory Athelhurst was greatly
upset by this sudden and unlooked for blow, it seemed
to have rather the contrary effect upon his friend De
Montford, who had his own little schemes on hand, and
the appearance of Mr. Murray Cresenworth upon the
scene was not so great a surprise to him as it had been
to poor Sir Gregory.

After the first awkwardness had passed, Mr. Murray
Cresenworth had been warmly welcomed by the sporting
element in the county, and he soon found himself a
welcome guest among the country squires. One of these
was a certain Captain Lane, who, for some reason or
other, appeared to greatly dislike De Montford, and
one day, from idle curiosity, perhaps, Mr. Cresenworth
jokingly asked his new friend why he was so bitter.

"Because I know the man is a villain!" was the quick
reply—"and *you*, Cresenworth, should be the one to
know it before it is too late."

"Why, what do you mean by that?" says the unsuspecting Murray.

"I mean," answers the captain with emphasis, "that
your wife is in love with De Montford, and you are so
blind that the only man in the country who doesn't
know of it is the lady's husband. If you want proofs I
can give them! Here is a letter which fell into my
hands, fortunately, and which is proof positive that De
Montford and your wife are more than mere friends."

Mr. Cresenworth at first is furious with the captain for
daring to attack his wife, whom he loves and trusts, but
at the sight of a letter in Elra's handwriting, evidently

written to De Montford and couched in tender language, such as it was impossible for a woman to use except to her husband or lover, he allows himself to be convinced, and thus unconsciously becomes the tool of the men into whose hands he is ready to play. Not only is the letter shown him, but a receipt for a large sum of money, its acknowledgment by De Montford, and love and thanks to his darling Elra.

This last document sets fire to the kindling mass of his resentment, and, without a word to his unsuspecting wife, Murray Cresenworth hurries up to London and holds a consultation with his lawyer, preparatory to taking steps for a divorce.

In the mean time the ladies at the Grange, all unsuspecting of the danger which threatens one of them, pursue the even tenor of their accustomed life, now brightened by the presence (to Topsie at least) of Roanwood Offington, who seems to find his quarters at the Grange so comfortable that he is loath to tear himself away. He has noticed, however, a certain restraint and avoidance of him exercised by that young lady, and, manlike, the more he is repulsed, the greater his ardor in pursuit of his object. Some days have now passed, Mr. Cresenworth is still absent from home, and Roanwood Offington is stopping at the Inn Bramber, as he is fully determined to have a satisfactory interview with Topsie previous to his departure from those country parts. With this end in view he enters the library one morning at a time when he knows Miss Topsie is usually to be found there, and taking a book, and a seat in a distant corner of the room, calmly waits for her appearance.

It was true that Topsie had purposely avoided him, for

she could not fail to notice his growing admiration, which had soon deepened into love; and she dreaded an explanation which she felt would have to come sooner or later, if once she allowed herself to listen to his words.

Mr. Offington is beginning to grow weary of his enforced retirement from the cheerful fireside, for the days were now cold enough to warrant the luxury of a bright wood fire on the hearth, when he hears at last the sound of voices in the hall, and presently Topsie enters the room alone, and running to the fireplace with a little shiver, throws herself down on the rug before the cheerful blaze.

Here the gentleman with the dexterity of an old huntsman quietly stalks his prey, who, unconscious of his presence, is gazing into the bright flames with a sad and troubled look on her young face.

"A penny for your thoughts," he says gently, at last, and the girl gives a great start while the color rushes to her cheeks as she looks around in evident confusion.

She sees it is Mr. Offington and knows that her hour has come, for there is a look of determination on that young man's face which tells her instinctively that she must give her answer now.

I am glad to find this opportunity of speaking to you alone (with emphasis upon the word) before I go. You have so evidently avoided me, and been so constrained in my presence lately, that I am almost fearful of speaking to you now, but I cannot leave the Grange, dearest, without a word from you. Can you not say that word, and bid me hope that I may one day claim you as my wife?

Topsie had risen to her feet and now stood facing him with downcast eyes, and lips that trembled as she whispered,

" Please say no more; I must not listen to you—yet."

" Then you do bid me hope, my darling," he cries, eagerly trying to seize her hand.

" Yes ! if ever the clouds are cleared away," she murmurs, and with one look of radiant love and hope she tears herself from his arms and hurries from the house.

On her way through the gardens she hears Elra's voice calling, and hastily drying her tears, she turns to meet Mrs. Cresenworth, who comes to her with an open letter in her hand and a look of anxious bewilderment on her face. " Just listen to this new freak of my husband's," she says to the girl ; " he writes me saying, ' am I prepared to advance any good reason why he shall not institute proceedings for a divorce against me ?' I know Murray's jealous nature too well by this time, but I never thought he would dare to be so insane as this. What can he mean ?"

But here Topsie suddenly drags Elra into the shade of some shrubs to avoid meeting two men who are walking in their direction, and they recognize De Montford in an earnest and amicable discussion with his erstwhile hater, Captain Lane.

" I do not know why I so distrust both of these men," says Elra, after they have passed—" I never feel safe when they are anywhere near."

" Your instinct tells you right," says Topsie, pale as the colorless roses at her throat. Heaven help you if you lie in their power, one of them at least will know no mercy."

And Elra knows at last that Hugo de Montford it has been who has wrecked her loved Topsie's life. " He is a friend of my husband."

"Then," says Topsie, reflectively, " I see it all—it is he who has worked you wrong with your husband! I feel it, I am sure of it, for some purpose of his own, and Heaven befriend you, Elra!"

CHAPTER XXII.

CLAD IN ROSE AND GRAY.

It is Thursday—a brisk winter's day—and a day of surprises it proves to be for more than one family in the neighborhood of Ravenstowe, for what begins with a comedy of errors may end before long in a tragedy!

That terrible condition of misery and discomfort called house-cleaning is being carried on at the dower-house, now occupied by the dowager Marchioness of Ripdale and two of her elder daughters; and the ladies have been driven from one room to another, from the dining-room to the hall, where they are now occupying the window-seat looking out on to the wintry avenue.

"I wish ma could regulate things better, and not have everything miserable for the short time that we are home," snapped Psyche; and though you may think I speak of a little dog, I refer in reality to a gaunt maiden lady, written of in Debrett as fifth daughter of Edred, Marquis of Ripdale, and of his wife Lenora.

"I'm sorry for you, my dear," says the dowager lady, tartly, "but you are not obliged to stay, Amabel, and I can manage to exist without you! I suppose you think *we* do not feel the inconvenience as well as yourself."

Lady Psyche was heard to mutter crossly to herself to the effect that the dower-house was not a cheerful place, that she felt her usual attack of rheumatism approaching, as she walked away from her mother and sister to reconnoitre the premises and see if her room was still in a state of chaos.

"What a temper Psyche has," sighs the dowager—always finding fault; this is not Ripdale Castle, with its retinue of servants! By the way, Amabel, when did you last hear from Artrale?"

"I showed you her last letter," answers Amabel, who is as fat and lazy as her sister is gaunt and restless; "she mentions Lenore."

"Oh, indeed!" says Psyche, joining in the conversation, "and what does she say about *her*? I really think Artrale ought to know better than to even mention her to us; though she was our sister, she has disgraced the family, and I, for one, never wish to see her again."

The dowager sighs; but Psyche continues: "I always thought Lenore was a little mad, her mind always leaned towards the startlingly eccentric. Don't you remember, ma dear, when she caught those two little mice and harnessed them to the toy steam-engine, and allowed them to run away with it? Such peculiar ideas in anybody else would have been accounted insanity!"

Here she is interrupted by the entrance of a maid-servant, who comes to ask her mistress what is to be done with the contents of a large oaken bureau, which is to be relegated from the lumber room to one of the apartments.

"It's full of papers, my lady, bills and such like, or law papers maybe," says the maid.

Oh, burn them, Hester! answers the dowager indifferently, but Amabel suggests that they should first be looked at, and the maid retires, returning presently with her apron full of musty-looking papers, which she deposits on the hall table as requested.

" Where did they come from ?" says Psyche, gingerly
touching the dusty documents with the tips of her
fingers.

" The old bureau was bought two years ago, at a sale
from the vicarage; these must belong to Mr. Grey most
likely."

" Here is a strange document," says Amabel with
interest, " and it looks like a marriage certificate !"

" Show it to me," says her sister, and the two unfold
the paper and commence to read it.

"It is a marriage certificate," cries Amabel, excited-
ly ; " here, let me read the names. Why—Lenore Allesmere and Hugo de Montford ! It cannot be," she gasps,
" it can't mean that Lenore is really married !"

" Let me have it !" says the dowager, imperiously ;
" this must be some trick ; I will never believe it ; after
these long years to find that Lenore was really married
to that man !" But when the document is in her hand
she sees at once that Amabel's words are true. There
stand the two names, though the corner of the register
has been torn carefully away, and the name of the
clergyman is missing.

" Girls, this matter must be seen into at once," cries
the dowager, in great agitation ; " this document must
be placed before that man, and he must be made to con-
fess whether this be true or no. Poor lost Lenore !"

" Here is the very man we want," says Amabel, from
her post by the window-seat. " Dr. Warder, mother, is
now coming up the avenue; let us tell him, and ask for
his advice."

The good old family doctor is soon put in possession
of the astonishing revelation made by the old bureau,

and he is intrusted with the precious paper with which to confront De Montford.

"No time is to be lost," he says, as he bustles into his long overcoat. "Give me authority to meet the fellow with this in my hands, and I will soon know whether the villain has all this time been deceiving that poor child or no. For all your sakes," he adds, "I pray that this piece of paper will win back your sister; though, if she were really married to that man, Heaven help her, to be in the hands of such a scoundrel!"

He forthwith loses no time in calling at De Montford's cottage, and finding that gentleman out, resolves determinedly to repeat his call on the morrow.

"A note for you miss," says Anatole, entering the drawing-room at the Nest late that same afternoon, and handing his young mistress a suspicious looking three-cornered letter, which Maudie seizes on with joy, recognizing her dear marchioness as the writer thereof. "Oh, mamma!" she says, after hastily glancing at the contents, "her ladyship wants me to meet her at the ruins at four o'clock, and have a good 'spin on the downs,' as she calls it. I am so delighted that she has kept her promise of returning to Ravenstowe in the winter, and of course I will meet her. We may be late, so don't wait for me, but have your dinner at seven as usual."

Then Miss de la Roche hurries to her room, and having donned her bloomer costume, according to directions, she sallies forth to meet her friend at the ruins.

Maudie is first at the rendezvous and has to wait some minutes before her ladyship appears, but she is used to this, and knows that she mustn't grumble at whatever it may be her friend's caprice to inflict upon her.

" Hello, Maudie !" says the new-comer, "quite on time, as our transatlantic friends say. I told you I would be here again, and after three days at Ravenstowe with my elderly sisters-in-law, to say nothing of a gouty, dyspeptic husband, I thought a smart run across country would do me good, and clear the cobwebs from my brain ; moreover, I want to talk to you, and to find out all I can about the beautiful Mrs. Eldmere, or Mrs. Cresenworth, whichever it is; she interested me that day when I saw her at your house, and I believe you know something about her."

Maudie was only too willing to tell all, and more than she knew about the fascinating lady who had robbed her of Sir Gregory's attentions, and the two set off at a smart trot through the fields, which the marchioness declared led, by a short cut to the downs where the " spin " was to be taken.

But, as often happens, the short cut proved a long one ; and having leaped small brooks, clambered over fences and gates, and made themselves both hot and tired, they at last emerge onto the high-road again, where they sit down to rest on some stones, and to consult as to what is best to be done.

" I believe we are lost, Maudie !" says her ladyship in great glee; she looks as calm and cool as when they started, and is a great contrast to her poor friend, who is still panting from her recent exertions.

" What fun that would be ! I haven't an idea whereabouts we are, so let us sit and wait here till something turns up."

Presently the stillness is broken by the sound of cart-wheels, and a gypsy caravan comes slowly down the road.

Tied to one of the vans is a poor hungry-looking dog, and when the marchioness catches sight of his woebegone face and drooping tail, a wicked little thought flashes through her mind; and going up to one of the men she asks, abruptly, "Will you sell me that dog?"

"Yes, my lady," the man replies with a grim smile of humor; "he is a fine watch-dog, and a high bred un, but, being a lady, I will let you have him for a half sovereign! He's worth a deal more," he continues, thinking perhaps he has not been greedy enough.

"Well, here is your money, my good man, and at the same time I want a penny rattle, one of those wicker toy things."

"Maudie, you shall go shares with me in this," she whispers; "I mean to have no end of fun. Do you think that animal could possibly be made to run, even with a rattle tied to his tail? if so, we can both have great diversion for a ha'penny, a penny being the price of the rattle, and I won't charge you for the dog." Maudie is well used to her friend's vagaries, and is willing to submit to all she proposes, though to tell the truth she is now thoroughly tired, and only wishes herself at home again.

The dog and rattle being paid for, the caravan moves slowly on, and the two ladies are left in solitude again. The marchioness has tied the animal to the fence and is now engaged in endeavoring to fix the rattle to one of his extremities, which he resents with a low growl, and Maudie, who is terribly afraid of all strange dogs, stands watching in an agony of fear, as she is not sure if she will be asked to hold the brute or not.

"It's getting very late, isn't it?" she remarks, timidly;

" had we not better wait till another day? I am sure we must be miles from home."

"I suppose we are, or at least you are," says her friend, coolly, " and I mean to take a drive in the next conveyance that comes along. " Why, here is the very thing," she continues, mischievously, as a small cart, commonly called a kreel, is seen approaching. In this kreel is some clean straw, and lying on the straw are some half dozen little pigs, who blink and wink and squeal at intervals. The marchioness stops the bundle of rags which directs the footsteps of the donkey who draws the cart, and after a short parley room is made for the two ladies in its interior, and in spite of Maudie's protestations she is forced to mount and take a seat beside the pigs, while the dog is tied to the back of the cart, and is dragged an unwilling victim in their wake.

"What fun!" says her ladyship, looking round with intense amusement depicted on her face, partly at Maudie's disgust, partly at the novelty of their position.

"These horrid pigs!" says the girl, plaintively.

"They won't hurt you, missie," answers the old crone. "They is as knowing as can be; look for all the world, the impudent little things, as if they could tell fortunes."

"Here is a carriage coming," cried Maudie, in a tone of despair.

"All right," tuck your head down," says her friend, boldly, and the next moment a handsome phaeton and pair is driven rapidly past. No sooner is it out of sight than the marchioness gives vent to a peal of silvery laughter. "Did you see them?" she asks. "My lord and master, whom I left at home suffering from an attack of gout and temper, driving with a fair unknown!

This will suit me finely! How glad I am we were hidden here."

"Was it really your husband?" says Maudie, in an awe-struck tone.

"None other than the noble marquis himself. I told him I might be going up to town to-day, so I suppose he thought it was a good opportunity. I declare, Maudie, we are having a lovely time this afternoon, and if it were not so late we might have the dog chase after all." By this time, however, the sun had set, the shadows were lengthening, and both ladies began to feel ready for their accustomed meal, so it was decided that the dog should be reprieved till the following day, and that they should leave the kreel at the next farm-house, where the old crone told them the pigs were to be delivered.

"It's quite nigh the Grange," she said, to Maudie's delight, as she saw some prospect of reaching home that night, for the Grange and the Nest were within a mile of each other. Just then the cart turns a bend in the road, and reveals the figures of two people, a lady and gentleman, standing just in front of them. With a gasp of horror Maudie recognizes De Montford and Mrs. Cresenworth, and buries her unfortunate head in the straw as she whispers the same to her companion. As they pass them in the growing dusk the marchioness notices that Mrs. Cresenworth is clad in a long gray cloak, richly embroidered and trimmed with beads and feathers, and as she turns, apparently to dismiss De Montford with a haughty gesture, they hear her say, "I must beg you not to come any farther—I am going into these cottages—so I will wish you good-bye.'

They watch her as she walks smartly up the lane

towards the farm-house, and, before entering, see her loosen her rich cloak, which she hands to a little girl who is standing near the door, for she is going in to see a sick woman, and knows by experience that the interior of the cottage is neither clean nor comfortable, and that the windows have not been opened all summer.

If Maudie has recognized Mrs. Cresenworth it was the keen eyes of the Marchioness of Ripdale which first saw De Montford, and by the time Elra Cresenworth enters the cottage door she has formed a plan which she at once proceeds to carry into execution.

"Maudie," she says, in an imperious way, "I am going to leave you, but don't dare to move or speak—watch me, and follow me at a distance after I have spoken to De Montford;" and the next moment she has sprung out of the cart and is walking towards the cottage. When she reaches the door she says quietly to the girl who is still waiting there,

"Give me my cloak, child;" and, handing her a shilling, takes the garment from the astonished little maiden, and throwing it around herself, walks quickly down the lane to where De Montford is still lingering, as if loath to tear himself away. She has found a thick lace veil in one of the pockets of the cloak, and, having tied this over her face, she trusts to be able to pass for Mrs. Cresenworth without detection. They are both tall women, and the marchioness is a good actress, so she has no fear of successfully duping De Montford, especially as it is now so dark that it would be impossible to distinguish features.

. De Montford gives a start of surprise when he sees the supposed Mrs. Cresenworth returning so quickly, and he comes forward at once.

"I am afraid you found your invalid out or up," he says, significantly," and now it is too dark for you to walk alone; may I not offer you an arm?"

To his surprise his arm is at once taken, and, is it his fancy, or does Mrs. Cresenworth press it gently as she murmurs a reply? Can it be that she relents, and after such a cold and stubborn resistance, has at last fallen a victim to his seductive looks and words?

"But it's always the way," thinks this conquering hero complacently, "these great beauties give in to one in the end with a much more startling brevity than their less sought sisters!" and deeming he has his grasp on the beautiful, coveted, forbidden fruit, he passes his arm gently around her waist, and draws her to him, and is not one whit surprised when she secedes and comes to him with very little resistance, but with what he deems an hysterical little sob. He endeavors to search her eyes, but these are strictly averted, and for fear lest so magnificent a prize should slip from his grasp, he deems it his best plan to strike while the iron is hot.

"My darling," he says, "you have consented at last! You will come with me, and I shall protect your fair name with the last drop of my heart's blood! My dog-cart is here waiting, and my cottage is not far away; let me escort you thither, where malice cannot penetrate to make your hours bitter. None will dare to molest you there! We shall be safe from all intruders. You will come then, dearest one?" For his only answer he catches the sound of a second smothered sob, and it is with renewed pleading in his voice that he says: "How unhappy you are, and yet how beautiful! Come with me, Elra, and allow my heart's worship to be laid at your feet, to make you happy as the lark that sings in a summer sky. Come!"

The lady seems reluctant to accept his proposition, but at last suffers herself to be handed into the dog cart, which is drawn at once in the direction of De Montford's shooting cottage. In the mean time Maudie is chafing and fuming at this new freak of her ladyship, though she dare not disobey her tormentor, and when she sees the dog-cart drive rapidly off, she knows she has to follow it as quickly as the donkey can be urged along; though she is heartily tired of the present comedy, she has a still greater fear of her ladyship's displeasure. Very little conversation takes place between the occupants of the dog-cart. De Montford can scarcely believe that this is really Elra Cresenworth by his side, but though her face is veiled, he recognizes the long gray cloak she had been wearing; and the marchioness, scarcely trusting herself to speak, except in whispers, holds her head down and pulls the lace veil still further over her face. On their arrival at the cottage a man steps out of the shadow, and coming to the side of the dog-cart, whispers a few words to De Montford which make him bite his lips and change color.

"Wait here," he says in a hurried whisper to the unknown, as he hands Mrs. Cresenworth from the carriage.

"Here we are, dearest. You are quite safe now. Wait one little moment while I see my agent, and then I will be with you." So saying he hands the lady into the house, and, locking the door carefully behind her, puts the key in his pocket. A brief, sharp battle of words ensues between the two men outside, and then De Montford reluctantly mounts his dog-cart, the stranger taking the seat beside him, and drives off in the direction of the Manor-house.

Maudie and the donkey-cart have by this time made their appearance, for in spite of the old crone's assurance to the contrary, she has insisted on being driven in pursuit of De Montford. When they reach the cottage Maudie hears her friend's voice calling to her, and, looking up, sees that lady standing at the window of a room above, and jumps down, much relieved, from off her bed of straw.

"You can't get in," says the marchioness, who seems to be enjoying it all hugely. "The door is locked, and you will have to climb in at the window. Look about and see if there's a ladder handy that will help you."

Maudie obediently looks about, and finds an old ladder leaning against a tree in the little garden. This she brings to the window, and, putting it in position, proceeds cautiously to mount the steps. All goes well till Maudie nearly reaches the top; then there is a crash and a scream, and the frail support gives way under her ample weight. But she is at the window-sill, and the marchioness, catching hold of her, drags her into the room. Then, realizing their ludicrous position, she flings herself into a chair and bursts into a peal of laughter.

"Well, you're a friend in need," she says, as Maudie goes to the window and ruefully gazes at the ruins of the ladder, which are reposing in a heap on the flower-beds.

"Now that you have removed our only means of exit, we shall have to remain here all night, I suppose, for the door is locked, and I don't mean to break my ankles by a leap from that window; so we must stay here and make the best of it."

CHAPTER XXIII.

THICKENING, DARKENING, CLOUDING.

After De Montford has driven away in the direction of his cottage, with Mrs. Cresenworth by his side, an angry head is thrust over the hedge along which she has just passed with her companion, and a few muttered oaths are heard.

"I vow by Heaven," says Murray Cresenworth's hoarse voice, "she will make a fool of me no more! She will have to reap the reward of her treachery and her sin. I shall stay proceedings no longer."

His loud tones have the effect of scaring a few little rabbits close by, and he sees a very red tumbled head of hair peep from a warren lower down, and the next moment the legs that belong to the head are scampering affrightedly across the fields towards the Grange; but poor Mr. Cresenworth is too preoccupied to care how many little bundles of rags he may have the pleasure of seeing bowling along in that direction.

"I had come to offer her a last choice between honor —with a sigh—or dishonor. She has chosen the latter; and—she was my wife!"

This was said as sadly as a man might speak who resigns all right to happiness henceforth, for Murray well knew that his wife had been the very light of his eye and life of his heart, and that his existence without her was a void.

He loses no time in despatching a boy on horseback to the nearest telegraph station with the following despatch, written by him in feverish haste lest his resolution should fail:

"Finish up proceedings, and let the journals be apprised as ordered.

"(Signed)   MURRAY CRESENWORTH."

A long night of agony he spends in a room of the inn at Bramber, and daybreak finds him up and about again, glad to put away the horrors of a night unequalled in suffering by anything he has been through in his previous life.

Had he, however, been in the mood to notice anything that night, he might have seen two men enter a room in the village inn, not so very far from his own; and he would have recognized De Montford in the one, while the other we will describe as the stranger who had so inopportunely interrupted De Montford's tete-a-tete with the fair lady of his heart.

There is evidently a dispute between the men, as loud angry words are spoken by them, which have some relation to a large financial scheme that one of them has in hand.

"It would be bad, would it not," says the stranger, in mocking tones, "to let them know of that embezzling matter practised upon your father-in-law—by whom we shall not say?"

"Hold!" cries De Montford; "who is my father-in-law? tell me that."

"People would not confide large sums to the keeping of *your* banking concern, would they?" continues the stranger, not noticing the interruption.

"An impudent blackmailing scheme," rages De Montford; "I know your purpose, you cowardly rascal, but you will find that the law can gag you sooner than you might desire!"

"And the man you shot—"

But here ensues a violent altercation between the two men. At first De Montford is proud and overbearing in manner and speech, but by degrees, helped by the stranger's powerful arguments, he assumes a milder tone and is at last forced to yield, as those who knew his haughty nature did not think it possible for De Montford ever to have done.

But Cresenworth notices nothing, and next morning disdaining breakfast, he mounts his horse, impatient to call at the post-office for any mail that the morning may bring. The post-mistress hands him a telegram from his lawyer, which had evidently crossed his of the previous evening, but which had not been delivered earlier to Cresenworth, owing to no particular address being given. It contained the words:

"Divorce granted yesterday at 2.59. Morning papers will corroborate.

"(Signed) CLARKSON, RYFE & CLARKSON."

He staggered ever so little when he read the message —it was so strange—so unexpected—so soon. What though he himself had ordered his lawyers to proceed with the utmost despatch in the matter?

"It is finished then, and a beautiful woman, once noble as she was beautiful, has been trained at my wish through the slough of the Divorce Court! Poor little Elra! your sufferings have begun."

Touching with his lips a glass of some strong stimulant, he mounts his horse in a dazed way, and rides down the frost-hardened road towards the Grange, not knowing what new developments Fate has in store for him—just as the hale and hearty man goes forth in the morning and sees not the death's-head that hovers round and follows him to his fate.

If we go back but a few hours, and follow the apparition that had rather startled Murray Cresenworth by popping at an inopportune moment from a rabbit burrow and shooting off in the direction of the Grange, we shall find the same strange apparition arriving at its destination in haste that is more hot and hurried than graceful.

Alone at the Grange, and feeling her nerves rather shattered from all she has lately learned, Topsie retires to bed (though it is still daylight), under orders from the doctor, where a strong injection of morphine is administered.

"You must be kept quite quiet for a few days, my dear young lady," he says, "and then I hope you will be feeling yourself again."

Ere she lays her head on the pillow, however, for a much needed sleep, her room is suddenly invaded by Daddy Dolan, who has been watching outside during the doctor's visit, and on his departure makes her way into Topsie's room and rushes to her bedside.

"Oh, Miss Topsie, dear!" she half sobs, "are you going to die? I saw the doctor here, and thought maybe he was murdering you, and I having so much that I must tell you!" All this is said in a burst of grief from Daddy, whose devotion to Topsie is well known, and who is a privileged intruder at the Grange—so that the girl's presence in the house did not cause much astonishment or curiosity. Topsie had been in the habit of teaching her young protégée, and though the result has not yet been great, she knows she has won a faithful and trusty friend in the poor neglected, simple-minded country girl.

"What is it Daddy? tell me dear," she says, as Daddy continued to sob, her head buried in her apron. "What has happened?"

"I was in the rabbit warren, miss, a while ago, sitting on the bank a-thinking of nothing when I see that bold black man a coming down the lane" (this was Daddy's name for De Montford, whom she cordially detests for some reason or other). "I crouched down for him not to see me, and then I heard voices talking, and one was a lady's. I didn't listen, miss, but I couldn't help hearing what they said; leastways he spoke so loud and she in whispers."

"What did they say? tell me," cries Topsie, sitting up in bed with wide open eyes, "tell me, Daddy, quickly!"

"They whispered some first, and then he says: 'Well, come with me *now!* everything is ready, my carriage is waiting, and we can soon be at my hunting cottage, safe from all intruders; they will never think to look for you there; come, my darling!' The lady seemed to be saying 'No' at first, then he persuades her some more, and they go forward and get into a carriage and drive off; she seemed to be frightened somewhat; leastways she cries out 'No! no! how can I trust you?' But he whips up the horses and off they go; then I comes across to tell you, miss, and on my way I meets the poor gentleman, Mr. Cresenworth; he must have been there and heard it too; and she such a pretty lady!"

" Who was it ?" almost shrieks Topsie, seizing the girl roughly by the arm.

" Why, Mrs. Cresenworth, miss ! I told you there was no other lady as I see."

With a wild cry Topsie flies from her bed, all thought of sleep is dashed in a moment from her mind. She hurries into her riding habit in hysterical haste, and orders Irish King to be instantly saddled with the child's basket saddle which had been recently purchased for little Miss Offington. The saddle has a high back, rather like a chair, and to this, as she mounts her horse, she has herself bound (in a moment of strange inspiration) by a leathern strap. The next instant she is dashing rather wildly down the sweep of lawn towards the tower gates.

Mrs. Cresenworth, returning a little later, hears from her maid that Topsie is out riding, and is satisfied with the explanation of her absence, until finding it grows very late and there is no appearance of Topsie she becomes alarmed; and is rendered doubly so on being told of the dose of morphia administered to that young lady in the afternoon. It is therefore in a sad state of alarm lest the young horsewoman may have been overtaken suddenly by the effects of the narcotic, that Mrs. Cresenworth orders a search to be made—of which, however, nothing comes.

CHAPTER XXIV.

BY TISDALE BRACKEN.

"Dolan, go and attend to those earths; see that they are stopped," said Sir Gregory that evening as jumping from his horse he ran briskly up the stone steps leading to his well appointed bachelor's abode.

"'Pon my soul," cried he, irritably, looking round the old halls, hushed in gloom and silence, "I must get married to enliven this old tomb! How sweet and bright that little Eldmere could make it all for me. I wonder will she have me when I ask her? or more, I wonder will she even give me the chance of taking her prim little hand in mine and proffering my request? By my faith if she doesn't—" and here, to signify the strength of his fierce intentions in case of such trying circumstances, he quaffed a full goblet to her honor, for which act of appreciation she would no doubt have felt flattered and grateful, particularly had she seen him stagger a little towards the comfortable settee in front of the cheery log fire and stretch himself there, the while murmuring her praises in very thickening speech, quite oblivious to the important fact that his Mrs. Eldmere had been claimed by another man.

"Poor master, it isn't his fault!" said the long limbed daughter of the red-haired Hibernian, Dolan; it isn't his fault. She had him worked up to that same, and sure she must be a heartless thing, for master he be the

grandest—" and forthwith her thoughts revert to last
Michaelmas, and the largesse slipped in her hand by the
master of the manor, accompanied with a—well, we won't
mention, for the sake of that dignity which I have heard
affirmed (rightly or wrongly I dare not say) belongs inva-
riably to scions of the old, old stock.   Be that as it may,
the recollection of it made the cheeks of the fair Hibernian grow a little pinker under the freckles, and it made
her feel justly indignant against any "rediculous stuck
up thing" who might affect to despise the master she
chose to champion.

"What could she want better?" asked she scornfully.
"She thinks she has it, but she hasn't, that's sartain,
the poor crathur."

Now this daughter of a red-haired race boasted, besides
freckles, a true womanly heart, even if it was inclined
to admire in her master what she considered was the
highest type of manly beauty, and everything else besides
that was good and noblest in her estimation; but that
did not prevent her being a sensible, comfortable, every-
day, commonplace girl—one who never indulged in day
dreams, although she did commit the folly of giggling
when "the master" had slipped something in her hand,
accompanied with a—well, it is not fair, and I won't tell
what!

She, Miss Dolan, also rejoiced in several names, and
among others the soubriquet of Daddy Long Limbs
(translated legs) was her especial property, owing to her
peculiar length of nether limbs; and this particular
evening, when the master of the manor was happy in
his rather maudlin dreams concerning his hard-hearted
goddess, there came a ringing cry through the yard at

the rear of the manor: "Daddy! Daddy Dolan! come out if ye want to see for yourself sich sport—and quick."

The long-limbed maiden, with dishevelled hair flying in the wind, rushed out at what she deemed a very irresistible appeal from the small boy Dolan, her brother; for she knew it meant that there were rats and terriers in the wind, or rather in the yard, ready for any number of exciting encounters.

"Fadder is goin' for to stop the erts, so if we sneak and make no noise, we can have the rabbits to ourseffs, and steal a march onknownst to de ole man. Daddy doan yees be like a girl and make noise like a girl, its silly; and if yees doan we'll have roas' rabbit on de quiet."

Daddy of the long limbs had a lingering fondness for rabbit cooked in this outlaw fashion, so she vowed in a piteous way that she would not be a bit like a girl, and that she would sneak, and, positively, make no noise; whereat they started for the fox and rabbit coverts, taking care to "sneak" at a careful distance from Dolan the elder, who preceded them by the length of about a field.

It was a moonlight night, and once within the shadow of the woods the little outlaws diverged into a track of their own, with their eager terriers throttling themselves in their detaining arms, in rebellious endeavors to steal off for a scamper and a tear after the timid little rabbits. At last, and only when they believed themselves fairly out of ear-shot of their revered parent, they gave themselves unreservedly to the intoxicating pleasure of slaughtering any foolish little beast who was simple enough to stand and play until caught and worried to death by Boxer and Foxer.

Of these there were not many, indeed I do not think any timid rodents gave them the opportunity of "roas' rabbit" that night; but for all this the little Dolans were enjoying themselves to the top of their bent when Boxer struck up a low wailing howl, a long "keening," such as dogs are wont to indulge in when death is hovering around a house. In a moment the piercingly sad note was caught up by Foxer, while the Dolan children stood rooted where they stood, prevented by a paralyzing fear from articulating a syllable with their trembling lips. The climax came in the trampling of a horse's hoofs on the mossy turf, and scarcely daring to look at the dark figure which, distinct in the moonlight, loomed above them in the saddle, they turned with as genuine a howl of terror as even their beloved Boxer or Foxer had been capable of and faced for home, scampering all the way. There they arrived, to their astonishment, in safety, and I do not think that ever after they cared exactly to disturb the gentle little rabbits on moonlight nights.

Had they stayed in the woods with their parent they might have heard still more weird sounds while that person was applying himself diligently to the stopping of the earths. Two of these had been securely fastened against the matinal return of the fox, when suddenly he had occasion to whistle for his dog. This was a noble greyhound, black as coal, neatly and cleanly built, and fleet of limb; the pride and delight in fact of the sport-loving Hibernian, who never went anywhere without his much esteemed canine companion. But to-night, although he would not have sacrificed his dog's companship, he could not help thinking, with a slightly uneasy feeling, for he was a superstitious man, how weird and ghostly appeared the spectre-like hound, as in and out of the tangled undergrowth of tree and shrub he glided with noiseless foot-fall. When, therefore, the hound dropped himself suddenly prone on the earth a few paces ahead of him, and stretched his limbs and tail to a stark, rigid stiffness—the while setting up so partly fierce, partly dismal a howl—the right-hand man of Sir Gregory Athelhurst, in a moment of nervousness, seized his double-barrel breech-loader, and in an instant had his finger on the trigger.

Not a moment too soon, he told himself, had he placed himself, on guard, for down one of the open glades intersecting the woods came a horse at full gallop, which gave him but scant measure of time to spring aside, as with frantic speed the animal tore on through the woods, hushed till now in the still midnight. The moonlight flooded his pathway, and in the moment when he had to spring aside so deftly or be trampled upon, Dolan had caught sight of the flutter of a lady's riding habit.

"Be krapes! who can be out in the woods this awful hour?" he cried angrily to himself, although his teeth did chatter a bit—"and a lady too, who ought to be warm and snug in her little bed at home; but it's a sorry trick, and I wouldn't choose to be the lady," he concluded, scornfully, feeling indignant enough to hold the said lady up to the ridicule and gossip of the whole country around.

However, he did not have much time to plan vengeance, when a sudden and appalling thought froze his blood. "She might be a sperret, the Lord presarve me!" Whereat his teeth fairly rattled in his head, and his knees shook beneath him. However, these mental terrors were mild to those which seized him a moment later, making his blood freeze, and leaving him entirely undecided whether he was suffering from an attack of delirium tremens, or whether he was really standing in the moon flooded woods by Tisdale Bracken, for through those woods rang out clear and wild and full of music, in the dead stillness of the midnight, a cry which made the woods resound, from end to end as it were, with the thrilling blast of the huntsman's bugle, as he puts his treasures, the fox-hounds, into covert to begin their search for their appointed prey.

"Hi, get in there; get in, get in! Now you're on him, brave fellows, my beauties, now you're on him; Neptune, get in there. 'Ware, hound!" This last ejaculation being emphasized by the loud cracking of the huntsman's whip, and then there followed a startlingly ringing cry of "Tally-ho! tally-ho! tally-ho! gone aw-a-ay!" accompanied by a long and cheery blast of the horn.

Echo answered echo from the neighboring hills, until the silvery tones were caught and hurled back from the old tower walls of Bramber, rousing the answering call again into mocking life amid the stillness of the slumbering woods, until at last, in weird ripples of bell-like notes, it died away in the dells, leaving all things steeped in solemn repose once more. Eerie the whole thing was, and savoring highly of the supernatural, in the opin- of Dolan, whose cap refused to lie any longer on his bristling hair, and with the assistance of which he was fain to dash some beads of moisture from his brow. Had he been capable of framing a few thoughts on the occasion, he would have quickly built up a pretty little romance, and told himself that the "leddy was out for a lark." But with the demoniacal sounds of huntsman's whip and horn ringing through the woods, there was nothing could persuade the solitary terror-beset Dolan that the figure on horseback was other than that of a "sperret," and when next the wild black horse came careering down the wind, dashing full upon him as though he himself owned a spirit's claim to invisibility, Dolan stepped aside, and raised his gun to his shoulder. He knew that the horse was a valuable one, and that there was nothing of the spirit about it, but the figure sitting so straight in the saddle, what was it? This was what Dolan wished to glean, when, raising his breech-loader to his shoulder, he took deliberate aim. The report rang out as the unknown horsewoman dashed by, and Dolan saw by the large tear in the flimsy veil that the shot had struck her over the ear, glancing off, then in the direction of an old oak, where it lodged, and was afterwards found by Dolan. Of the bullet having struck her Dolan was certain. Judge, therefore, of his surprise when, without a groan or even a sound escaping her immovable lips, and sitting erect as ever in her saddle, she continued her reckless course through the woods. But something more than mere horror was now running through Dolan's mind, for in the moonlight he had seen the lady's face.

"Krapes, it's the lady of the Grange or her sperret!" and Dolan *pere* scurried home just as precipitately and about as gracefully as had his long-limbed daughter earlier in the night.

"Confoundedly awkward this prejudice in the Hibernian mind against harmless spirits," thought Sir Gregory next morning on hearing the ghostly story. "I myself would not mind being beset by half a dozen supernaturals, but here is this blockhead, Dolan, will never stop the earths for me in future, because a horse galloped by him in the dark, which is deucedly stupid." But so it was for years after, Dolan could scarcely be coaxed outside his doors when once darkness had fallen, and more especially did he shun the glories of a moonlight night, for he had seen and could affirm with his dying breath that it was moonlight nights that the spirits most affected.

The next morning—after Dolan had seen a ghost—dawned intensely cold. The hunting men at the Manor-house, looking at an early hour from their windows, beheld a spreading expanse of white, frost-covered fields, hard and stern enough to defy any ray of sunshine to soften them to-day, and they turned from the view with a disgusted whistle and the exclamation of "No hunting to-day!" Daddy Dolan, who has spent most of the night out-of-doors, sliding on various little sheets of ice that came in her way—which pastime she would not miss for anything—has called early at the Grange, and finding that neither Mrs. Cresenworth nor Topsie had spent the night there, she becomes alarmed, and stands thinking for some moments with her mouth open. The determination she then comes to may be described in the manner she puts it into action. After one or two wise nods and grunts she suddenly takes to her heels and runs as hard as her legs can carry her, till, out of breath and dishevelled, she arrives at the Manor-house, and rushes into the breakfast-room, where Sir Gregory and Rutland Borradale are enjoying their morning meal, reading the newspapers and cursing the weather alternately. Dad-

dy's appearance, like a bombshell in their midst, considerably startles both men, and Sir Gregory swears a little
as he asks impatiently :

"What the deuce does Daddy mean by this inopportune appearance ?"

The girl pants for breath, and then rushes into her
story with incoherent haste.

"I knew as something were going to happen," she
says, "for a many things had warned me this last night.
Pat and I were out in the woods, and we see the stran-
gest being riding on horseback, while the crazy huntsman followed, crying, 'Tally-ho ! tally-ho !' It were
neither man nor woman," says Daddy, dropping her
voice to an awe-struck whisper; "it were a spirit, and
Pat and me felt our flesh creep when it flew past. They
seemed to be riding towards the Grange, and maybe it
was a token, for the ladies is missing, both Mrs. Cresenworth and Miss Topsie, and the Lord knows where they
may be by this time, with wild horses and crazy huntsmen after 'em."

"What under heaven do you mean, girl, by all this
rigmarole ? Speak out and tell the truth !" thunders the
baronet.

"It's the truth I've told ye," Daddy answers, sullenly.
"The ladies are missing. They haven't been seen at the
Grange since yesterday, and were not there last night."

This news greatly alarms Sir Gregory, who, leaving
his breakfast unfinished, rushes out to have a horse saddled, leaving Rutland Borradale alone in the room with
the girl.

No sooner is Sir Gregory out of sight than Daddy rubs
her hands together with delight, and says to herself:

"I knew that would bring him out. He thinks a powerful deal of the ladies, but what would he say if he knew that Mrs. Cresenworth is running away with that bad man, De Montford?"

"Mrs. Cresenworth — De Montford!" says Rutland Borradale, in a horrified whisper, catching hold of Daddy. "Tell me what you mean, girl!"

"Just what I say," answers Daddy, wrathfully. "I can't tell you no more, as I don't know no better than you do. What with ghosts and missing folks, I'm that dazed I don't know nothing to-day, and that's a fact."

This is all Rutland Borradale can extract from Daddy, and so he, too, has his horse saddled and roughed, and, springing upon his back, he gallops him across country in the direction of De Montford's cottage.

CHAPTER XXV.

"DONE ONCE—DONE TWICE!"

At De Montford's cottage in the early morning a dainty head protrudes from a small lattice, and two handsome laughing eyes are coquetting with the duller ones of the ploughboy, who, supposed to be engaged at that hour in weeding the flower-beds on the terrace, is instead gazing with open eyes and mouth—into which his goddess has already shot three little missiles of dust and water—at the unaccustomedly lovely vision above him. Suddenly, however, to the surprise of the ploughboy, the head of his enchantress disappears very quickly, and looking around for the cause he sees the master of the cottage approaching in company with a stranger. Finding himself taken as much notice of as if he were a shrub or a stone, he stays to overhear some significant words spoken by the stranger in a dry, meaning voice.

"What has been done once, my dear fellow, can be done twice; we shall see if you have duped the lady, or if the lady has not duped you!"

Ere they have time to turn the key in the lock, however, they are precipitately joined by Sir Gregory Athelhurst, arriving from one quarter in a painful state of manly alarm for the safety and well-being of his admired one, and a moment later, from another direction, by Murray Cresenworth, who looks feverish and purple about the eyes, as he comes to seek for he knows not what har-

rowing confirmation of his wife's guilty shame. It is
early morning yet, and intensely cold, as the four men
stand on the threshold of De Montford's shooting cottage, which is, by common consent, to be the next moment ruthlessly invaded.

Sir Gregory precedes his friends, and by doing so receives a greeting ovation in the shape of a solid mass of
treacle on just the right part of his bald head! Next
comes De Montford, who divines that the penalty inflicted upon his forerunner is meant for him, but whose
emotions are too powerful to allow him to smile; and
lastly comes the determined-looking stranger and Murray Cresenworth. A little scream and a succession of
giggles are heard, and a suppressed cry of " Mon Dieu,
quelle horreure !" and when the men emerge from the
gloomy stairway into the sunlight of the room they see
a very charming sight, but one which nevertheless has
the effect of petrifying De Montford as he gazes, spellbound, at the apparition of the two ladies, who have
evidently shared the privacy of his apartment. Hitherto
throughout all that has been happening he has held his
head very proudly, as that of a conqueror, for he has had
reason to tell himself that the one being who to him was
worth all things else was waiting for him at his cottage,
and could not be torn from his arms. But now his
head almost sinks to his broad chest with aggravated
rage and disappointment; he clinches his hands and sets
his teeth, for he sees it all—how he has been duped;
and, moreover, he now tells himself he will have to strain
every power of his ordinarily active brain to extricate
himself within the next hour from the tangled meshes he
finds hampering him on all sides.

Flung carelessly over a chair he sees the costly mantle which he knew was owned by Elra Cresenworth (another such, to his knowledge, was not to be found in Paris or London), and in whose folds of silken gray and rose he had vainly imagined himself to be gathering in his arms the beauty and wealth and worth he would give half the world at that moment to own.

Standing beside the chair is a vision of dainty piquant loveliness attired in Tam o' Shanter cap and silken sash and kirtle, such as the hardy Highlanders wear, and which made no effort to conceal a finely moulded limb, while at a little distance, farther in the shade, was what appeared to be another figure clad in the same costume, rather a caricature upon her companion.

If De Montford had been startled by the revelation thus made to him, Murray Cresenworth's sensations upon learning the true state of affairs can better be imagined than described. As the truth flashed upon him he was able to comprehend the full meaning of the situation, and, with a low groan of agony and despair, he buried his face in his hands.

Here the marchioness breaks into a ripple of malicious laughter as she sees Maudie's evident mortification, and notes with delight the tragic faces of the men before her.

"Maudie, tell the gentlemen what a royal time we have been having," she says. "Is not the suspicion of wickedness often a much more palatable and enjoyable ingredient than mere wickedness itself? It is so much more spicy and so much more dangerous. Now, although Maudie and I have borne our misfortunes with the sanctity of angels all night (we caught a rat to while away the time), I have no doubt that if my husband—dear little Cupid, you know!—were to insinuate his fat limbs up that narrow stairway and see me here, he would certainly be unkind enough to knock one of you gentlemen down or to shoot another! As for me, he would get a divorce this very day if he only knew he could get it annulled to-morrow."

She says this with a quick look at Murray Cresenworth and then laughs softly to herself, for that gentleman has been writhing beneath her words, and is now calling for a glass of water with all the helplessness of a fainting woman previous to sinking on a chair, with an ugly ashen-gray look about his mouth and eyes, while he holds a hand to his side, as if he suffered pain in the direction where he had been shot.

For a moment no one speaks; but the painful silence is broken by Sir Gregory, who whispers something to De Montford, and then goes out to fetch the needed stimulant for Mr. Cresenworth, while De Montford looks in vain for the stranger, who, somehow, has evidently contrived to make his escape, as he is nowhere to be seen.

"Here he is," thinks De Montford, with a sigh of relief as a quick, heavy footstep is heard upon the stair, and the next moment the Marquis of Ripdale comes upon the scene, to find himself face to face with—*his* wife.

She calmly smiles as she surveys the intruder, who, with a furious look, grunts out a series of oaths between his teeth at the gentlemen around; and turning to his wife with as disgusted an air as Napoleon might have worn when at a ball he told his sister, who was dancing in full dress, "Pauline, go and put on your ch—s—e! the Marquis of Ripdale exhorts his spouse to cover her limbs a little more, and not to show so much of her shapely ankles. Whereat she robes herself in the lovely gray cloak which has been the innocent cause of all this trouble, and with a sprightly air of extreme indifference she takes leave of Maudie, and is about to gain the stairway, but in passing by the window she glances out and sees so strange a sight that her exclamation of surprise brings the other occupants of the room at once to her side to see, in their turn, two horsewomen, one rather in advance of the other, careering aimlessly over the hill that protects the back of the cottage from the northern blast. All crowd to see it save, indeed, De Montford, who has quietly slipped from the room, ordered his horse to be saddled, and springing across his hunter's back, has, in an incredibly short time, gained the side of one of the ladies who had been seen from the cottage window. But he is not unfollowed.

"My business here is not ended yet," mutters the stranger before mentioned, as coming up with De Montford he overhears that worthy, with all the telling eloquence of desperation, pleading for Elra's love, very much as if he were pleading for his own life. He hears him cruelly urge upon her her bitter position as the divorced and despised wife of Cresenworth; he urges likewise upon her that it had been with his name she had been compromised, through no fault of hers, of course, but that fact a malicious world will not credit; and he concludes by entreating her to silence all bitter tongues by becoming without delay his loved, respected and adored wife. Elra listens to his words in silence for some time, and then suddenly pointing to the other lady on horseback at a little distance from them, whose figure her eyes have never wandered from, she says, quietly:

"You shall have the only answer worthy your loyalty and devotion when we hold yonder lady's horse by the bridle." Her manner was so softly, dangerously sweet, with so much alluring languor in her eyes, that De Montford could scarce trust his senses, and dared not indulge in the swift hope that shot through his frame, making life turn to a rose-color once more for him.

"Oh, if it could but be!" he thinks, distractedly, and carrying her gloved hand reverently to his lips he kisses it with a fervor which he gladly thinks must have impressed Elra, as she turns quickly from him. "My sovereign queen, command me unto death," he whispers, ere breaking into a gallop they follow up the unknown lady on horseback.

Scarce five minutes later the stranger, who had been a silent witness of the above scene, was startled by the sudden appearance and wild air of a younger horseman on the ground, who asks him, in breathless tones, "Elra— De Montford—where are they?"

"Gone to the railway station yonder, I presume," retorts the stranger, coolly pointing towards the retreating figures of the two equestrians.

"Powers of heaven, if that be true, he'll die first!" and driving the spurs savagely into his horse's flank, he strikes across the fields rather wildly after them.

"Her spirit is perhaps crushed, poor little soul, and she may even do this in her desperation. Oh, for a hand to help her! Shall I be there in time! Can I possibly?"

This is said in horror, as he sees the railway cars circling along like a serpent in the valley, within ten minutes' course from the halting-place, and he looks over the fine wide fields of stubble and turnip ridge, besides the yawning ditches that he must put behind him ere he can arrive in time to save his loved one from her imminent danger. He puts spurs to his horse, and with an encouraging word cheers on the noble brute to show his mettle now or never. On they go, at a mad gallop over fields and hedges, till they reach the last obstacle which separates them from the road beyond. Here, alas! they are less fortunate, and Borradale perceives when too late the mass of ice which, slippery as a sheet of polished glass, is waiting to receive them. He clears the fence with a tremendous leap, but as his horse's hoofs strike on the glittering ice he stumbles, and falling heavily, with a dull crash, rolls helplessly, like a log, backward into the dark yawning ditch behind. In his frantic struggles Borradale knows that it has fared badly with his gallant horse, but he has not time to help him out in his distress.

"Poor noble brute! you have saved my angel! no breath can touch her still," he cries. But he was not a moment too soon. The train had drawn up to the platform, and De Montford, after a word of coldly received entreaty, becomes desperate. Fearless of consequence he has now placed his arm on her waist, and is drawing her forcibly along. Appalled by this unlooked for danger, Elra cannot force back the little shriek that is startled from her lips, and which begs very eloquently for manly assistance in her hour of need. In another moment De Montford finds his arm struck more roughly and forcibly than politely from its position about Elra Brookley's waist, and turning he encounters the flaming eyes of what he considers a madman. Then, while they are amiably looking at one another, the train passes on. It is well that the two men have not much time for lengthy conversation for they are both stammering with rage, when Dr. Warder, with De Montford's strange companion of the morning beside him, drives up alongside them, and following timidly, as it were, comes a horse down the road, at sight of which Elra wrings her hands. "It is Topsie! quick, quick! catch her horse!"

The animal that had evaded all pursuit by Elra during the morning appeared now in rather an exhausted condition, and, having once come within range, was cautiously circumvented by the gentlemen's united efforts. Dr. Warder seizing the bridle, and with an exclamation of horror, and "I have come too late!" leads the horse close to Elra.

"Dearest Topsie, speak!" cries that lady, aghast at the deathly pallor of the girl's face, the starkness of her limbs, while from those around her burst exclamations of 'Who is she?' 'Dead!' 'Can it be?' 'Topsie!' 'As I live, Lady Lenore Allesmere!'

"Quick, Warder, for the love of Heaven save her! save her!"

"Is this, indeed, Topsie, and have I come too late?" says a new arrival on the scene, and turning they see that the group has been joined by Roanwood Offington, with rather a distracted look in his eyes.

"I fear," says Dr. Warder, solemnly, "we have all come too late. Lady Lenore *de Montford* is, if I mistake not, far beyond our assistance."

"De Montford!" "De Montford!" "De Montford!" is repeated around in all the tones of the ascending and descending scale.

While this conversation has been taking place, the

doctor has been busily engaged in loosening the straps that bind Lady Lenore to the saddle, and, while Elra is placing some cordial to her lips in a vain hope, the physician turns to the assembled group and says, warmly:

"Yes, gentlemen, this cruelly calumniated lady has been all these years the wife of that *brave* man yonder!" and he scornfully indicates De Montford, "as may be seen by her marriage certificate; and now help me with those cords on the far side!"

So saying, he hands to Elra a paper, the reading of which strikes a great wonder into her soul. Turning to her erstwhile suitor, she says, in icy tones:

"What greeting has De Montford for his lost bride?"

De Montford looks at her as coldly contemptuous as a man who appreciates her mental powers as very small.

"Yarns — if you will excuse me"— he retorts, "are believed by mere women, but a man must see the signature of the officiating clergyman before he begins to believe anything so impossible as this stupid concoction;" and to himself he thinks, "So that is the trick that was practised on me that night. I had feared something of the kind, but it will avail her nothing. Part of the certificate is lost anyhow." But suddenly he remembers a little piece of torn paper which he had seen in Mrs. Cresenworth's possession, dated and signed by the Rev. George Grey, and which might very well answer for the torn corner of the certificate before him; and even though the wife with whom he has so suddenly and unexpectedly been confronted has the every appearance of a corpse, De Montford loses a little of his assurance. Suddenly a happy idea seems to strike him. He is will-

ing to accept Lenore as his wife, since public opinion is
so strong on that point, and he thinks of a passage in the
last will of the late Marquis of Ripdale, his wife's father,
in which, to his beloved daughter Lenore was left the
sum of £30,000. " By Jove!" he thinks to himself, " it
cannot be possible that you have had a wife's capital at
your command all this time and did not make use of it."

Roanwood Offington had listened in silence to the doctor's explanations, for he can scarcely realize the full
extent of the misery it has brought him. That Topsie's
real name is Lady Lenore, *and above all that she is another
man's wife,* seems to him impossible of belief. In the
mean time the doctor has disappeared, but some one has
caught the words " Frozen to death while still under the
influence of the morphine," dropped from his lips, as,
gathering the stark form of Lady Lenore in his arms, he
carried her towards the station-master's little cottage,
and once in its cosy rooms, dismisses all useless attend-
ants and spectators, while using all the means in his
power he applies restoratives.

Outside the cottage the conversation in the group
waxes loud and stormy.

" My wife, indeed! So that was the trick practised
on me by clever Lenore Allesmere, was it?"

" Don't dare to breathe her name, you in—or I'll
knock you down!" and the stranger steps towards him
menacingly.

" Knock me down for speaking about my wife? I'd
like you to remember that I have the right to demand of
you why you mention the lady. As for me, with regard
to her, I speak and act as I choose, without consulting
you."

" Will you ?" says his strange friend of the previous night, as he closed his mouth with an ominous snap.

" I will, if it so please you, my lord," retorts De Montford, caustically. " To begin with, my wife's £30,000 will go immediately to capitalize the little scheme you are interested in."

. "Naturally," laughs the other, " when you get it between your fingers."

"You will see how quickly the law of England will enable me to touch my bride's dowry. A dead wife is ready money, you know," he says, rubbing his hands softly together.

" Before you avail yourself of the wealth at your disposal, you ought to learn a few facts which will enlighten you as to the way in which you stand with regard to your wife."

Here the stranger dashes off into a recital which holds his listeners spellbound.

CHAPTER XXVI.

"BRAVE LITTLE HEART."

I was a clerk in a London bank, and had returned to witness the ceremonies and festivities which were to follow the nuptials of our own Lady Artrale Allesmere and Redstone, Earl de Brun. The marriage had not been announced publicly, as the family were in mourning, but that would not prevent the people on the estate from celebrating it in jovial fashion. So I had got off from duty on a four days' holiday, and intended to share in the fun, while I stayed with my father, who used to be Jack, the valued huntsman of the old Marquis of Ripdale, but was now superseded. What happened to me then on the night before the wedding was this:

Standing in the shrubbery, under the pale light of a young crescent moon, which was slowly rising in the heavens, I overheard De Montford's conversation with Lady Lenore :

" Where is Artrale ?"

" Not to be seen to-night."

" That is not true. I must see her, if I have to brave it all and walk into her father's library to demand her. I start for Brussels early in the morning, and as I love her tenderly, and have no intention of trusting to her changeable disposition, I mean to have the ceremony of our promised marriage performed this very night, even if I have to spill my heart's blood for it."

" Then," says Lenore, after a pause, during which she has sought to gain time, " your last letter should have arrived earlier, for Artrale, having had a previous engagement at the 'Firs' for the masquerade ball to-night, went there this afternoon in time for an early dinner."

"Not doubting your word, of course," retorted De Montford coldly, fearing a ruse, " but being quite determined to see and speak with Lady Artrale this night, if even in the presence of her assembled family, I shall beg your excuses for passing on towards the castle, or may I hope to have your escort?"

His determination evidently strikes rather a chill to Lady Lenore's heart, for it is in a slightly unsteady voice that she replies : "As you do not credit my words, perhaps you will believe this," handing him a note in Lady Artrale's handwriting. This confirms what has already been told him, and at the end of it are the words,

" I wish so much to see you, if only for a short while, and nothing will please me better than to have you come to the ball to-night. Pray be there, just to please your little Artrale, whom you will recognize by repeating twice the word Adelaide to the lady wearing the colors which are enclosed in my letter. But on speaking to me you must promise to call me by the name of 'Adelaide.'
Yours, in haste,   ARTRALE."

De Montford pauses as he finishes reading the note, and with a dark look at Lenore says, brusquely, " I suppose you are ready to corroborate what is said in this letter ?"

"Yes," says Lenore bravely, thinking of the danger which threatens the life's happiness of her sister.

" Then come with me, seek out your sister at the ball,

you will know her dress better than I, and bring her to me. If she be not there I shall return without delay to her father's house and demand fulfilment of her promise. Will you come now ?"

Lenore grew paler under the moonlight, which was now bright, and hesitated, as if these may have been her thoughts: How can she save Artrale ? What shall she say to this man who is so sternly bent upon the destruction of all her sister's present joy and happiness ? What would her fiancé say to find that his future bride had promised to wed another, had even now arranged to meet him upon the very eve of her wedding day ? The intimacy so lightly begun, the intrigue so thoughtlessly entered into by her careless sister, where had it brought her ? And then the proofs, her letters, were still in De Montford's hands ! The next moment she had made a desperate resolve.

Seeing her falter, De Montford coldly lifts his hat and advances towards the house. " I will come," she says ; and he turns, upon hearing her voice.

" So you are ready to answer for the truth of this letter ? Then come, we lose time," and he hands her into his waiting carriage which is driven rapidly away.

As they drove off I stepped from out of the shadow ; an overpowering curiosity, mingled with a desire to be on hand if my respected Lady Lenore should require my help, impelled me to follow them. I never had much hard cash in those days, but what little I had went to hire a horse and light wagon, and in a short time I too was on the road leading to the Firs. Arriving there, after some little delay, I had no difficulty in tracing De Montford, whom I saw in earnest conversation with a beautifully robed lady; but, in the meantime, the following events, as I learned afterwards, had been happening:

Lady Lenore, on arriving at the Firs, had at once hastened to the dressing-rooms, where, by the means of some judicious bribery, she had been enabled to robe herself in the disguise of a monk's cloak and hood; and, with the latter well drawn over her face, to escape recognition, she joins De Montford in the shrubbery; and, leading him to one of the ball-room windows, which is left invitingly open, to give air to the crowded rooms, tells him to stand in the shadow of the palms and ferns which decorate this egress to the garden, and she will send Artrale to him. She plunges in among the crowd of dominoes. Having gained the greatest crush of the dancing-room, she exclaims, in a loud, well-heard whisper, "Adelaide! Adelaide!" but nothing comes of her little ruse, and going still farther in the crowd she repeats it. This time it was crowned with the following success: A lady, clad in the most delicate shade of lavender, trimmed with a richer, deeper purple shade, tinged here and there with red, impersonating "clouds at sunset," turns quickly towards what she imagines to be the form of the man who had challenged Adelaide.

"What will you with Adelaide?" she murmurs as softly as music from the harp-strings.

"That Adelaide will follow me," says the unknown, still in a whisper, and presenting her his arm he leads the way through the crowded rooms to the open windows by which De Montford stands expectant.

During their progress through the crush the monk has, unseen by his companion, managed to fasten to her shoulder a knot of ribbons similar in color to those which had been enclosed to De Montford in Artrale's fictitious letter, and, with a sign in the direction of De Montford, the monk bends towards her and whispers :

"A devoted slave of yours, he, and longs to lay his heart at your feet," and so saying, disappears.

"This rather amuses me. I must carry on the farce," thinks Adelaide. "But my voice may not answer unless, indeed, I have so hoarse a throat as to have it unrecognizable for that of any particular person. Yes, I shall have the influenza, and that very severely." In the conversation that follows she delights her adorer every short while with a mournful frog-like croak, which, notwithstanding its beauty, elicits great sympathy on his part.

De Montford, standing outside the windows, had begun to doubt whether he was not on a fool's errand, and had repeated in his thoughts many unspellable, naughty words, when, suddenly catching sight of the knot of colors similar to those he wears, he springs forward with the challenge, "Adelaide! Adelaide!" and this being, to his delight and surprise, answered as he had hoped for, he had straightway poured a volume of impassioned words into his companion's ear. The lady in question is rather dazed at first by the fervor and (to her) incoherency of his earnest pleading but entering into the spirit of what she considers "an intrigue entirely worthy of a masquerade," she appoints a spot in the grounds to meet the "unknown," as she terms her ardent admirer.

The rendezvous is to be at midnight, and on her way back to the cloak room for a wrap she meets a friend to whom she divulges the little plot.

" If you want to be amused, my dear," she says to that young lady, "come with me."

" Where do you propose to go ?" asks her friend, Lady Muriel, cautiously.

" To the vicarage, dear."

" This cold night, and why ?"

" To be married, of course," laughs Adelaide. " You may scarcely believe it, but I have an admirer whom I never discovered before."

" And his name ? I fear you are very wild, Adelaide," says her friend, laughing also.

" That I shall find out in goodtime. Bet you half a cookie he never finds out my name, though. Wild, you say ? What can I do, dear, if the poor, crazy fellow is so deeply enamoured ? The unhappy man is awfully in earnest, and would think nothing of shooting himself, and me in the bargain, if I did not consent on the instant. He wants to be married just here to-night. Nothing else will please him, and to fall in with his humor I intend to go through with the ceremony, so here goes. Come along and see me married, dear," she says, with a dry humor and gleam of mischief in her eyes that fairly startles her companion.

" But your husband !" she gasps, although at the same time she is intensely amused at this wild project.

" Dear Cupid is at this moment vastly enjoying himself in his way, and 1 can't see why I mayn't have a little fun on my own account. He is now discussing ortolans, surrounded by some of the prettiest and most rapid of our beauties, and I am sure not even the announcement that his wife has eloped with a dark unknown would for one moment trouble his digestion, or

interrupt his little amours with the fair ladies who con-
stitute his court. No! I mean to see this through, as I
believe the whole thing will prove vastly entertaining,
and my being already married adds a piquant flavor to
the romance."

"Are you not afraid of being recognized?" suggests
her friend, who is evidently more cautious than herself.

"Do you think it possible to recognize me for any particular person?" she cries, removing her domino and
displaying a head and cheeks swathed to the very eyes
in cotton wool. "It is fearful to be growing old, but I
must only bear it, and fight my hardest against cold,
cough, influenza, sore throat, bronchitis, and rapid con-
sumption, all of which I am at present suffering from.
However, before the night is out I intend getting some
of *Uriah Levi's* sarsaparilla, and I shall be instantly
cured of everything."

The young lady evidently seems impressed with her
friend's capabilities as an actress, for she makes no further remonstrance. They both depart together to find
the gentleman of the colors at the appointed place of
meeting.

He is there in waiting, and hurries them off to the
vicarage close by, where a hasty ceremony is performed
without interruption, save for an occasional little giggle
from the heavily veiled bride.

At the conclusion of the service the wheels of a carriage are heard on the road outside, and De Montford,
looking at his watch, exclaims:

"It is even later than I thought; I must leave you
now, my darling, but shall come to claim my own within
two days." Then he would have lifted the veil which

shrouded the face of his new-made bride, but she drew back with a little scream and gesture of refusal, and evidently wished to avoid a caress.

"Always wilful, he whispers, but the next time we meet you will give me what you deny me now."

"Not wilful, dearest," replies in hoarse tones the happy bride, "but it is my neuralgia, which is so painful that to have my head touched is torture indeed, dearest; but all that will be for next time, as you say." However, he cannot part without some kind of caress, and pressing his lips tenderly to her uncovered brow, he whispers, with infinite compassion, "You are in pain, dearest! how I wish I could stay to alleviate your sufferings." So saying he jumps into his carriage and cries to the coachman, "To the nearest station — like lightning!" and is gone after having signed his name to the marriage papers. In the meantime the name of Lenore Allesmere had been written down by that lady herself as a substitution for that of the bride, while Adelaide had glided from the room. This substitution of signatures being unnoticed by the clergyman in the confusion of the bridegroom's departure, the reverend gentleman proceeds to exhort the bride to be a dutiful and loving wife, and promises to forward the certificate of her marriage within a few days.

Her reply rather staggers him. "Do not trouble, the certificate will be valueless to me."

"Ah!" he says in great surprise. "Evidently you are very young and inexperienced or you would know the worth of a marriage certificate !"

"You can keep it then until I want it, since it may prove more valuable than I had thought !" and, with many thanks to the good minister, the rather hilarious bride and her chaperoning friend take their departure back to the ball-room, to indulge in *Levi's* sarsaparilla to cure her cough, cold, etc.

———

Lady Lenore, whom I had not once lost sight of during all this time, seeing that her sister's future happiness was at last quite safe, suffered me to escort her on her homeward way. The Hall gates at Ravenstone being now closed, however, I invited her to take shelter in my mother's cottage, which she accepted, and was kind enough to return to for several nights following upon the ball at the Firs.

"And behind all this mummery, who was the bride?" bursts in De Montford savagely.

"Adelaide, Marchioness of Ripdale," says the silvery tones of that young and beautiful and thoroughly imprudent peeress. "You were cheated in a bride, De Montford. Ha! ha!" But in the mean time the young stranger points to where Lenore has disappeared in the doorway of the station-master's cottage, and says, in a voice that trembles with emotion:

"She saved her sister with no thought of self in her young heart, and to-day you have seen her dead in her youth and loveliness—at rest at last, brave little heart!"

As the young man finishes his recital Roanwood Offington omes forward, however, and astonishes him, for he wrings his hand warmly, almost to the point of dislocation of the bones.

"To you I owe my most earnest thanks; you have given me a very beautiful, peerless bride. In that cottage yonder Lenore still breathes, and in my arms but a

moment ago she justified my thanking you for your devotion. Friends till death, old fellow, and may I have
the chance of doing as much for you as you have for me."

During this little announcement Rutland Borradale
has been, to Murray Cresenworth's evident dissatisfac-
tion, hovering around his goddess, and is very unhappy
that he cannot soothe the apparent misery depicted on
her ordinarily bright riante face : in his soul it must
be said he curses the erstwhile husband who did not
know how to appreciate the adorable being he had won
for his wife. While Cresenworth, now more unwilling
than ever to resign the beautiful prize which is slipping
from his grasp—especially when he sees that the jewel
of untold price, which he has spurned, is likely to become the property of another, strikes a bold stroke on
his last stake and—loses.

While for a moment Borradale is out of ear-shot, he
catches sight of Elra standing a little apart from the
others, with her shapely head resting against the glossy
shoulder of her horse, and in her eyes he sees there is a
wistful look, as of a dumb animal in pain. "Can she
then know ? Has she heard all ?" thinks Murray, and
bending swiftly towards her, he but dares to whisper
the one word "Elra !" in a tone so abject that she could
not help but pity him. "Elra !" he repeats, seeing she
is silent, "have you no word for me ?"

"You forget Miss Brookley," she says, in such meas-
ured, cold tones that his hopes go down with a rush.

"Never that for me," he says, passionately. "Elra,
give me one word of forgiveness, of command, of permission to protect your name, to reinstate it where is
properly its place, among those of noble women—as I

unfortunately alone can do it—and it shall be done with my dying breath."

But she turns away with scorn on her parted lips. "All England," she says, " has been this morning advised of my—my crime."

On catching her words a cold moisture breaks over Cresenworth's forehead and the thought strikes him that the events of yesterday, followed by a harrowing, sleepless night, and clinched by what had very nearly proved the tragedy of the morning, have been too much for him, and, with his hand to his side, he staggers for support against her horse.

" Come away, darling," tenderly whispers Borradale to her at this moment, but Cresenworth, with all the dogged determination of a man who has never been beaten before in his life, comes quickly to her side.

" Elra, stay and hear me !" but here he gasps, for a terrible pain has shot through his heart. "I feel I am going ; Elra it is in death's agony that I entreat you to be mine once more, my honored wife !" One look he cast at her pale, cold brow, one piteous look, as might a dog who was suffering death at the hand of its loved master, and ere her glorious eyes could soften, ere a word of gentle womanly love could tremble on her lips, time has slipped into eternity, and fear, love, hate mocked at her—for Murray Cresenworth, with a long, long shiver of agony, a stagger and a groan, stretched himself dead at her feet !

"Courage !" says Rutland Borradale, tenderly supporting Elra Cresenworth's form ere she totters against her horse. " My wife! my darling! now, forever ;" but weakened though she be, she recoils in horror from his touch.

"Never!" she cries, pointing to her husband's form stretched stark at her feet. "It is by your hand he lies there—"

"Murdered, she would say," and turning quickly Borradale beholds the flashing triumphant eyes of Adelaide, Marchioness of Ripdale.

"You will never own her," she pursues, maliciously. It was the shot sent home so straight by you that has killed him, and she will not marry his mur—

"Adelaide!" he cries, savagely eying the beautiful woman he has once loved; but in a moment he is calm again and master of the situation.

"That will not prevent me from giving her my heart's adoration and love to my dying day."

"Oh, my God!" comes in a moan from Elra's lips, while Adelaide looks on with a rather disdainful shrug of her shoulders.

_____

"Are you Mrs. Cresenworth, madam?"

"Yes," says that lady, rather startled, as she turns to the speaker, who proves to be a youth of some eighteen summers, who had but a moment ago arrived on the scene.

"Then, ma'am, I've been charged to deliver you this note from Clarkson, Ryfe & Clarkson, and to explain to you, in case you don't fully catch its meaning, that there was no divorce granted yesterday in your case. There was, it is true, one given between a certain Mr. Greselwirth and his wife, one of whom is a client of your lawyers, and Mr. Ryfe, who had prosecuted the case, being unable to get back from court to the office, wired word to the effect:

" 'Greselwirth's divorce granted, 2.59 ; advise him and wife immediately—RYFE.'

" The name, transmitted in a hurry, read wrong, and thus the mistake which you know of occurred."

" You have said enough," Elra answers faintly, " you have come too late; my husband is beyond learning of what has been done."

For the physician, having been called from the side of Lady Lenore, has officially pronounced Murray Cresenworth to be dead.   The old shot-wound he had received on his wedding morning had come against him at last, causing a very sudden failure of the heart.

" Here comes your train, De Montford," says the much injured Marquis of Ripdale, touching that worthy briskly on the shoulder, " and if in six hours "—taking out his watch and looking determined—" you are not off English territory you will be arrested for—what—you yourself best know.   Go or stay, as best suits yourself and that praiseworthy banking scheme of yours."

" Bluster, my lord, mere bluster !" says De Montford with a proud curl of his lip, " but you will find I am no coward, and here I stay as long as it suits me to remain where I am, indifferent to bullying from peer or pauper."

" Then you are prepared to answer a charge of forgery substantiated by this paper, which you will easily recognize, as it was stolen by you from the vest-pocket of the man whom you shot almost to death for that express end two years ago—Murray Cresenworth—and whose death now lies, without a doubt, at your door."

The marquis holds in his hand the while a piece of blood-stained paper, torn at one edge—the very one which Daddy Dolan had carried from her fortress of refuge under the Athelhurst china cabinet, and which she had afterwards sold at what she considered a "skinning bargain" to a stranger who had been kind to her, but whom she had considered afflicted with lunacy.

De Montford, when he sees the paper, grows cold and very white, but he is no coward, and though he stands in imminent danger he feels he has ground for some hope; he knows that a peer of the realm will sacrifice an amount of rancor rather than have his wife's folly and imprudence aired in court—which must eventually be the case in this matter of his forgery—therefore he feels reassured.

With a muttered imprecation, and the words "the banking scheme must go to the dogs!" seeing he has met his master, De Montford does what many a bigger villain has done before him, in similar circumstances, *i.e.*, slips into the train and gets quietly out of the way.

CHAPTER XXVII.

MOONLIGHT ON THE MOUNTAINS.

It's no use denying it, Fortune is a fickle jade!

During the early days of his passion for Mrs. Eldmere Sir Gregory had never doubted of the ultimate success of his suit, and he had begun even to hope he was making advances in the lady's favor, when, through the untimely advent of Mr. Cresenworth, he found himself "completely knocked out," as he described it; and as a solace for his blighted affection the worthy baronet betook himself to hard riding and hard drinking, hoping to find consolation in the deep and flowing bowl!

One evening when riding home with his friend the Earl of Darcliffe (who is himself a black sheep and a boon companion of the baronet), after a good day's racing and many pints of sparkling champagne, they reach the Manor-house at a late hour, and Sir Gregory insists upon his friend accepting his hospitality for that night at least.

"Come in, old fellow," he says with a boisterous laugh; "don't refuse a good thing! I can give you such a bowl of punch as you never tasted before;" and as the earl, who is also rather the worse for what he has imbibed, willingly assents, the two men turn in at the gates and gallop up the avenue. Just before reaching their front door Sir Gregory's horse shies violently at some object on the road, and lands his master in the middle of a flower-bed at one side of the carriage sweep. This completely sobers that gentleman, who picks himself up with many groans and bad words, and then goes to see what the object may be that can have so startled his tired horse—who, to his knowledge, has never done such a thing before, and who is warranted to stand firm at a cannon, or a threshing-machine, or any other foe to equine nerves.

What he finds is a child's wheelbarrow, full of white sand, into which is stuck a goodly array of paper flags, and which has evidently been used by the children in some military demonstration. This formidable obstruction is planted full in the middle of the carriage drive. Sir Gregory silently curses Mrs. Dolan and her family as he rubs his shins, and explains to his friend that he is not hurt, only bruised.

" Confound those brats!" he mutters as they enter the house, and then he takes his friend off to his own particular den, where we will leave them to " make a night of it."

As the result of the latter festivity, Sir Gregory wakes next day in a particularly bad frame of mind ; and, as he slowly dresses, he thinks of the wheelbarrow of the previous night, and resolves to go down and give Mrs. Dolan a gentle reminder, both as to the breakfast for himself and friend, and the desirability of keeping the little Dolans out of his and his horse's way. He has worked himself up to a proper state of mind in which to deliver the lecture; but, on his appearing at the head of the stairway leading to the hall, his anger is changed into speechless indignation. Mrs. Dolan, who is usually the most untidy and dirty of mortals, with a holy horror of water and brushes, has apparently changed in this respect, for the hall is now at least two inches deep in water, while the young Dolans, with shrieks of delight, are engaged in swimming boats, and upsetting pails, and other diversions. At the sight of their master they turn and fly, and he picks his way across the wet hall to reach the shelter of the dining-room. Here, too, all is in confusion. The carpet is rolled up, the furniture is tied and bandaged, and even the mirror and pictures are swathed in yellow gauze.

"What the devil does all this mean?" roars Sir Gregory, in a fury, as he rings the bell violently and swears in audible tones. "Where is that woman?"

"Do you allude to me, sir?" says Mrs. Dolan, appearing in the doorway, clad in a costume that would have delighted the baronet at any other time, but which now exasperates him all the more.

"What do you mean by turning my house topsy-turvy like this?" he cries. "Are you mad? You look it, I'm sure!"

Mrs. Dolan, who is attired in a short gown of doubtful color, well drawn up to escape the wet, thus showing a generous display of ankles, a calico jacket, and with her head tied up in a duster, and a large feather-broom in her hand, looks more like an Indian squaw than a respectable house servant. But there is the fire of determination in her eye, and a toss of her head shows her master that she means mischief. ~

"Sure it's yourself that's mad," she says in reply, "to take objections to the cleaning. It's little enough the house ever sees, and I thought it would be all the better for a touch of soap and water. Sure it's me that should

complain at the extra work and not yourself. What
with your friends to stay, and your late suppers and
early breakfasts, I declare I'm worn to a thread already."

"That will do, woman!" roars Sir Gregory. "You
may pack up bag and baggage and leave my house at
the end of the month—do you hear? Dolan can stay if
he has a mind to, but I will not stand another hour of
this—so now you know. Take down all this rubbish,
cart away all your pails and brushes, and have breakfast ready for us in half an hour."

Mrs. Dolan sees that her master is in earnest, and retires precipitately to do his bidding and revenge herself by falling upon her husband and giving him the
greatest "talking to" he has had for many a day; but
the breakfast-table is ready at the hour Sir Gregory
mentions, and when the Earl of Darcliffe makes his appearance all signs of house-cleaning have disappeared
for good.

After the meal the earl takes his leave, and Sir Gregory, who has been silent and taciturn all the morning,
brooding over his wrongs, accompanies him to the station, and then turns his horses' heads towards the
Nest. Calling in there he asks for Miss de la Roche,
and is ushered into that young lady's presence.

"How delighted I am to see you, Sir Gregory," cries
Maudie, with eyes of great astonishment at the early
visit; for since Sir Gregory's infatuation for Mrs. Eldmere Miss Maudie had been entirely neglected by the
baronet. "Mamma is not up yet, she has been suffering
much lately, but I will let her know that you are here."

"Pray don't do that, my dear young lady," says Sir

Gregory earnestly. I came to speak to you, and am glad to find you alone, and forthwith the baronet goes on to relate that his domestic happiness is so imperilled by the aggravations of his house-keeper, Mrs. Dolan, that he has come to ask Maudie to be his protectress—and his wife.

The unexpected news is almost too much for poor Maudie, who sighs and blushes with delightful embarrassment as she says, with a little smirk, "Dear Gregory! how did you find out that I loved you all along?" And to this the baronet wisely answers nothing, though he sighs as he thinks of Mrs. Eldmere and her beauty, even as he presses his new fiancée's fat little hand to his lips in a lover's first caress. "It had to be," he murmurs to himself, "I couldn't stand that woman any longer." And thus it was that Maudie wooed and won Sir Gregory at last, and despite even her envious sisters Odile and Pauline—who had flown to England on hearing the happy news, to do all the mischief they could—became the happy bride of a comfortable English baronet, who could actually hear, see, and speak like most of us.

It is a lovely summer night; a bright moon sheds its lustre upon the landscape, sometimes disappearing behind a fleecy cloud or snow-clad peak, at others shining in dazzling splendor upon the wooded valley beneath, and lighting up the tiny villages that lie nestling in the heart of the Bernese Oberland, now quiet and hushed in sleep. A gay party is assembled on the mountain's brow, and bright talk and merry laughter fills the air, for they are waiting with some impatience for the first sounds of the distant bugle blast, which was to acquaint them with the famous echo of this region; an attraction of this lovely spot which the travellers had come to hear, at this hour of the night, thus adding a strange charm to the beauty of the scene.

Somewhat apart from the rest stand two figures, who, though alone and in silence, appear to be well content to have their solitude thus undisturbed. They, too, are listening for the first faint sounds of the distant horn.

Presently the lady moves away from her companion, and, going to the edge of the precipice, peers down into the darkness beneath. Her light figure stands poised there but for a moment, for the gentleman advances, and, throwing a protecting arm around her waist, leads her back to higher ground.

"My darling, what a risk to run!" he says, tenderly, though reproachfully, gazing at the beautiful face. "How dare you? It is well that I am at hand to protect you, and I suppose you will now admit my right to shield my own from danger."

"Yes, I suppose I must own you for my lord and master," she answers, with a happy little laugh; "but it is, I assure you, a most *unwilling* slavery. However, for all that, though these chains are constraining," touching the firm arms still held around her, "I do not care yet to break them."

"I would not attempt it if I were you," he says, dryly. Then, "My own Elra!" he murmurs passionately, and catching her to his heart, he kisses the lovely lips so near his own, and reads all the love and tenderness shining in her eyes as she answers, softly:

"God grant us happiness, my dearest one!"

And then the first faint sounds of the bugle call steal softly through the valley, ever growing louder, till it dies in a gentle murmur, as the echo repeats the sound of its tones.

THE END.

WORTHINGTON COMPANY'S

CATALOGUE

of Standard Books that every one ought to have; they are all handsome and attractive, and will be a valuable addition to any one's library.

NEW EDITION, NEW PLATES.

ALICE ADVENTURES IN WONDER-LAND.—12mo. $1.25.

Above are the most charming fairy tales of the 19th Century. Exquisitely amusing, deliciously illustrated. Nursery classics translated into most of the languages of Europe.

AYTOUN.—Lays of the Scottish Cavaliers. By Wm. E. Aytoun, late Prof. of Literature and Belles-Lettres in Univ. of Edinburgh, and Editor of *Blackwood's Magazine.* 16mo, extra cloth, $1.00.

BAILEY, PHILIP JAMES.—*Festus :* A Poem. (New Aldine Edition.) 16mo, vellum cloth, $1.00 ; do., do., three-quarter calf, extra, $2.50 ; do., do., flexible, or tree-calf, $3.50.

This great dramatic poem exhibits a soul gifted, tried, buffeted, beguiled, stricken, purified, redeemed, pardoned, and triumphant. It is interspersed with delightful songs. Has been praised by Bulwer, Thackeray and Tennyson as a remarkable poem of great beauty. The present edition is very handsome, the type is large and elegant, the paper is excellent, and the steel engravings are of exceeding grace.

BON GAULTIER'S BOOK OF BALLADS.— By W. E. Aytoun and Theodore Martin. A new edition, including "Firmilian." Cloth, $1.00.

In all his poems Prof. Aytoun has put forth a sustained power and beauty of expression which have placed him in the foremost rank of the poets of his time. "His Lays" have all the historic truth and force of Macaulay, expressing noble thought by a delineation of generous and lofty natures stated with fluency, vigour and movement. His ballad themes are selected from striking incidents and from stirring scenes of Scottish history, and he has thrown over them the light of an imagination at once picturesque and powerful.

BURTON (Dr. J. Hill).—The Book Hunter, with Memoir and Index. NEW EDITION, with Portrait and Engraving of Interior of Library. Crown 8vo, Roxburgh style, $3.00.

Burton's "Book Hunter" is indispensable to every owner of a library; it will be found of incalculable aid in classifying, studying, collecting and the preservation of books. It abounds in reminiscences of noted Bibliophiles and Book Hunters. We offer in this edition a volume that for general excellence of typography and binding will delight the heart of every book hunter.

CAMPBELL (Sir George, M.P.).—White and Black. The Outcome of a Visit to the United States. By Sir George Campbell, M.P. Being a Bird's-eye View of the Management of the Colored Races, with the Contents of my Journal. Crown 8vo, cloth extra, $1.75.

We have in this work the views of a prominent Englishman on the relative positions occupied by the Black and White Races in the United States. Several suggestions and opinions are given toward solving the Race Problem that will be read with lively interest by all who desire the caste question amicably settled.

CARROLL (Lewis).—Through the Looking Glass, and What Alice Found There. With fifty illustrations by John Tenniel. 1 vol. 12mo. $1.25.

CHILD'S OWN BOOK OF FAIRY TALES. —Containing Aladdin or the Wonderful Lamp, Beauty and the Beast, Children in the Wood, Goody Two-Shoes, Gulliver, Jack the Giant Killer, Jack and the Beanstalk, Puss in Boots, Robin Hood, Tom Thumb, White Cat, Yellow Dwarf, and others. With upwards of one hundred illustrations, after designs by eminent American artists. Square 16mo, cloth. $1.50.

The best collection of the famous old-fashioned Fairy Tales contained in any one volume, many of which can only be found in this edition.

CHILD'S TREASURY OF FAIRY TALES. For Little Folks. Containing The Six Swans, Little Hunch - Back, Hop - O - My Thumb, Blanch and Rosalind, Dummling and the Toad,

Fortunio, The Fox's Brush, The Three Wishes, Cinderella, Whittington and his Cat, and many others. Printed with extra large type. Illustrated with 60 engravings by the American artists, Twaites and others. Cloth, black and gold, square 16mo, $1.50.

This edition of the more popular and best known Fairy Tales is especially commended for the profusion and beauty of its illustrations.

CHILDREN'S BIBLE PICTURE AND STORY BOOK.—With sixty full-page illustrations. Square 16mo, beautifully printed and bound in cloth extra, $1.50.

A real beautiful book—one that ought to be placed into the hands of all, even the youngest children. It is a complete history of the principal events or stories in the Old and New Testaments, written in remarkably clear, simple, unaffected language, extremely well illustrated. It brings out into bold relief the singular charm of the book of books, and leads on to the study of the scriptures.

CRAIG'S DICTIONARY.—A Pronouncing Dictionary of the English Language. Based upon the Works of Webster, Worcester, etc., etc. Containing 30,000 Words and 750 Engravings. Edited by C. H. Craig, LL.D. 12mo, cloth, $1.00.

"Every one ought to own a dictionary,"—and the low price at which we offer this edition places it within the reach of all. It is, undoubtedly, the best cheap dictionary made; it contains all the words in general every-day use, with their most standard definitions and pronunciations.

CRAIG (A.R., M.A.). YOUR LUCK'S IN YOUR HAND; or, The Science of Modern Palmistry, with some Account of the Gypsies. Numerous illustrations. 12mo, cloth, gilt extra, $1.25.

A recent revival of interest in this fascinating study has certainly proven the fact that Prof. Craig's Palmistry is the most complete and satisfactory work on the subject extant—it shows the careful work of a master hand. Should there be a single "doubting Thomas" who does not believe "your luck's in your hand," let him read the convincing arguments in this work and be converted.

CYCLOPÆDIA OF BIBLE ILLUSTRATIONS, being a storehouse of Similes, Allegories, and Anecdotes. Edited by Rev. R. Newton, D.D. 12mo, cloth, $1.25.

A treasury of spiritual riches borrowed from nature, art, history, biography, anecdote, and simile, by Christian authors of all countries and ages. A book full of wisdom and of the happiest illustrations of points of doctrine and morals.

CYCLOPÆDIA OF THE ARTS AND SCIENCES:

Botany, Zoology, Mineralogy, Geology, Astronomy, Geometry, Mathematics, Mechanics, Electricity, Chemistry, etc., etc. Illustrated with over 3,000 wood engravings. 1 vol., 4to, cloth extra, $6.00 ; sheep, $7.50 ; or, in half morocco extra, $10.00.

This popular Encyclopædia is more than a first-class book of reference, it is a library of popular scientific treatises each one complete in itself, which places into the hands of the reader the means to procure for himself a thorough technical self-education. The several topics are handled with a view of a thorough instruction of these particular branches of knowledge, and all statements are precise and scientifically accurate.

DANA (R. H., Jr.). Two Years Before the Mast. 1 vol., 12mo, $1.50.

One of the most fascinating and instructive narratives of the sea ever written for young folks. The reader's sympathies are enlisted with the hero from first to last, but the hardships and hairbreadth escapes he meets with would prevent most boys from emulating his example.

DUFFERIN.—Letters from High Latitudes.

A Yacht Voyage to Iceland, Jan Mayen, and Spitzbergen. By his Excellency the Earl of Dufferin, Governor-General of the Dominion of Canada. Authorized edition. With portrait and several illustrations. 8vo, cloth extra, $1.50.

The titled author has given us in this work a narrative of a voyage replete with incident in the yacht "Foam." His impressions of the countries and people visited in the far North are written in a fresh and original style, in the purest English, and the account of the whole voyage is as pleasing and interesting as a work of fiction.

ELIZABETH BARRETT BROWNING'S POEMS.—The most satisfactory American edition issued, printed from excellent type on paper of superior quality, with introductory essay by Henry T. Tuckerman. 3 vols., 8vo, gilt tops, $5.25 ; half calf extra, $10.50.

The highest place among modern poetesses must be claimed for Mrs. Browning. In purity, loftiness of sentiment, feeling and in intellectual power she is excelled only by Tennyson, whose works it is evident she had carefully studied. Nearly all her poems bear the impress of deep and sometimes melancholy thought, but show a high and fervid imagination. Her *Sonnets from the Portuguese*, are as passionate as Shakespeare's, all eminently beautiful. Of her *Aurora Leigh*, Ruskin said "that is the greatest poem which this century has produced in any language."

FESTUS.—A Poem by Philip James Bailey. With choice steel plates, by Hammett Billings. Beautifully printed. 4to, cloth, gilt, $3.00; do., do., full gilt and gilt edges, $5.00.

GAUTIER (Theophile). One of Cleopatra's Nights and Other Fantastic Stories. Translated from the French by Lafcadio Hearn. 8vo, cloth extra, gilt top, $1.75.

A brilliant and intensely fascinating collection of stories from the pen of the inimitable Gautier, they are excellent specimens of his work in his brightest and happiest vein; the scenes are audaciously limned, and distinguished for their conscientious fidelity to nature.

GRAY.—The works of Thomas Gray, *in Prose and Verse*. Edited by Edmund Goose, Lecturer of English Literature at the University of Cambridge. With portraits, fac-similes, etc. 4 vols., crown 8vo, cloth, gilt top, $6.00; half calf, $12.00.

"Every lover of English literature will welcome the works of Gray, the author of the immortal 'Elegy written in a Country Churchyard,' from the hands of an editor so accomplished as Mr. Gosse. His competency for the task has been known for some time to students of poetry, and the present edition is now considered to be the most careful and complete ever published."— *London Athenæum.*

GUNNING (William D.).—Life History of Our Planet. Illustrated with 80 illustrations by Mary Gunning. Crown 8vo, cloth, gilt extra, $1.50.

From this work, more so than any other, we probably gain a clearer idea of the almost incredible changes Nature has wrought on our planet and still more wonderful changes we may expect in the future. We are given several interesting pages—with illustrations—on the mammoth creatures of pre-historic times, whose mummified bones alone remain to tell their story. It should be read by every one who desires to know more about the world we live in.

HARDY (Lady Duffus). Through Cities and Prairie Lands. A most interesting book of Travels in America. 1.vol., crown 8vo, cloth, gilt top, $1.75.

Recollections of a most pleasant trip made by this distinguished lady through America. She has many warm words for the kind manner in which she was treated, and altogether the work is a most pleasing and pronounced contrast to the average hastily written English impressions of America.

HISTORY AND ANTIQUITIES OF FREE-MASONRY, as Connected with Ancient Norse Guilds, and the Oriental and Mediæval Building Fraternities, to which is added the Legend of Prince Edward, etc., by George F. Fort. A New Edition. 1 vol., 8vo, $1.75.

This work is the result of years of labor on the part of the author, whose original and persistent design has been to arrive at the *truth*, and, at the same time, supply a want long felt by members of the Masonic Fraternity, as well as the uninitiated. That he has fully accomplished his purpose is demonstrated by the fact that it is now looked upon as the most standard and authentic history of Freemasonry in existence.

HOW? or, Spare Hours Made Profitable for Boys and Girls. By Kennedy Holbrook. Profusely illustrated by the author. 8vo, cloth, gilt, $2.00. do., do., full gilt extra, $2.50.

The most interesting and instructive work of the kind ever issued. By the help of their plainly worded and fully illustrated instructions, any bright boy or girl may devise unlimited entertainment and fashion many acceptable and useful presents for playmates and friends. The directions are for working with wood, paper, chemicals and paints, with knife, pencil, brush and scissors, and for the performance of sleight-of-hand tricks.

JERROLD (Blanchard). Days with Great Authors. Dickens, Scott, Thackeray, Douglas Jerrold. Selections from their Works, and Biographical Sketches and Personal Reminiscences. Numerous illustrations. 8vo, cloth, gilt extra, $2.00.

To the hosts of admirers of these great authors this work will prove of absorbing interest, as it contains many reminiscences never before in print. Considerable space has also been devoted to their public speeches, and short, characteristic selections are given from their best works.

LA FONTAINE'S FABLES.—Translated from the French by Elizur Wright, Jr. Illustrations by Grandville. Crown 8vo, cloth extra, $1.50.

La Fontaine's Fables—there is magic as well as music in the name : they have been deservedly popular for years, and they will be read with ever increasing pleasure by young and old, "as long as the world rolls round." This is the only moderate priced translation of these charming fables published.

LE BRUN (Madame Vigée).—Souvenirs of. With a steel portrait, from an original painting by the author. 2 vols. in 1, crown 8vo, red cloth, gilt top, $1.75.

"An amusing book, which contains a great deal that is new and strange, and many anecdotes which are always entertaining." It is written in a reminiscent and chatty style, and relates many "choice tid-bits" of the distinguished historical personages with whom the authoress was acquainted.

LOUDON'S COTTAGE, FARM AND VILLA

Architecture and Furniture.—Containing numerous Designs for Dwellings, from the Villa to the Cottage and the Farm, each design accompanied by analytical and critical remarks. Illustrated by upwards of 2,000 engravings. In one very thick vol., 8vo, $7.50.

One of the most useful books on architecture ever issued. Gives valuable hints to anyone contemplating building either villas, cottages, or outhouses, and may save thoughtful and practical men hundreds of dollars.

MACAULAY'S LAYS of Ancient Rome.—With

all the antique illustrations and steel portrait. Beautifully printed. 4to, cloth, extra gilt, $3.50 ; do., do., full gilt and gilt edges, $5.00 ; do., do., 12mo, cloth extra, $1.00.

When the famous historian issued these lays, which have since become classics, it was a literary surprise, for no one thought that he was also a poet of such high degree. His poetry is the rythmical outflow of a vigorous and affluent writer, given to splendor of diction and imagery in his flowing prose. Stedman said of this volume, " the lays have to me a charm, and to almost every healthy young mind are an immediate delight."

NAPOLEON.—Las Cases' Napoleon. Memoirs of

the Life, Exile, and Conversations of the Emperor Napoleon. By the Count de Las Cases, with 8 steel portraits, maps, and illustrations. 4 vols., 12mo, 400 pages each, cloth, $5.00 ; half calf extra, $10.00.

With his son the Count devoted himself at St. Helena to the care of the Emperor and passed his evenings in recording his remarks. Commenting in a letter to Lucian Bonaparte on the treatment to which Napoleon was subjected, he was arrested by the English authorities and sent away and imprisoned.

NAPOLEON.—O'Meara's Napoleon in Exile; or A

Voice from St. Helena. Opinions and Reflections of Napoleon on the Most Important Events in his Life and Government in his own words. By Barry E. O'Meara, his late Surgeon. Portrait of Napoleon, after Delaroche, and a view of St. Helena, both on steel. 2 vols., 12mo, cloth, $2.50 ; half calf - extra, $5.00.

Mr. O'Meara's works contains a body of the most interesting and valuable information—information the accuracy of which stands unimpeached by any attacks made against its author. The details in Las Cases' work and those of Mr. O'Meara mutually support each other.

NAPIER'S PENINSULA WAR.—The History of the War in the Peninsula. By Major-Gen. Sir W. F. P. Napier. With 55 maps and plans of battles, 5 portraits on steel, and a complete index. An elegant Library Edition. 5 vols., 8vo, $7.50 ; half calf, $18.00.

Acknowledged to be the most valuable record of that war which England waged against the power of Napoleon. The most ample testimony has been borne to the accuracy of the historian's statements, and to the diligence and acuteness with which he has collected his materials.

NELL GWYN, The Story of, and the Sayings of Charles the Second, related and collated by Peter Cunningham, F.S.A. With fine portrait and 11 extra engravings. 8vo, cloth extra, $3.50.

An exceedingly interesting memoir relating to the times of Charles II. Pepys in writing about Nell Gwyn called her "Pretty witty Nell," was always delighted to see her, and constantly praises her excellent acting. Cunningham states that had the King lived he would have created her Countess of Greenwich, and his dying wish to his brother, afterwards James II., was : "Do not let poor Nelly starve."

PICTURESQUE IRELAND, Descriptive and Historical.—Comprising 50 full-page engravings on steel of its picturesque scenery, remarkable antiquities and present aspects, from original drawings by W. H. Bartlett, and a complete account of its cities, towns, mountains, waters, ancient monuments, and modern structures by Markinfield Addey. 2 vols., 4to, cloth extra, gilt edges, $10.00 ; or in half morocco extra, gilt edges, $20.00.

These two handsome volumes will make the reader better acquainted with the picturesque features of the "Emerald Isle" than any work that has ever preceded it. Only by a combination of both pen and pencil was it possible to give an idea of the beauty of Ireland, its marvelous lakes, mountains and valleys, romantic streams, mysterious round towers, giant's causeway, waterfalls, stately castles, magnificent religious and public edifices, etc., etc.

PURITANS. History of the Puritans and Pilgrim Fathers. By Professor Stowell and Daniel Wilson, F.S.A. In 1 vol., 8vo, cloth, $1.75.

Stowell and Wilson's history is acknowledged everywhere to be the best and most exhaustive history of the Pilgrim fathers. A full and complete account of the rise of the Puritans under the Tudors to their settlement in New England, which is herein given, makes this a most valuable work of reference and study.

STAUFFER (Frank H.). The Queer, The Quaint, The Quizzical. A Cabinet for the Curious. With full index. 8vo, cloth extra, $1.75.

" Oddities and wonders,
Antiquities and blunders,
And omens dire ;
Strange customs, cranks and freaks,
With philosophy in streaks "

are all to be found between the covers of this book. It certainly is the completest collection of odd and curious events ever made.

TAINE, H. A.—History of English Literature. Translated by H. Van Laun, with Introductory Essay and Notes by R. H. Stoddard. 4 handsome volumes. Cloth, white labels, $7.50.

It is *the book on the subject*, the more wonderful that, written by a French critic, it should be accepted by English-speaking people—everywhere—as *the* authority on the literature of their own language, universally prized for its clearness, terseness and comprehensiveness, and yet as interesting as a work of fiction.

THE APOCRYPHAL NEW TESTAMENT, *Being all the Gospels, Epistles, and Other Pieces now extant attributed in the First Centuries to Jesus Christ, His Apostles* and their Companions, and not included in the New Testament by its compilers. Translated from the original tongues, and now first collected into one volume. With numerous quaint illustrations. 1 vol., 8vo, cloth, red edges, $1.25.

As a literary curiosity this work has excited the greatest attention all over the Christian world. There is nothing in it contradictory of those truths which have been accepted as *revealed*, but every chapter and verse goes to confirm the undoubted writings of the apostles and evangelists.

WALT WHITMAN.—Leaves of Grass. Original edition. Year 85 of the State. Foolscap 8vo, cloth extra, $3.75.

We offer here the Fine Original Edition of Whitman's Poems. Recognition of the wonderful power and charm in his rugged verse has been freely given by all who appreciate the grand and beautiful in poetry. The " Good, Gray Poet " is gaining admirers daily; his *Leaves of Grass* is destined to live forever as a representative classic of a bold and rythmic style of versification peculiarly his own. .

9

WATERS (Robert). William Shakespeare Portrayed by Himself. A Revelation of the Poet in the Career and Character of one of his own Dramatic Heroes. By Robert Waters. 1 vol., $1.25.

In this able and exceedingly interesting book on Shakespeare, the author shows l ow the great poet has revealed himself, his life, and his character, besides refuting conclusively the ciphers of Donnelly and other Baconian theories. Altogether the best life of Shakespeare, remarkably well written in vigorous English. "An original, wholesome, scholarly, and plainly sincere book on Shakespeare. It is after all something new about Shakespeare, which Lowell feared could not be said."—E. C. STEDMAN.

WILSON'S NOCTES AMBROSIANÆ.—The Noctes Ambrosianæ, by Prof. Wilson, J. G. Lockhart, James Hogg, and Dr. Maginn. A revised edition, with Steel Portraits, and Memoirs of the authors, and copiously annotated by R. Shelton Mackenzie, D.C.L 6 vols., crown 8vo, including " Christopher North," A Memoir of Prof. Wilson, from family papers and other sources. By his daughter, Mrs. Gordon. Cloth $9.00; half calf $18 00.

This series of imaginary conversations were supposed to have taken place between Christopher North (Wilson), the Ettrick Sheperd (Hogg) and others in the parlour of a tavern kept by one Ambrose in Edinburgh, hence the title Noctes Ambrosianæ. A too literal interpretation is not to be given to the scene of these festivities, however, but the true Ambrose's must be looked for only in the realms of the imagination. It is one of the most curious and original works in the English language, a most singular and delightful outpouring of criticism, politics and descriptions of feeling, character and scenery of verse and prose, of eloquence and especially of wild fun. It breathes the very essence of the Bacchanalian revel of clever men. Prof. Wilson is a writer of the most ardent and enthusiastic genius whose eloquence is as the rush of mighty waters.

YOUNG FOLKS' HISTORY OF THE RE-BELLION. By William M. Thayer. Illustrated. 4 vols., 12mo, cloth, $5.00.

Fort Sumter to Roanoke Island.
Roanoke Island to Murfreesboro'.

Murfreesboro' to Fort Pillow.
Fort Pillow to the End.

A faithful history of the late war, which by its attractive presentation is especially adapted to youthful readers. Its narrative is full of dash and adventure, the military events are recited vividly and thrillingly, it is interspersed with individual heroism, suffering and daring, and on the whole renders a better account of the war and its causes than any other book that we are acquainted with. The author's style is perfect at all times, either delicate, pathetic, or picturesque, but always in simple language that any young reader can fully understand.

ÆSOP'S FABLES. New edition, profusely illustrated. 8vo, cloth, gilt, $2.00; do., do., full gilt extra, $2.50.

Æsop, born in the sixth century before Christ, while traveling through Greece, recited himself his home-truths, which in the shape of fables are full of wisdom that will teach and live forever. He did not collect or write them down, but they were easily remembered, became universally popular and were passed on from mouth to mouth, and from generation to generation.

ANDERSEN'S FAIRY TALES.—By Hans Christian Andersen. New plates, large, clear type, handsomely printed and illustrated. 12mo, cloth, black and gold, $2.00; do., do., full gilt, $2.50.

The most charming fairy tales of the world, full of earnestness, humor, pathos, and fresh inventiveness, written in a style of carefully studied simplicity. They have become familiar to children in all countries.

ARABIAN NIGHTS ENTERTAINMENTS.—New edition. Edited by E. O. Chapman. Profusely illustrated. 8vo, cloth extra, $2.00; do., do., full gilt, $2.50.

A very pleasing edition, with most attractive illustrations of the oriental fairyland over which Queen Shehrazad reigns. It is now and always will remain a classic.

BARON MUNCHAUSEN.—The Life, Travels, and Extraordinary Adventures of. By the Last of his Family. 1 vol., cloth, gilt, $2.00; do., do., full gilt extra, $2.50.

The original Munchausen was an officer in the Russian service, who served against the Turks. He told the most extravagant stories about the campaign till his fancy completely got the better of his memory, and he believed his own extravagant fictions. The wit and humor of these tales are simply delightful.

BOY'S OWN BOOK.—A Complete Encyclopædia of all Athletic, Scientific, Recreative, Out-door and In-door Exercises and Diversions. Beautifully illustrated. Crown 8vo, cloth, gilt, $1.50.

The best present anyone can make to bright boys. One ought always bear in mind the adage " all work and no play makes Jack a dull boy."

GRIMM'S FAIRY TALES. — Translated by Lucy Crane. Profusely illustrated by Walter Crane, Wehnert, and George Cruikshank. 8vo, cloth, gilt extra, $2.00; do., do., full gilt, $2.50.

The most entertaining fairy stories ever written, singularly fascinating, the delight of children, young and old.

GULLIVER'S TRAVELS for Children. Specially edited by E. O. Chapman, with over 200 illustrations. 1 vol., 8vo, $2.00; do., do., full gilt, $2.50.

The most original and extraordinary of all Swift's productions. While courtiers and politicians recognized in the adventures of Gulliver many satirical allusions to the court and politics of England, the great mass of readers saw and felt only the wonder and fascination of the narrative.

ROBINSON CRUSOE for Children.—Edited by E. O. Chapman, with over 170 illustrations. 1 vol., 8vo, cloth extra, $2.00; do., do., full gilt, $2.50.

How happy that this the most moral of romances is not only the most charming of books, but also the most instructive!—*Chalmers.* Was there ever anything written by mere man that the reader wished longer, except *Robinson Crusoe.*—*Dr. Samuel Johnson.*

HENTY SERIES.

A TALE OF WATERLOO; or, One of the 28th. By G. A. Henty. With full-page illustrations by W. H. Overend. 12mo, cloth extra, $1.50.

A boy's story which covers the period of the Napoleonic wars, and particularly describes the Waterloo Campaign. It is written in Mr. Henty's best style, skillfully constructed, highly enjoyable and full of exciting adventures.

IN THE REIGN OF TERROR.—The Adventures of a Westminster Boy. By G. A. Henty. With full-page illustrations by J. Schönberg. 12mo, cloth extra, $1.50.

"The story is one of Mr. Henty's best."—*Saturday Review.*

"The interest of it lies in the way in which the difficulties and perils Harry has to encounter bring out the heroic and steadfast qualities of a brave nature. Again and again the last extremity seems to have been reached, but his unfailing courage triumphs over all. It is an admirable boy's book."—*Birmingham Post.*